Friends of the President

mervyn curran and Rachel Curran

Published by mervyn curran, 2022.

FRIENDS OF THE PRESIDENT

First edition. December 8, 2022.

Copyright © 2022 mervyn curran and Rachel Curran.

ISBN: 979-8215369654

Written by mervyn curran and Rachel Curran.

Special thanks to Rachel O' Connell Curran and to Catherine Loughran for reading the work-in-progress and for coming back with copious notes! You were a great help.

JFK airport, New York.

2019

The man forced a smile onto his face as he approached the TSA desk in JFK airport. Behind the smile, the man gritted his teeth while handing over the passport for examination. He hated this airport, and he hated the country he was now entering. It had not been his intention to be here, but circumstances elsewhere were not conducive to completing his original plan. He hated the agents of law enforcement that stood guard at every port of entry, and he despised the over-polite manner with which the agents greeted everyone. The illusion of freedom permeated every part of this society. But it was one of the most policed nations in the western world. The man kept his false smile in place, answering politely, while being questioned by the TSA agent sitting behind her attack-proof screen. To show his true feelings at this point would be to invite closer scrutiny by more agents. The man knew he needed to be discreet, to go unremarked and unnoticed by officialdom. He collected his passport, thanked the agent, and moved on.

The world would notice him soon enough.

JFK airport
Same day.

TSA agent Domingo Santos, standing beyond the booth in a position to scan the queue for any aggressiveness or suspicious behavior, looked at the lone man as he presented his documentation. Domingo noted a sudden change in the man's face. The man, middle-aged or older maybe, smiled at the desk agent as he walked to her station, but as soon as the agent looked down at the man's passport to compare it to the on-screen details, the man dropped the smile and looked annoyed. People got stressed while travelling, something probably caused this guy to disagree with someone in the car park outside. He sure looked peeved, though.

The next guy in the line, a young man whose face shone with sweat, grabbed Domingo's attention. The airport halls were nice and cool because of the air conditioning, so there was no good reason for a guy to be sweating so much while simply standing in line. The agent radioed an alert to his colleagues and prepared to pull the man out of line. This passenger would have a chat in a small room in his immediate future. How he answered their questions or didn't, the next step would be luggage search and a pat down of his person. After that, a body cavity search. He would not be making his flight, that was for sure.

The agent forgot all about the man that lost his smile a few minutes earlier. Drug arrests were far more interesting. The lone man, having cleared through to the arrival's hall, moved away down the corridor. He stopped at the doors leading to the main airport buildings. A voice called out from behind him, and he turned to face a woman as she came striding up the corridor from another arrivals area. The couple embraced, exchanged a few words, and moved off together into the hall. The man, although still not smiling, at least no longer looked angry at the world.

JFK airport.
Same day.

As a patrol officer in the Port Authority Police Department, John Corcoran thought he'd seen everything twice already. Having been a street patrol cop for his first couple of years on the force, he shared a patrol vehicle with a more experienced officer. This older cop taught John the vital street knowledge that wasn't covered in the training courses. John and his police mentor were first-on-scene at a few serious crimes. His senior officers commended him in the reports on a couple of headline cases. They spent their time assisting the detective division at those crime scenes. To be in such close contact with senior investigators had given John an appetite for more involvement in detective work. Posted in JFK airport this past year, John was enjoying the more relaxed environment. He knew he did not want to be a street cop for many more years. It was getting more dangerous out there each year. He would apply for his detective badge as soon as possible. He would serve a few years in that division to gain as much experience as he could. Then he would look at a move into the management side of the police department. Something in an office, with little chance of getting shot while working.

At JFK airport, one of the infrastructural facilities managed by the Port Authority, Officer John Corcoran walked and watched. The airport fascinated John by how it was a constantly shifting kaleidoscope of humanity. He observed people as they entered the departures hall from the outside world. He watched them as they moved through to catch their flights and he watched them come back again a week or fortnight later through the arrival's concourse. He saw the excited tourists starting their holidays, and he saw the stressed businesspeople commuting to start their workweek in

American cities. John enjoyed being here and knew every inch of his patrol areas.

His usual duty in Terminal four at JFK was one of law enforcement, but was mainly helping lost, confused passengers who needed directions or advice. These interactions took up a large part of his working day. The constant questions and requests from tourists do not bother John too much as he enjoys helping people. As a teenager, John spent most of his summer holidays working in restaurants and in supermarkets to help pay for his education. Burned forever into his brain was that excellent customer service is vital. He believed that everybody at every level in an organization should work to ensure customers have a positive experience. If customers got treated well, they would return to buy goods and services from the organization again and again, securing future employment for everybody. It is his job at the airport, along with his fellow officers, to be the people at the front of the house. Behind the scenes are the food people, the custodial crews, and many other people, that are essential to making JFK one of the most successful airports in the world.

The day John met Gerard and Alice Nolan started out relatively quiet. That would change later as, over the past three days, there had been heavy fog on mainland Europe, which delayed a lot of planes trying to take off or land at European airports. A dozen of the morning flights from Europe to the US were behind schedule leaving their origin points, which meant they were late arriving at LaGuardia, JFK, and Newark airports. Because of the bunched-up arrivals, there would be a higher than usual volume of travelers milling around the hallways all at once instead of being spread across the entire day. This meant the afternoon and evening were apt to be busy with hundreds of stressed and tired passengers coming through. Airport staff were enjoying these quieter hours early on, knowing it might be chaos later.

John was counting the minutes down until it was time to resume patrolling through the shopping mall and food courts. Hitching up his uniform trousers and straightening his tie, he used his two-way radio to check in with his colleagues around the airport, making sure at least one officer was watching each of the key areas of the airport. They assumed JFK to be number one on the list of potential terrorist targets. Department of Homeland Security personnel support and oversee this police protection. These agencies are on constant alert for attacks such as occurred on September 11th. Officers like John Corcoran were the public face of a massive operation which was in place to protect America and her interests.

John turned away from his visual study of incoming passengers to begin a walking patrol and saw a couple coming through the doors. The pair caught his eye and, out of habit; he watched their entry. As John watched, the man got through the opening and, stepping to one side; he reached back to hold the door open for the woman coming behind. He then stayed in place, holding the door for a group of older women following the woman. There were smiles and nodded thanks from all concerned. The lone woman, having gotten through, stepped to the side to wait for the man, and the four older ladies moved forward to continue their journey into the airport halls.

John nodded approvingly at these chivalrous gestures. His own Mother had raised him always to hold the door for women. He gave up his seat to women of any age on public transport and he always offered to help the elderly of either gender across the street. He had been on the receiving end of feminist rants about equality for his efforts and on one occasion he had offered a seat to a woman only to be told that 'she' was in fact a 'he' and the man did not appreciate the gesture at all. But more often, the person whom he had helped had thanked him. It sometimes seemed to John that the battle for equality of the sexes had only resulted in a reduction in niceness by everybody toward everybody else. Men were reluctant to aid a woman out of fear of being verbally abused for the perceived chauvinism. Rather than winning any sort of battle, in John's opinion, it won nothing for anybody. Instead, it only coarsened human relations. The world could not have too much human decency in his opinion. Knowing he held these sentiments only further convinced him he should aim to get out of the police force as soon as possible. He wasn't really cut out to be the cynical smart-ass that the job was trying to mould him into.

His attention, taken by the arriving man's courteous action at the door, meant that John kept the couple in sight as they went into the building. As they walked, their wheeled luggage followed behind them like matching pet dogs. They reached the sanctuary of an empty circular bench and the man sat down. He gathered both sets of luggage in close to his feet. The woman remained standing while a brief conversation took place between them. Then the woman went walking towards the Starbucks concession on the far wall.

John amused himself for a moment in trying to guess what sort of drink the man would have requested. Probably a latte, but maybe an Americano. The woman would have a cappuccino. They both looked to be edging toward old age so would add neither sugar nor milk to their beverage, probably following doctor's orders to do with cholesterol and blood pressure. But then again, the couple looked European, so maybe they did not have the same health concerns as American people; maybe they both took lots of sugar and cream. The man took a phone from his pocket, checked its screen, and then replaced it inside his jacket. He then sat back on the bench, let his head roll back on his shoulders and closed his eyes, resting in classic weary tourist mode. Almost immediately, though, the man stood up and began pacing around the seats.

Officer John, having a patrol circuit to complete and having daydreamed enough, set off on his well-worn walking route. Soon, he was stopping to chat with people or being stopped by tourists looking for restrooms or a coffee stand. Just another day at JFK airport.

Along with the police officers like John, there would also be plain-clothes Federal agents mingling with the crowds and these agents carried iPads with a constantly updated list of the FBI most wanted list of criminals plus pictures of suspects on the no-fly list. Anybody suspected of being a person of interest would have their face captured on a few dozen cameras. They would then run the images through the database for possible matching with photographs of known terrorist or criminal suspects. Agents would approach the person and ask them to provide identification. If the person was a match to a suspect on file, an agent would handcuff the person. A powered mini truck would transport the suspect to a service corridor. The operation would take just minutes. The travelling public were none the wiser that agents removed a threat from their midst.

Citizens in towns and cities across America attended town hall meetings of their local representatives and someone asked what they spent their tax dollars on. Federal agents in attendance would reply in whispers behind a cupped hand, we spend them on us risking our personal safety intercepting potential threats to allow you to fly anywhere in the world without us stripping everyone naked before boarding your plane. We keep these arrests out of the public eye as far as possible to avoid the scenario of small-minded people refusing to fly if they see a turban or a Burqa on a fellow passenger.

Officer John Corcoran, assuming he would never see the chivalrous man and his travelling companion again, dismissed them from his thoughts and set off across the wide expanse of tiled floor. Dealing with the usual requests for directions from stressed passengers in his usual efficient manner, John completed his sweep of the hall and corridors. Steadily making his way back to his starting position in the wide-open hall at the front of the building, he got himself a small cup of coffee from the self-service machine at the snack bar. Spending ten minutes chatting to the two women working on the counter while he drank the steaming brew would serve as his break for now. There was hardly a day in the airport's life that did not have drama or salacious gossip to be spread, dissected, and laughed over among the employees of the massive complex. John Corcoran enjoyed the company of the service staff and was popular with them.

He finished his coffee, bid adios to the counter staff, and made his way across the hall, moving in the general direction of the entrance area. There was now a noticeable increase in the mass of humanity streaming through the halls. This was the start of the expected swell in passenger numbers as the airlines of the Western world played catch-up on the delayed flights of the past couple of days. Stress levels and the sound of crying children increased all around the place. John again hitched up his trousers and waded into the flow.

To John's mild surprise, the same grey luggage still occupied the floor around the seating area as when he left this area a while before. Among all the hurrying, bustling, stressed passengers moving from one gate to another, this couple was not in any hurry to make a connecting flight. When John got closer, he saw there was at least one difference to the earlier scene in the seating area. The couple appeared to have swapped places. Now it was the woman sitting with her feet lost among the huddled luggage, while the man was now absent. On the table space between the seats sat two beverage cups.

While John looked on, the woman, in unknowing mimicry of her male companion's earlier actions, took out a phone and checked its screen before returning the device to her pocket. She then stood from her seat to look around the hall, a frown on her face. Officer

Corcoran guessed she was looking for the man with whom she had come in. Catching her eye as he passed through her field of vision, he raised his eyebrows to check if she needed help. She responded by shrugging her shoulders and smiling, as if to say that no, I don't need help, but I might need help in a moment. I'm not sure yet.

John guessed from the frown on her face and the way she was looking around, that her male companion had been gone longer than usual. John wondered if the man had gone to the bathroom and maybe fallen or become ill while alone in the cubicle. Or maybe he turned right instead of left upon exiting the bathroom and was now wandering down unfamiliar corridors.

Then, right at that moment, as if John thinking of him had summoned him, the man came striding purposefully towards the bench. The woman remained standing to greet his return. The man reached his female companion, leaned toward her, and put his hand on her arm. He spoke to her quietly while darting glances over his shoulder. He kept looking past John, back towards the public restrooms.

Glad to see the two of them seemed okay, or at least that they did not seem to require the help of a police officer, John turned away to continue his sweep of the area. He had taken just a couple of paces when his sleeve was plucked from behind. Turning, he saw it was the male half of the couple with whom he had just interacted. Up close, John could see the guy was not as advanced beyond middle age as John had earlier thought. He had looked older from a distance because his hair was grey and his bland, generic clothing somehow seemed to suggest a person of a much older age. John could now see the man was possibly only middle fifties in age.

The man leaned in close to John and said in a whisper, "Make it look like I'm asking you for directions. Just pretend alright?" The man then made exaggerated hand gestures as if he was indeed asking the police officer for help in getting to a destination. However, instead of asking how many lefts and rights he told a surprised John, "Excuse the dramatics; they might be watching me. My name is Gerard Nolan, the woman there is my wife, Alice. We are English, British citizens. I was waiting for Alice to come back with the coffees, and I was walking up and down and just, you know, people watching, I like to do that.

I saw a man come through the same door we used earlier. As he entered this hall area, another man came across the room and met him. This second man was wearing full traditional Arab clothes, including that little headband they wear; I think it's keeping their headscarf in place. When the men came together, they reached out to one another to shake hands. However, just as they were reaching out, the one with the Arab clothes removed an object from his sleeve and passed it across to the newly arrived man. He did it so that it was concealed within the handshake. I only saw it because I happened to be staring right at them at precisely the right moment and from a convenient angle. When they separated, the Arab man went across the hall and down that corridor over there".

At this point, a clearly anxious Gerard Nolan pointed across the hall to the corridor along which John had just performed his patrol. John thought he recalled passing a man with flowing robes walking in the opposite direction in one hallway earlier. Even in the ethnic mixture that was the streets of New York or the halls of JFK, those white, flowing robes stood out from the background.

Gerard Nolan continued with his tale. "I saw the other man putting the object into his jacket. Then he walked over to the bathrooms. He went inside and I followed him. I don't know what made me do that. I was curious but I think also suspicious. Because of the way the Arab man gave him the object, I suppose. And yes, because of the Arab clothes his contact was wearing, I'm a victim of Hollywood stereotyping, I'm afraid. If it's not Arabic looking men, it's shady Russian or Albanian gangsters who are the bad guys in the movies. In the toilets, I saw he had gone into a cubicle, so I went into the adjacent stall. I could hear him moving around on the toilet, the seat creaking, and the shuffling of clothing. Then I heard small mechanical noises and clicking sounds and I could see shadows on the floor just under the partition. I got down on the floor of my stall and I looked under the dividing wall. The man was kneeling on the floor in his cubicle, and I could see he had spread a few layers of toilet paper on the tiles, presumably to keep from touching the bathroom floor. On the paper were small objects, white and grey, plastic looking things. There was also a short length of thin electrical cable with the copper ends already exposed. As I watched, he made minor adjustments to the parts and then he pressed two of the objects together and I heard a clicking sound. Once these pieces became joined, I saw a tiny green light glowing from one side of what was now a small box shaped object.

When the guy picked up the little box and folded up the tissue and left the stall, I flushed the toilet and came out to the row of basins to wash my hands. He was there ahead of me, washing his hands. He nodded a greeting to me in the mirror and I said hello right back, just two lads meeting in a bathroom. I dried my hands and came out here to tell Alice what was happening and to find a police officer and I saw you. I have to tell you, I worked in factories in my younger days and that thing that he put together looked like the kind of assembly that you would make for a doorbell or maybe an alarm system controller. I think you need to find out why this one was being put together in an airport toilet. It can't be anything good, is what I think. `

Officer John Corcoran had served six years as a police officer. He'd seen and done many interesting things and had experienced some exciting days on street patrol. But he also suffered through countless boring days walking around the halls and corridors of the airport. On many of those days, he idly wondered if this was the day when he would be tested like so many were tested in New York a few years before. On those days, he simply hoped he would be up to the task if, God forbid, another terrorist attack happened.

Today, right here and now, something suspicious was happening and Officer John was finally being put to the test. In his head, he reviewed his training for this type of situation. He tried to force his brain to focus on who he was supposed to call. What were the words they trained him to say to anybody that he called? Had the cops on 9/11 been this way when it all began that morning? What were the protocols for this situation? As the on-scene officer, he needed to secure the witnesses. He needed to identify the suspect. What were they suspected of, though? John knew he needed support and back up, but he was not sure if he should send that request over his two-way radio. It wasn't the most secure network, and it seemed there was always someone listening these days. He did not intend to give any warning to anybody in the vicinity that he knew about the little plastic box. Nor did he want to have his babbling distress call getting recorded by some hacker and then broadcast on YouTube for all to laugh at. That shit was a career killer, for sure.

With all these thoughts and more going through his mind, the situation began to seem big and overwhelming to John. He was hearing too many voices and he was losing track of the correct sequence in which to proceed. He could feel himself beginning to panic when Gerard Nolan put a cool hand on John's hand and spoke quietly. The English man had seen John's eyes darting about in their sockets and the beads of sweat on the officer's forehead and he had known the cop needed help. Gerard helpfully suggested that John should first, get the three of them to the Airport security office. He reminded John they had dozens of cameras in the airport and once they got to the office, they could look at the monitors in the office. Gerard could use the security screens to pick out and identify the man he had followed to the toilets. John's colleagues could then intercept him in the corridors. A quick search of the man's clothing would reveal what exactly was the object in his pocket. They should also try to pull the Arab looking man in and search him.

Officer John Corcoran, just for those initial seconds, his brain was stuck in a roaring confusion of thoughts, but he was calmer now. This citizen, who looked like the sort of man that would take a cup of milky cocoa before retiring to bed early in his favourite pyjamas, was running rings around a trained police officer. Embarrassing, but true. It was the sort of thing that John thought he might neglect to include in his official report of today's incident. He just hoped nobody asked Gerard Nolan for his version of events.

John thanked the Englishman for the helpful suggestions, gave himself a mental shake and asked Gerard to gather his wife and their luggage and to follow him. Now that Officer John had calmed down, his training kicked in and made him a far more dynamic figure. He escorted the couple across the hall and over to the far wall. Set discreetly into this wall was a door marked 'Airport Personnel only beyond here'. There was no regular keyhole, nor was there the type of key code pad into which you might enter the correct digits. Instead, there was a small plastic oblong at chest height beside the painted steel doorframe. John pulled an I.D. card attached to an elasticated cord from inside his body armor and held it up to this wall-mounted oblong. When the card touched the plastic box, a red light flashed, then faded and a green light showed. There was a metallic click deep in the door's guts, and John pushed it open. He held the heavy door while the Nolans passed through and he followed them, pushing the door shut behind him. He never fully trusted those hydraulic arm door closers; he had seen too many movies where a bad guy simply followed the hero through the swinging door and caused mayhem.

When all three of them were on the other side of the door, Gerard Nolan mentioned the plastic gizmo on the wall that John had scanned his card on, and he said that it was almost the same as the little gadget he had seen the man in the toilets assembling. John nodded and noted grimly that he agreed with Gerard Nolans' earlier assessment of the gadget. The thing being assembled in an airport toilet wasn't going to be used to ring a doorbell. It was for nothing so innocent. Clearly, a person would activate the device somehow and this would affect something else. Taking Alice Nolan's suitcase from her and leaving her with just a small handbag to carry, he gestured for them to proceed straight ahead.

Sensor activated lights set into recessed holders along the walls came on in response to their approach to light the way. The small group hurried along the corridor that lay beyond the door. As they walked, John explained they were now heading into the deep bowels of the airport building, a part of the airport complex unseen by the travelling public. The air in the corridor smelled clean but stale, a sign of how infrequently this route was used. The roughly plastered walls and bare concrete floors were testament to the assumption that this corridor would only ever be utilised by people in the employ of the airport. Paying customers of the facility or passengers of the many airlines that operated from the airport would not have access to it.

At a T- junction in the draughty corridor, John told them to make a right turn which brought them to a service elevator, the steel-clad doors of which were well marked with scratches and dents from countless trolleys and carts that bumped into it over the years. Again, using his id card on a wall scanner, John opened the elevator doors and bade them enter. The interior of the lift held an electrical odor, as if a circuit was overheated. It reminded Alice of the time she had gotten stuck in a failed lift in a hotel in Budapest. Gerard had been left sitting at their table in the dining room, unaware of the drama being played out just yards from his seat. Once they were in and the elevator started moving, John was secure enough to use his radio to inform the people upstairs of his approach and that he was bringing civilian guests. He told Alice and Gerard that strictly speaking, he was breaking rules by bringing them up to this security room. However, he felt it was appropriate in the circumstances. John explained he wanted Gerard himself to explain the incident to the more senior officer upstairs. As Gerard had guessed downstairs, they would want him to watch the security video to pick out the man he had seen in the toilet. They would also want to identify the man's Arab contact if he was still in the building. If agents could not locate the man, outside units of the port authority police department and the federal agencies would be on the lookout for the man.

Unexpectedly for Gerard and Alice, when the lift doors slid apart, they opened directly into the security office instead of into another corridor. They stepped out of the lift and found themselves facing a massive bank of security monitors. There were a couple of dozen screens, all showing different images and different viewing angles from all over the airport buildings, cargo yards, and maintenance sheds. The screens showed the runways and taxi areas with aircraft either parked or in motion to and from the aircraft stands. Seated in front of these screens were seven people. They were dressed in regular office attire, but they also had a firearm in a holster, either under their armpit or on their hip. All had a police ID badge on their belt or on a lanyard around their neck.

A couple of these screen watchers turned their heads to appraise the new arrivals disembarking noisily from the secure elevator. They saw it was civilians escorted by a uniformed police officer, so the operators dismissed the visitors. The heads swivelled back to their scrutiny of the screens. The other operators had not allowed themselves to be distracted at all as they examined something of interest on their screen. Every few seconds, one of them would key in a note on a pad on the desk in front of them.

As Gerard and Alice watched, the picture on the screens changed in response to input from the operator, who had a computer keyboard and what looked like a gaming control stick. The operator could change the view from a particular camera as required. Each police officer wore a headset with an earpiece on one ear while the other ear remained uncovered. All officers wore their earpiece on the same side so that their supervisor only had to speak from one end of the room, and all would hear the words without turning their head from their respective screen.

Officer John, leading the three-person procession into the room, beckoned Gerard and Alice through to another section of the office. In here, they met the commander of the airport security department, Barry Kennedy. A tall, heavyset man with flushed cheeks and sweat shiny forehead, Kennedy shook their hands and told them they were most welcome in his little kingdom. He joked they would have to excuse the mess; the cleaning people only came in once a week. The joke had the tired sound of a phrase that Barry probably uttered every time a new person entered the room, but the Nolans both laughed dutifully. Barry thanked them for their help so far and told them there were other people he wanted them to meet.

Two agents, dressed in well styled suits and armed with black handguns in hip mounted holsters, joined them in the room. Barry introduced them as Federal agents, Rachel and Suzanne from the Department of Homeland Security. Barry Kennedy offered coffee, invited everyone to sit, and asked Gerard Nolan to describe the whole incident from beginning to end. There was no taker on the coffee as they all sat down in vacant chairs pulled from under desks at unused workstations.

The agent named Rachel placed a small digital voice recorder on the edge of the desk close to Gerard. Before pushing the power button, she asked Gerard if he was ok being recorded. He assured her he had no issues with that. He was most anxious that she and her colleagues get his report as clearly as possible.

Gerard went through the story again, being careful to ensure he missed no part that might be important.

The Agent named Rachel interrupted his telling only twice, once to ask Gerard to clarify a detail regarding just how he had observed the surreptitious hand-over of the device between the two men. She noted the men had been standing in the arrival's hall entry way and Gerard and Alice were sitting in the center of the hall, which meant there was a lot of distance between the two positions. How could Gerard's eyesight possibly be that good? She explained she was not casting doubt on his truthfulness but was merely playing the role of a defence lawyer in a future court room, assuming this ever got as far as a court. She wanted nothing in the report that could cast doubt on the rest of the details.

Gerard smiled, an embarrassed blush rising in his cheeks, and explained he had been pacing the floor, counting tiles. He suffered from obsessive-compulsive disorder which caused him to count tiles on walls or on floors in any unfamiliar buildings in which he might find himself. It was a coping mechanism that helped him relax. He had been at the far end of a particular line of tiles, was busy counting, and adding the total to the previous line count when the Arab robes swept past his downcast eyes. The man passed so near to Gerard, he could hear the man's leather sandals creaking and could smell his expensive aftershave. Gerard, startled by this apparition, had looked up and had lost count of the tiles he had already tallied. He was about to turn around and begin recounting the tiles leading back to his seat. Instead, in the half-turn and still distracted by the robed man, he was in the perfect position to observe the exchange between the two men.

They were standing only a couple of meters away as they shook hands and made the exchange. Gerard recalled his thought at that moment was that he didn't think Arab men shook hands. He thought they embraced and kissed cheeks. Agent Suzanne had kept her head down and was making notes through this tale, but she looked up with a thoughtful expression on her face. When Gerard asked her if she had a question for him, she said that Gerard might have a valid point about the embrace versus the handshake. It might suggest the Arab man was merely playing a role rather than being a traditional Arab. Then she said with a grim determination, `we'll be asking him to his face soon enough, I guess`.

The second time Rachel broke in was to ask Alice Nolan if she had seen any part of this hand-over. Alice explained she had been in line to buy coffee when the Arab man and his contact came together. She still had not returned to the seating area by the time the men had gone their separate ways and Gerard had followed one man into the bathroom. It was her initial assumption upon taking her seat once more that Gerard had been taken with a sudden urge to use the toilet and hadn't been able to wait for her to come back with the coffee. She had taken a seat to wait for Gerard's return. It was at that point that Officer John had encountered her and, seeing her concerned expression, had checked if she needed assistance. John Corcoran smiled to hear his impression of her being nervous about her companion's absence had been the correct one. Alice further explained that she knew nothing about the small object being exchanged until Gerard returned from the toilets and told her the basic story before he approached the airport police officer to seek official help.

On the heels of the explanation by the Nolans, John Corcoran realised he had missed a detail earlier, and he asked now if Gerard, before deciding to follow the man to the toilets, had thought of the fact that their luggage might have been picked up by a security patrol and removed for security reasons while he was in the bathroom spying on the man with the device. Gerard had left the seating area before Alice had returned from the coffee shop, which was a considerable distance from their seats. Gerard confessed he hadn't thought of that. He was so intrigued by that interaction between the two men and with the object he had seen them exchange. Then he laughed and said, `it all worked out fine though. Nobody took away our underwear to be destroyed as a terrorist threat`.

When Gerard completed his recounting of the entire incident and sat back, Barry and the two female agents looked across the desk at each other, and Rachel nodded. Without saying a word, all three got up from the table and moved away for a private conference, apart from the seated Nolans and John Corcoran. Gerard whispered to Alice and John that he reckoned the agents weren't just ordinary agents. They were some types of specialists, presumably in anti-terrorist investigations. After a murmured conversation with Barry Kennedy, the two Homeland agents returned to the group and told Gerard they would like him to join them at the camera monitors to find the man from the toilets. Gerard nodded grimly at this and said, `I have a feeling he won't be too hard to spot. He wore the most horrible yellow tie I have ever seen. And his mate should be simple to find, too. He looks like an extra from the Lawrence of Arabia movie set in those robes`.

That proved to be the case when only minutes after Gerard had begun to scan the moving crowds and the static lines of passengers at the check-in desks, he spotted his target. Gerard stabbed a finger at one screen and exclaimed, `there he is, that's him! `. In the high-definition images on the screen, a male figure wearing a yellow tie was visible. He was standing with his back resting against a wall, sipping from what looked like a coffee cup and looking like he hadn't a care in the world.

Agent Rachel had taken charge of the situation. She spoke into the small radio handset clipped to her jacket lapel. She gave orders to move forward. She described the suspect and gave his location.

She emphasized agents were to take the man into custody without harming him.

To Gerard and the others in the control room, Rachel pointed to the screen upon which Gerard had identified the suspect, and she pointed to her operatives among the moving crowds of passengers. She explained that two plain-clothes cops posing as a tourist couple would get close to the man. At that point, agents disguised as cleaning staff would be ready to pull down the steel shutters on that section to enclose the suspect in a small area. This was in the event of the man having a weapon or explosive device. It would ensure injury or damage being kept to the smallest area. To get several agents close to the suspect, the agents posing as tourists would start rotating their positions, interchanging with two other officers. They were not wearing any obvious disguises but were dressed in suits and ties. This was to prevent the man from becoming suspicious from seeing the same couple in his immediate vicinity too often. The idea was to enclose him in a loose circle of agents before the arresting officers could step up to arrest him.

In the security office, everybody watched in a tense silence as the drama played out on the screen. The only audible voices now were the comments and updates from the agents down in the airport corridor as they stalked their prey. Rachel trusted her officers to do their job. There was no need for further instructions. Both sets of agents walked past the spot where the man was waiting and then circled back to watch him from the other side of the corridor, once with coats on and fully buttoned, then in the other direction without coats. The officers posing as a couple, standing together to take a selfie with the JFK departures board in the picture, succeeded in getting a clear picture of the suspect's face in their photo. They transmitted the photo to the CIA and NSA analysis sections to be run through all known databases for identification. They also sent the photo to the phone of Agent Rachel Connor in the security office. She showed it to

Gerard Nolan, who quickly identified the man as the same guy he had stood beside in the toilets earlier. The yellow tie was visible in the photograph, and everyone agreed it was indeed hideous. This was the man that Gerard had seen assembling the plastic device. Standing up from her chair with a broad smile, Rachel shook Gerard's hand and said, `well done, thank you. I am Rachel Connor, and my beanpole partner is Suzanne Clarke. We are from the Department of Homeland Security, and our focus is on JFK airport. Right now, I'm very interested in the other man, your movie extra guy in the robes. Please keep looking at the screens and call out if you see him. Once we have him located, we can scoop both men up at the same time`.

Gerard resumed his earlier stance in front of the camera monitors and as he did, the agent at that screen looked up at him from the operators chair and said brightly, `if you can nail this second guy before he either walks or flies away, we can wrap this entire thing up in a single afternoon. ` Agent Rachel heard the remark and rolled her eyes to the ceiling, `I wouldn't bet money on that just yet Harry, these things can stretch out in directions you can't even see at this point. `

There have been people in various levels of society throughout history that have made predictions, which later turned out to be inaccurate. The prediction by Harry, the camera operator, turned out to be one of those inaccurate predictions. The prediction by Rachel was right on the money however, the incident unfolding in JFK airport that day did indeed stretch out in every direction. It went around the world, stopping in various places along the way but, eventually it returned to America. And it left a trail of turmoil, blood and broken lives in its wake.

Turning to Barry Kennedy, Rachel told him she wanted his best operator in front of a console to show recorded camera footage. She wanted them to run the CCTV recording back to a point just before the time that Gerard had seen the two men meeting in the hall. Rachel wanted to focus on the meeting at which the Arab man had covertly passed the electronic device to the other man. She felt sure the sleight-of-hand passing technique used by the Arab man was something he would have practiced; he would be proud to have done it so smoothly. If he had practiced it to where he felt confident enough to use it at JFK, he would be likely to use it more than once. Rachel suggested they could track the man in the Arab robes from that meeting point. Not only would this tracking allow them to discover his current location, but it might also show them if he had met with anyone else. If he had met others, had he passed over more devices? Those robes might be voluminous enough to carry more than just the single device they knew about. When Rachel suggested there might be multiple devices, every agent and officer in the room turned to stare at her, expressions of dawning horror on their faces. The implications were sinking in fast; they were now in a major incident. By arresting these two men and any others, further escalation would be halted.

At the bank of monitors, all the heads swiveled back to their respective screens, eyes narrowed, and foreheads furrowed with renewed focus. This had gone from a suspicious meeting of two men in an airport to a clear and present danger. The scenario was something they all trained for, but few of them expected to have to deal with. Three of the agents at the screens reached down to their holstered firearms and touched their gun, just to reassure themselves of the lethality of the weapon. Then they turned to focus on the task in front of them.

When Alice Nolan and her husband first entered the security office, Gerard had become closely involved with the activity at the monitors and left her sitting alone. She had moved over to the couch against the far wall and had gathered their luggage on the floor beside her feet, much as her husband and then she herself had done downstairs earlier. Alice took out her phone and began playing the brain training games she used to entertain herself and pass her spare time. She figured she and Gerard would be in this office for quite some time yet. They would miss their connecting flight and their holiday plan would need to be changed. They had flown into JFK on separate flights because of Gerard having business in Paris. She herself had been busy with a charity fundraiser in her church group at home in England. But she consoled herself with the thought that they hadn't had a strict schedule to follow. They had flown from place to place, enjoying various cities and tourist attractions and had bought tickets as they travelled. This security alert that Gerard had sparked was an interesting deviation from the normal routine, and at least they would have a travel story to tell friends back in England. She just hoped it wouldn't take too long to resolve. She enjoyed travelling and wanted to get back to that.

The camera screen operator had brought the video footage back in time to where the two suspect men were meeting and clasping hands just inside the doors of the airport building. The agent asked Gerard to confirm if this was the meeting he had witnessed. Gerard was amused to see himself in the video footage, first as a distant figure sitting on the bench downstairs and then as the camera footage advanced, he was the lone figure moving against the tide of incoming passengers, head down and hand moving as he pointed at each tile and counted. In the early part of the video, he was in the seat with their luggage clustered at his feet. Six feet away from him right now, Alice sat on a couch with that same luggage at her feet. Bringing his wandering mind back to the present, he confirmed that those were the men he had seen earlier.

From that meeting point, it was a simple matter for the camera operators to follow the path of the robed man as he moved around the airport. Simple, but also very disturbing to everyone watching on the video screen. Barry Kennedy, Rachel and Suzanne plus Gerard Nolan, and half a dozen federal agents tried to crowd around the one screen to see the Arab man's progress as he roamed through the building. It became impossible for everyone to watch the video together, at which point Barry instructed the operator to project the camera feed onto the large briefing screen high on the wall at the end of the office. They all turned to watch and there were gasps and exclamations as the very recognizable suspect, looking as innocently friendly as it is possible to look, met various people while he appeared to stroll up and down the halls.

He met three lone men and four lone women who were wearing business suits and carrying briefcases.

He met two men together wearing matching football shirts.

He met two men wearing traditional Arab robes like his own, but with different coloured headbands.

He met a woman that was carrying a young child in a front mounted sling.

He met a casually dressed man that was with a petite woman and chubby child, both looking like they bought their outfits in Gap for kids. The Arab man embraced the woman and shook hands with the man.

He met two men wearing hiking boots and knee-length shorts that were carrying huge rucksacks festooned with rolled sleeping bags, tents, plastic bowls, and metal cups.

He met two men in the garb of Christian priests who showed no hesitancy in their embrace of this gentleman.

He met a lone young man who was dressed in a cracked leather jacket with peeling badges on the lapels. The jacket was only half zipped, and a smudged t-shirt was visible underneath. He wore greasy looking jeans and was wearing dirty sneakers on his feet. He did not appear to have any sort of luggage or personal possessions with him and was smiling vacantly throughout the exchange.

In all, the Arab robed man met, shook hands with, embraced, and likely, handed across one of the plastic devices to nineteen people. Nineteen individuals were now carrying small, soon-to-be-assembled electronic devices inside JFK international Airport. The purpose of the devices at this point was still unknown, but nobody in the upstairs office believed it was anything benign. Rachel Connor instructed her agents not to make any moves on any suspects. Agents were to keep suspects under close surveillance. It was necessary to determine the purpose of the small objects first. There might be other people involved in the conspiracy and Homeland security wanted to roll them all up at once if possible. A lot more agents would be required on the ground at JFK, and quickly too. It was time to alert the President.

Agents Rachel Connor and Suzanne Clarke again moved apart from everybody else, put their heads together and conferred. Rachel turned to address the people in the office. She announced they had now seen enough, and she was calling Washington DC. to inform the President she was initiating a full lockdown of all transport hubs in the Port Authority jurisdiction with immediate effect. She would impress upon the White House that a national lockdown of all infrastructure would be advisable. Rachel said it was now clear there was a full-scale incident developing right here at JFK and she was very much afraid there might be similar incidents happening in other airports.

Aviation authorities told all flights on approach to JFK to divert to their nearest airport. Flights waiting to depart JFK were grounded until all suspects were in custody and evident facts had been found out. There would be a full search of all aircraft to determine if there was anything suspicious on board.

The Homeland security agents offered their gratitude and commendations to Officer John Corcoran and asked that he report the situation by telephone to his commanding officers at Port Authority headquarters in Manhattan. Agents requested John remain in the office to provide escort and security to the Nolan couple until they increased the number of Federal agents in the airport. The Nolans were both now classified as material witnesses in an ongoing federal investigation. There might be terrorist conspiracy charges against the people identified on the security monitors. Witnesses would be required to testify in court. Homeland security would be briefing all law enforcement agencies as soon as Washington had considered their response to the security alert. All police officers and federal agents were to be placed immediately on high alert, all holiday leave would be cancelled and any agents not currently on duty were ordered to return to their local office for briefing. Until further notice, they were now in the middle of a national emergency. The lessons learned from 9/11 and from other incidents were being put into practice now. Nothing and no one would be allowed to slip through the net.

In the arrivals and departures halls, passengers waited at the gates, either to board their flight, or to meet people arriving at JFK airport. On flight status screens, they abruptly changed all flights to DELAYED. It was the same for every flight and experienced travelers seeing the changed status, knew that something serious was developing, or had already happened. An air crash was the presumed incident. The only question for these people now was whether their loved ones were on the affected plane.

Over an hour later, they would still be sitting and waiting. Unbeknownst to worried family members, the situation in the airport was still developing. Airline staff were afraid of jeopardizing an investigation and they incorrectly assumed Federal agents would brief the anxious passengers and families in the various lounges and waiting areas, so they did not pass on pertinent information. This lack of communication did nothing to alleviate the mental suffering of hundreds of people. In fact, it simply inflated the rumors. Social media lit up across various platforms, with people asking the internet if there had been any news of a plane crash or a hijacking or anything to explain the wait, they were enduring in JFK.

As nothing had happened yet, there was no real news and, in its absence, people naturally imagined the worst. People logged onto plane watching websites to attempt to determine which flight had been affected. The only thing they could find was a long list of delayed, diverted, and cancelled flights. Not one plane was unaccounted for on the status boards of the sky scanning websites. All planes had either returned to their original airports or they had already completed their journey and were on the ground at their destination airports. There was an absence of activity in the skies above the East coast of America. Because of a lack of answers from law enforcement, airports left aircraft sitting on the runway with engines idling to keep air conditioning running. Bottled water was handed around on board the planes. Flight attendants simply shook their heads, and shrugged their shoulders when passengers asked when they would be allowed to leave the plane.

Flight crews were bluntly told by airport authorities, we're not sure if it is safe to disembark the passengers just yet. When asked if it was the aircraft or the airport that was considered a danger, there were more shrugs of the shoulders from all involved. Don't fly or move that plane any closer to our airport buildings, don't disembark. The mystery deepened and spread and still the relatives and friends of passengers scheduled to arrive at JFK were left to wonder and worry and pray.

With dozens of flights in and out of JFK daily, the problem for the hordes of newly arrived federal agents now in the airport was how to search all those planes that had been scheduled to fly out over the next few hours. Investigators knew the nineteen devices were intended for nineteen separate planes. The entire airport was on lock-down and no planes could leave. The agents were worried that there might be explosive devices of some sort on parked aircraft. These might detonate at any moment. Parked at their stands, each aircraft was loaded with aviation fuel, which effectively turned each jet into a bomb.

Memories of September 11th were still fresh in a lot of minds, and the thought of all that aviation fuel just a few yards away from thousands of stranded passengers was nightmare inducing. If a person with a desire to damage and kill at JFK held a method for making that fuel explode, the damage to the airport and to the people gathered inside would be devastating.

A Transport Safety Authority technical specialist, considering the problem of how to search all the parked planes, realized that they did not have to search every plane. It had been decided early on that there were only nineteen devices and although nobody knew exactly what the devices were for; it was accepted that the devices were part of some sort of attack. But the fact of a definite count of devices meant that agents only had to search the planes on which the nineteen passengers were intending to fly.

As to which planes were the relevant ones, it was not long before Homeland security realized they would have nineteen answers to that question very soon. The nineteen people that had been seen meeting the Arab robed man were about to be taken into custody. However, before that happened, one of the nineteen suspects would have the distinction of being lifted first. The remaining eighteen would follow that person into custody soon after.

The idea was to snatch one of the nineteen and analyze the device he carried to determine the nature of the danger. If the device was not dangerous on its own, agents could then grab the rest of the suspects, safe in the knowledge that nothing was going to explode right then. The agents agreed that such a small object would not be explosive itself, but would instead be a trigger for a separate, larger device. Technicians mostly agreed the devices were not big enough to include any sort of antenna. So, these triggers, to activate a device, would need to be right up close to wherever the explosive devices were hidden. Either way, the agents knew they needed to capture one of the objects to be sure of all these facts.

While all flights were grounded with scores of people being left to worry, five federal agents entered a public restroom on Level 2. The agents surrounded the lone, scruffy looking male passenger using the toilet. The agents, guessing they might need to shoot the suspect if he attempted to activate the device in his pocket, had fitted their Glock 19 handguns with noise suppressors. They wanted the option of shooting the suspect without alerting the entire airport.

Inside JFK airport.

The plan with the silenced weapons and the five-man grab squad was to take this one suspect separately from everyone else. They did not necessarily need to keep the man himself alive; they only needed to keep the device intact for expert evaluation. It was assumed by now; the man had enough time to assemble his personal device and whatever the ultimate purpose of the gadgets, this one would be active by now.

The subject of their attention, oblivious to the agents' presence in the restroom, was whistling under his breath while he urinated noisily into the toilet. He strolled out of the toilet stall, looking down to button up his jeans as he walked. The man looked up to see a line of large figures, wearing FBI badges and standing shoulder to shoulder across the width of the bathroom. Each man was pointing a handgun at the scruffy passenger, and index fingers were white from the applied pressure on the triggers.

The agent standing solidly on the end of this terrifying wall of Federal beef spoke quietly, `unzip your jacket and let it slide to the floor, do it carefully, do it now`.

The suspect, a twenty-two-year-old restaurant cleaner from Brooklyn, had smoked some good quality crystal meth in the surface carpark after getting off the bus. He was on his way in to keep his appointment with the Arab man in the airport and was feeling proud he made it to the meeting on the correct day. He had kept himself together long enough to assemble his personal device, although stupidly, he had performed this task while sitting at a cafe counter drinking hot chocolate, in full view of anyone that wanted to look. With two hours to kill before his flight, he ground and snorted the last of his meth in a toilet cubicle and had gone strolling around the airport enjoying the sensations of being among so many people while meth buzzed through his brain.

Now in another bathroom, and still high, he was not sure if he was being accosted by a bunch of huge feds, or if he was hallucinating again. Nevertheless, he silently complied with the order on the off chance the federal agents were, in fact, real. It was getting harder to discern what was really happening and what was simply hallucination caused by the meth. He decided it was better to be safe than shot. These guys looked seriously pissed about something. He unzipped his filthy jacket and, as instructed, let the garment fall to the floor.

An agent moved forward and pushed the suspect in the chest, so that his back came to rest against the cold tiles between two of the urinals. Two agents then stepped forward and very carefully picked up the jacket. While one agent held the garment up, looking as if he was going to help his colleague try it on for size, the other agent reached into the inside pocket using two fingers held like tongs. When he drew out the plastic box, the agent holding the jacket then laid the jacket back on the floor. The device was placed very carefully on top of the jacket and one agent then left the bathroom.

The suspect, with a Glock handgun pressed against his chest, forcing him to lean against the wall, tried to speak but was ordered to shut the hell up. The senior agent stepped in front of the bewildered passenger and informed the man he was under arrest. The agent read the suspect his rights from a laminated card, after which the suspect was turned to face the wall and roughly searched from head to toe. In his rear trouser pocket, they discovered the man's passport and in the front pocket, a wallet containing a large sum of cash. As expected, there was also a plane ticket in a transparent folder. The agent that had performed the arrest then cable-tied the man's hands and left him standing facing the wall.

All four agents in the bathroom spun round with guns raised when the restroom door opened behind them. To their relief, it was their colleague returning to say it was all clear outside. This agent had brought a large janitor's cart up to the door of the restroom, and he now pushed it in through the double doors into the room. The agents picked the prisoner up by his arms and legs and bundled him into the cart, covering him up with a large paint speckled sheet. The man under the sheet was warned to remain silent until such time as somebody told him it was ok to talk. He was warned if he spoke or made any other sound, he would be shot through the sheet, and it would become his shroud in an unmarked grave somewhere he would never be found. The terrified man chewed his lower lip and tried to make himself even smaller inside the cart. The crystal meth had begun to fade from his brain, and he was acutely aware of being in serious trouble with this bunch of angry agents. He knew meth was illegal, but he had never heard that doing meth was such a big crime that they sent a whole team of federal agents to bust you for it.

The entrance to the nearest service tunnel was only yards away from the bathroom door, so the agents did not have to push the cart very far. The instant they entered the tunnel and were clear of the public areas of the airport, they began running with the cart in front of them. Around a bend in the drab concrete tunnel, was the first cluster of Federal agents and Police officers. Located here was the Homeland Security mobile command post, from which the entire operation was being coordinated. The janitor's cart was wheeled to this truck and the senior agent knocked on the door to announce their arrival. Other agents came out to remove the prisoner to a more secure holding area while the grab team from the toilets was allowed a few minutes to catch their breath. They would rejoin their colleagues in the airport as soon as the order was given to begin picking up the other eighteen suspects. Every agent wanted to be part of that operation.

The plastic object, carried from the bathroom still wrapped in the suspect's jacket, was now placed into the safe hands of a bomb disposal team. Their chief expert, a middle-aged and very serious looking woman by the name of Mabel Murielez had arrived at the command post before the device was delivered. She had been waiting impatiently for the device to arrive.

By a stroke of luck for the investigation, Specialist Murielez had earlier flown into JFK from Egypt, via Paris. She had been in Giza, seconded to assist the Egyptian National Security Agency in their investigation into a hotel bombing in Giza, in which three US citizens had died, along with a dozen Egyptian and European nationals. Miss Murielez had landed in JFK and was looking forward to a few days of rest at home in New Jersey.

Having landed just an hour before the lockdown of flights was initiated, she left the plane and walked across the tarmac to the airport buildings. She switched on her phone and began receiving messages from the various strands of the federal government with which she was on constant call in the event of an explosive threat, or when she was needed for consultancy on matters of explosive ordinance.

All the alerts had the FEMA logo as a header with a number scrolling across the top so that all responders would know they were receiving genuine Federal government messages.

Realizing she had landed at ground zero of a crisis in New York, Mabel had abruptly changed direction. She instead strode quickly away from the secure car park where her car awaited, and to which she had been headed until her phone messages interrupted.

Unsure as to where the command post would have been set up, she headed for the TSA police office, which was well signposted in the airport. She called her Homeland security supervisor as she walked and asked what to expect when she got to the command center in JFK. She also asked them to contact the Port Authority police officer in charge to arrange for her to be brought directly to where she could help most.

By the time Specialist Murielez arrived at the airport police office, she already knew where she should go. She just needed an escort from an airport officer so that she could get there by the quickest route. She breezed into the office and began to explain to the two police officers on duty what she needed. She did not get to finish speaking because a young and very eager female officer jumped to her feet, saluted in the general direction of Agent Murielez, and informed her that they had been briefed on the situation and knew she needed to get to the FBI command post at high speed. Sandra grabbed car keys from a board behind the cluttered desk and asked Agent Murielez to follow her.

Officer Sandra Whelan led Mabel out through the rear door of the small police building to a police car parked in the shaded yard there. With blue lights revolving on the car roof, but without sirens, Sandra drove at speed across a shimmering expanse of concrete towards a pair of huge steel doors on the North side of the airport complex. Stopping there, she jumped out and went to a keypad on the wall beside the doors. She keyed in the code and was back in the driving seat, with the car already edging closer to the doors before the electric motor had gotten started on the door opening process. She waited just long enough for the moving edge of the opening doors to allow the width of the cop car to squeeze through, and then she accelerated into the gloom of the tunnel beyond. Officer Sandra drove at forty miles per hour with the screech of the tires echoing off the tunnel walls until they came to a junction in the service tunnel. At this point, she finally slowed to a crawl to negotiate the turn. It was only a short drive to the point where the federal agency carnival had pitched its camp. Sandra turned to Mabel and smiling broadly asked, `was that fast enough madam? `. Agent Mabel Murielez smiled at Sandra, mirrored the officer's earlier salute, said thanks and farewell to her police escort, and jumped out of the car.

Mabel Murielez signed in with the agent in charge and asked about the device they had captured. The agent informed her the suspect, and the first captured device was right now in the process of being brought to their current location for examination. Murielez swore under her breath and stamped up the steps into the technical services trailer. She hated delays of any kind and right now she wasn't happy as she realized she could have gotten herself a decent cup of coffee before racing to the service tunnel.

Clearly, she had been too efficient in traversing the airport complex. She had gotten here before the suspect with his device had arrived. The coffee supplied to the front-line cops in these command set-ups was always horrible. She had hurried past at least four good coffee stands to get to the airport police office.

In times of anxiety or stress while trying to get to grips with a technical mystery, Mabel tended to be a mutterer. She muttered under her breath, and she muttered what sounded to people in her vicinity like a song or poem. What she was muttering was the periodic table of elements, from lightest to the heaviest elements, in a singsong rhyming cadence. It helped her focus and assisted in blocking out external noise while she mentally went through all the possibilities of a given situation. After a few minutes of sitting at the work bench in the trailer, simmering and muttering darkly, there was a shouted call from outside and as she reached for the door handle, an agent came scurrying up the steps and saluting her briskly with his free hand, very carefully handed the device to her. She took the gadget into the rear workspace area where her machines and computers were located.

She was now in the large, very well-equipped technical services van in which the rest of her explosive ordinance team had arrived ahead of her arrival. Earlier that day, there had been some confusion in her home office as to her current location when the initial alert was sounded to all federal agencies. In the event of her being unavailable, her agency simply assigned the next technical specialist on the duty roster. On today's roster, that agent would have been a middle-aged male bomb technician from the Delaware office, a very competent agent. But he was nobody's first choice for a national emergency such as the one unfolding here today.

Mabel Murielez was in constant demand because she had a gift for figuring out the mechanics of any electronic device or mechanical switching gear that was handed to her. Certain envious agents had, some years before, spread malicious rumors that she was directly descended from a long line of witches. She never tried to deny the rumors. She felt like her suspected magic powers helped the attending agents feel more confident when she was present at bomb scenes. She had been heard to emit the odd cackle during analysis of components, the better to encourage the witchcraft rumors.

Now, sitting in her favorite place on Earth, she placed the device on the sterile examining surface and turned it over, looking at the back of it, the sides of it, and then returned to what seemed to be the upper side. She inserted the slim blade of a tool into the seam along one edge and levered the two sections apart. She dismantled the casing so that the electronic component was left isolated. She attached voltage testers and noted the figures. She put the device under an x-ray scanner. She did a lot of transmission tests and examined it from every possible angle. She resolutely resisted the urge to press the inset button on the top panel of the device. There was probably no danger to aircraft from the distance at which she was sitting, but she refused to take any chances. Finally, after a short time that seemed to last an eternity to the agents waiting outside the trailer, she reached a conclusion.

Emerging into the service tunnel to brief the anxiously waiting federal agents and police officers, she announced the devices to be activators for something else. The purpose of that something, in the current context, was most likely an explosive device of some kind.

The range of the signal from the device would be short, most likely just a few yards. She was unable to state with complete confidence what the purpose of this little device might be, but she was able to state that the devices were not explosive on their own. She warned the agents not to press the inset button on any devices they collected. It was akin to pulling the trigger on a gun that might be loaded. And as nobody knew where the linked explosives might be hidden, one would be well advised not to take any chances. It was agreed that rolls of masking tape would be supplied to agents, so that the devices could be wrapped in tape to avoid any accidental pressing of the buttons.

The gust of air from the collective sigh of relief from those awaiting her analysis provided momentary competition for the cold wind that blew incessantly along the tunnels. A few agents touched religious symbols on chains around their necks and offered prayers of gratitude to their god. They were still left with the unanswered question of what exactly the devices were for, but at least they weren't bombs.

Now that they were sure the devices were not dangerous on their own, dozens of armed, angry police officers and federal agents went striding through the airport like a blue tsunami wave advancing silently towards an unsuspecting shoreline. Nineteen people on this particular beach were about to be picked up and carried away.

Agents and cops, advancing towards the crowds of passengers in the airport buildings, were fully expecting and were prepared for some level of resistance on the part of the Arab robed man plus the remaining eighteen suspects. In going to make each arrest, agents doubled up on each suspect. One agent stepped in front of the suspect, preventing the person from moving forward, and announced the person was under arrest while the second agent stood to one side with a gun at the ready to deal with any show of aggression by the person being arrested.

The agents were surprised, and in the case of a few of the more testosterone fueled male agents, not a little disappointed, to discover they merely had to walk up to each identified person and inform the person they were under arrest. The person accepted the situation without argument or complaint, indeed some even smiled at the officers as they raised their hands to be cuffed. It was as if each suspect had expected to be arrested and felt they were just going along with the arrest for appearance's sake. It was strange and unexpected behavior for people being taken into federal custody on terrorism charges.

A couple of the arresting agents remarked upon the relaxed nature of the arrests, but most agents took it as a rare case of the cop's job being easier than usual. Usually, these types of situations required a lot of physical effort, accompanied by the fear of getting hurt by a suspect that puts up a fight. This was just one of those times where it went smoothly in favor of the good guys. Why question such rare good fortune?

Agents took suspects to separate police vans, lines of which were waiting in the underground service tunnels normally used by airport employees for cargo movement and equipment transport. Fully briefed agents knew exactly what to look for on each suspect, and before putting each person into a bus, agents searched every suspect and were able to confirm that each of them was carrying a small plastic object, just like the one described by Gerard Nolan and the one examined by Mabel Murielez. Also, in each person's possession was a plane ticket plus cash. By using the plane tickets from the suspects as a guide, airline staff were able to tell agents exactly which planes should receive special attention from the bomb search teams. And now that they had the devices safely stored where nobody could press the button on the device, it should be safe to proceed with searches.

Homeland Security was, by now, confident they understood the nature of the terrorist plot. Each of the nineteen passengers was ticketed for a different flight. Once airborne, they would activate their respective device. Presumably this would trigger an explosion on board. Nineteen planes would be destroyed in mid-air, killing all those on board and causing catastrophic loss of life and damage on the streets below.

The targeted flights were scheduled to depart within a couple of hours of each other, all on the same day. It was assumed by investigators that the attackers on the first planes to take off would hold off on pressing the button on their device until all the flights were in the air. If any of the nineteen flights became delayed for whatever reason and were still on the ground when the devices were activated, blowing them up while the plane was parked at its departure gate would still be a major victory for whoever had organized the attack.

Now, though, affected planes having been identified were swiftly towed to a safe location away from the terminal buildings. Fuel trucks were connected to the wing tanks and most of the onboard fuel was quickly pumped back into the fuel carriers. Agents and airline crews worked at speed to make the aircraft as safe as possible in the time they were allowed. They were all aware that although the remote trigger devices had been captured, there might be a master switch somewhere close by, perhaps triggered by a mobile phone, that would detonate all the devices at once, if the controlling person realized their bombers had all been arrested.

Each aircraft, with crew and maintenance staff evacuated, was thoroughly searched by human and dog teams. To the utter mystification of agents, nothing suspicious was found in the passenger cabins or cockpits of these planes. Federal agents were standing around inside empty passenger jets, trying to figure out what the hell was going on. They had been convinced they would discover at least one bomb in a toilet or under a seat in each targeted plane. Separately, agents were busily combing through the lists of airport employees to discover which of them was responsible for smuggling bombs onto American aircraft.

Not having found any bombs, they now couldn't figure out what the plan was. The agents were standing around discussing their next move when an aircraft technician called Nigel stepped forward and shyly suggested they look inside the Aeronautics enclosure. The confused looks on the agents' faces and the way a couple of them looked towards the airport buildings as if the enclosure was some structure off in the distance made the tech guy smile. Nigel patiently explained he was referring to the interior of the aircraft fuselage where the fuel lines, electrical systems and hydraulics are routed from the nose of the plane through to the tail.

Nigel and a hastily assembled group of his colleagues were swiftly formed into search crews, each accompanied by two agents. Agents were warned to be alert during the search in case one of the technicians proved to be part of the terrorist plot and attempted to activate a bomb on a plane. The teams were sent into the interior of the aircraft where, as Nigel had explained, fuel lines, navigation and engine control systems were located. They had just begun to search when explosive devices were indeed found. A simple incendiary bomb had been hidden in an area of each plane in such a way, that as the agents were about to have explained to them by Nigel and his colleagues, demonstrated special knowledge of an aircraft's vulnerabilities. So, insofar as compiling a suspect profile went, it would be a much smaller group of suspects than previously thought. The agents might not have to question and examine the lives and families of every single employee at the airport to determine who placed the bombs. The pool of possible suspects had initially included the food service people, cleaners and the various technical people that serviced all and any part of an airplane. Now, though, knowing the bombs had been placed inside the guts of the planes, agents should only have to look at the aircraft technicians, those people with access to the inner workings of aircraft. These people would be the only ones with the security clearance required to place the bombs in these most damaging locations.

The search teams and agents were ordered to evacuate the aircraft to allow bomb squad technicians to gain access. Each device was removed very carefully and placed in evidence boxes. There was an explosive ordinance van waiting below on the tarmac, and all nineteen devices were placed in secure storage lockers on board the specially adapted vehicle.

A senior investigator, already thinking ahead to possible prosecutions and court appearances, strode down the aisle of the nineteenth plane to have been confirmed to be carrying a bomb, and grabbed the arm of the technician that had pointed them in the right direction. He demanded, `am I correct in thinking that people like you and your colleagues with specialist knowledge are the sort of people we should be looking at for the placement of these explosives?`

Nigel nodded in agreement and said he supposed it would be possible for someone to figure it out from books or from the internet, but he pointed out that the precise location of each bomb had been different on each plane. Aircraft were the same basic design inside and out, but there were some engineering differences in the interior workings between one plane and another. A Boeing might have two fuel lines or three valves or whatever, while a Lockheed might have a different number of fuel lines, or the wiring might be harnessed in a different way. Nigel said the explosives had been placed according to the fuel supply vulnerability of that specific aircraft. He smiled at the agents gathered in front of him and admitted, `I'm probably leaving myself and my colleagues open to Federal investigation here, but yeah, we would be the people that know the weak points on most planes. We've had to service and repair more than a few of them over the years`.

The senior agent clapped Nigel on the shoulder and thanked him for his help and for his information. He extended his thanks to the group of technical specialists who were huddled together like nervous children in front of a strict teacher. The agent gestured to his own team, and they trooped off down the passenger stairs attached to the plane aboard which they had finished their night's work. A few minutes later, while his technician colleagues were excitedly chatting about all the drama, that Nigel realized the senior agent had thanked them all for their good work, but he had not offered any reassurance that the technicians would not in fact, be intensely investigated by the FBI. He hadn't given reassurances about anything.

The agents had been briefed on the report compiled by Specialist Mabel Murielez, in which she had suggested it would be carried onto the plane in hand luggage or inside a pocket. Composed almost entirely of composite materials, they would not have registered as lethal items on the airport scanners and would probably not raise suspicions among TSA agents even if spotted in luggage. The device had clearly been designed to resemble a pillbox or an asthma inhaler.

When the targeted aircraft reached a certain altitude, or possibly after a certain amount of flying time, the passenger would simply press the tiny switch. The green light would glow brighter to demonstrate the device had sent its signal. In the aeronautics enclosure, the incendiary device nestled up against the plane's fuel supply lines would burst into flame.

The planes would likely be passing over heavily populated areas of New York and other US cities, which meant that the hundreds of passengers killed on board the aircraft would be added to the many more killed on the streets below. People in vehicles and in buildings would die in their thousands when the tons of burning aircraft tumbled from the night sky. Alongside massive numbers of deaths and injuries, the disruption to normal life would be devastating.

The attack would have wiped out public confidence in airline safety. The global airline industry would suffer catastrophic revenue losses as businesspeople refused to fly to meetings and conferences. Most people would cancel or alter their holiday plans and would instead drive by road to destinations to avoid flying. It would take years to repair the damage inflicted. Just the reports of this planned attack being made public would cause a massive drop in the numbers of people flying anywhere. In the absence of an actual explosion happening, terrorism still had the ability to cause utter pandemonium.

It had been noted on the day of the thwarted attack that nineteen, the number of people caught carrying the devices, were the same number as were in the group that had carried out the attacks on September 11th, almost twenty years ago. Might this be some sort of copycat event, or even a tribute to those nineteen hijackers? Agents were assuming the Arab man was the mastermind behind all of it, which suggested he was in the role allegedly played by Osama bin Laden in 9/11. In which case, the federal agents had cause for celebration as they had wrapped up the whole operation in one day with zero casualties.

They would not have to spend years searching caves and villages in Afghanistan for this terrorist. He had been caught at ground zero of his own failed attack. And it was all thanks to a sharp eyed, mildly prejudiced Englishman that liked to count tiles and watch people, especially people that looked like movie bad guys.

Agents in JFK and at other transport hubs around the country were allowing themselves a moment of relief, and self-congratulatory back slapping at having shut down a potentially massive terrorist attack. There was, however, a suspicion of things not feeling right.

It was being reluctantly admitted to by the agents carrying out the questioning of the nineteen people arrested at JFK.

Soon after the highly publicized arrests at JFK Airport, a strange story began emerging from the questioning of the nineteen alleged attackers.

They were not terrorists. Nor were they jihadists. They were not people with a grudge against America. They had not even been aware they were part of a genuine terrorist attack. They were, in fact, American actors, hired through online interviews by an international human rights activist group.

This activist group, calling themselves Free Humans, sought to prove the fallacy of western governments' obsession with the war on terror, with special emphasis being placed on the US government as the worst culprit in a seemingly never-ending shit-show of military interventions and attempted regime changes in foreign nations. Afghanistan and Iraq were merely the two most widely talked about at this point in history. The activist group wanted to show the world there was no foundation for arresting and imprisoning foreign combatants, captured in battle, and caged in Guantanamo Bay in Cuba without proper trial.

The group also aimed to call out the logic behind much of the security procedures in place at US airports and ports. Moreover, by demonstrating that successive US governments had exaggerated the terrorist threat for years to maintain their heightened security levels and to perpetuate the myth that America needed to maintain a high military readiness, both at home and abroad, the activists hoped to persuade people to write to their representatives to force comprehensive changes to the US Patriot Act. This Act, a particularly heavy-handed piece of legislation, was originally intended for emergency use in the aftermath of the 9/11 attacks. Left active on the statute books, the draconian law later came under fire when the NSA was caught listening to private conversations.

That agency used the wording of The Patriot Act to provide legal authorization for their illegal actions. Even with these findings of illegal actions, lawmakers implemented only light public safeguards as a result. Every year since, successive US Presidents renewed the Act and Federal agencies continued to use illegal surveillance methods to spy on citizens in the US and in nations supposedly friendly to the US, through the creative use of various sections of the Patriot Act.

In the aftermath of the aborted attack on JFK, the strange story that came out of the interrogations was this:

The nineteen actors had been approached on various social media platforms by a representative of the human rights group. This person, a very nice gentleman indeed, presented himself as a lawyer, hired to gather a group of volunteers. He had decided to hire actors. He said he had gotten their details from the various casting agencies to which each of them was signed. They were all aspiring actors and had signed up to the casting agencies in the hope of being selected for film and TV work. The actors were told by this lawyer they were each going to be paid $5,000 in cash to pose as airline passengers. They would be part of a controlled test to see if electronic devices could be smuggled through what was the second most stringent airport security in the world, that of JFK Airport. The devices were harmless but would prove how easy it was to get such a thing onto a plane.

On the agreed day, they were told to be strolling around the halls of JFK Airport whereupon a man dressed in Arab attire would approach them. Each of them would be covertly presented with their personally coded device in a public area of the airport by the Arab garbed man. The actual exchange would be done in a lightly disguised manner but would be carried out in plain view of other passengers and any watching security people so that it would be a real test of the alertness of airport security and safety systems.

Ahead of the big day, the actors had to log into a private YouTube channel using their social security number to watch a short video that demonstrated how to assemble the plastic device. Their return airline tickets, with destinations chosen by the activist group, had been emailed to them a few days before the big day. Three of the actors had to apologize at that point and explain they were temporarily too broke to afford a home printer and therefore they would need their ticket sent by alternative means. Their tickets duly arrived in their mailbox two days later. The envelope did not display a return address.

Instructions were that, after each plane took off and was in the air, they were to wait one full hour and then press the button on their device. Pressing this button, they were told, would record the location of the device to prove the group had successfully entered a passenger plane after passing through US security controls while carrying a device, said device not having been discovered by TSA agents at security screening.

The successful test would later be used to argue that most, if not all, the precautions in place at international airports could and should be removed. It would be shown that the nineteen passengers had been fully screened and their baggage searched but had still managed to board a plane with the device.

Not one of the actors ever questioned the morality or legality of their actions, not one of them seemed to have suspected anything was amiss. All nineteen of them, when asked by shocked and incredulous federal agents, confirmed they had every intention of boarding their plane and at the agreed time, they were sure they would not hesitate before pressing the button. It seemed the payment of five thousand dollars had been enough to ensure the unquestioning obedience of nineteen ordinary American citizens in committing possibly the worst act of terrorism in history.

During the questioning in separate rooms, five of these actors wanted to know if they would still be allowed to fly on their designated trip, as arranged. These people had never been on a plane before and were genuinely upset they might lose this opportunity to experience air travel. In three of the five interview rooms where these questions were asked by the suspects, Federal agents had to be physically restrained by their colleagues from attacking and hurting the innocent actors. The suspects hadn't meant any harm, they just wanted to go somewhere nice on an airplane.

Federal agents revealed to the actors that there were actual bombs on each plane, and that every passenger plus a lot of other people would have been killed if those buttons had been pressed in-flight. The expressions of shock and horror on the actor's faces were considered by interrogators to be completely genuine.

Although their tax returns listed them as professional actors, they were not considered good enough at acting to fake their dismay this convincingly. Eventually, due to no federal prosecutor being able to think of a charge to place against them, every one of the actors was released without charge. Federal agents held the interview room door open and bade the gullible idiots goodbye. Although, agents let them leave while also wishing they could slap some sense into every one of them.

The actors' joy at being let go free was offset by the letters they each received just a few days later. The IRS wanted to have a chat about a certain $5,000 in cash they had been paid recently. Also, there was a tax bill for the airline tickets they had received, as the actors had been hired to act. These were to be considered employment benefits, and therefore subject to taxation. Uncle Sam would have his pound of flesh, although every other agency was unable to find grounds upon which to press charges. Unfortunately, being a gullible fool was not prosecutable as a crime.

It is, however, considered taxable employment.

Federal and state investigations into Free Humans, the activist group, proved utterly fruitless. Such groups were required by law to register their name, logo, and their area of interest, but there was no such registration for this group. It seemed, in fact, there was no such group listed anywhere. They had not previously carried out any protests; they had never taken a lawsuit against state agencies or against any private enterprise. They had never written so much as a strongly worded letter of complaint to any government agency or office. The YouTube channel on which the actors had watched the training video was gone from the internet. There had been such a channel. The link was still present, stored in the email account servers for each of the nineteen duped actors, but the other end of the link led nowhere. The head office of the internet service providers involved were each visited by Federal agents carrying letters, signed by the US Vice-President himself, asking politely for full access to their server records. This gave the IP address of the computers that had operated the website and email service for the human rights group. That was traced to a sparsely furnished rented office in a commercial center all the way up in Putnam, New York County.

Federal agents were dispatched immediately to the office of the property agent that represented the commercial center, armed with letters of authority requesting access to all records pertaining to this investigation. The realtor dealing with the commercial property in Putnam was one Jade Chan. Jade worked from a tiny office that had been built on to the side of her home. A realtor for twenty-five years, she had managed to keep her business alive and breathing through the economic crash, and the bleak years that followed, by engaging in every variation of renting, leasing, selling and sub-dividing that she could envisage.

Some days, even now, Jade suffered anxiety attacks about some of the creeps she had personally shown around deserted offices and warehouses in the hope of making a sale, or of getting a rental contract signed and a deposit paid. Jade enjoyed watching TV shows and had watched the series `Breaking Bad` on TV. The scene in that series where the main character's wife opens the doors of a rented self-storage unit to reveal stacks and stacks of dollars in illegal drug money made Jade gasp aloud. Then she broke down crying. As part of carrying on her own business, she had opened the doors of similar storage units in isolated self-storage yards and, leaving the customer with a copy of the locker key so they could place their possessions inside at their own convenience, had never gone back to check on what exactly was being stored there. After seeing that scene in Breaking Bad, she had wondered what similar enterprise she had helped facilitate by never asking for references from potential renters.

Thankfully, though, those bad days were in the past. She felt times were now better, and she was not as desperate for clients as she once had been. But now here was the federal government asking about recent customers so, clearly, the bad days hadn't gone away entirely.

Although Jade always asked for references nowadays, she was of no help to the Secret Service agents when they asked who might have rented the office in question. She explained that sort of business was all done online, just like a thousand other such transactions these days. There was a constant flow of small business start-ups requiring serviced workspace or equipment storage. More so now than ever, America had become a nation of entrepreneurs since the horribly dark days of the recent recession. She truly wanted to help these nice Federal agents, but there were no records for her to hand over. Any CCTV footage from the business center carpark, would long since have been recorded over. She offered her laptop and home PC for them to be subject to forensic examination, but the senior agent dismissed these as useless. The agent said she was fed up looking at dead-end digital trails.

She thanked Jade for her time and the dispirited agents departed, unknowingly leaving Jade with a whole load of fresh anxiety.

Had she, in fact, rented an office to those horrible airport terrorists? Were they even terrorists, or had that attack been a hoax? She had read about them being actors and was confused about all the rest of it. Moreover, she thought those agents seemed to be just as confused as Jade herself now was. The whole world seemed to be a tangled mess of paranoia and anxiety. She would have a cup of herbal tea and do her breathing exercises before bed. And she would hope to never have federal agents in her home again. Even nice agents like those today.

The man that had been recorded on airport security cameras, handing out the trigger devices while dressed in flowing Arab robes, was now in custody and refusing to speak English to investigators. Arabic speaking interrogators were en route to the custody center, but nobody held much hope that the man would be willing to answer questions even if translated, any more than he had been in English. His fingerprints had been taken and put on every possible database available to the Federal government. There was no record anywhere of the man on criminal records or on civilian records. Facial recognition searches had failed to find any previous record of him, which might suggest he was a long-term terror operative. An operative ultra-careful to avoid ever being caught on camera.

He had no passport or identification on his person and agents had no idea of his nationality. Due to the clothing, he wore, and the sound of the language in which he had spoken just a few words to agents, it was assumed the guy was from the Middle east.

Even without actual evidence of the effect that this was an Al Qaeda or ISIS plot, most of the agents and officers were quietly confident in their initial assumption. They felt sure the primary organizer, and the funding for this attack, would eventually prove to be from one of those nations where sand and oil were the first two things most associated with them.

Left unsaid by agents was that terrorist bombs were the third thing most associated with those places.

Coast to coast in America.

Gerard and Alice Nolan were invited onto several popular American talk shows. Twenty days had passed since the failed attacks in New York. For the Nolans, there had been a couple of meetings and interviews with Federal investigators, but they had largely been left alone. Their statements had been recorded; they had walked the airport hall with agents to demonstrate where they had been when Gerard Nolan had witnessed the hand-over of the device. Federal agents were now satisfied they had all the testimony and statements they needed from the English couple.

The Nolans had been placed in the Four Seasons Hotel in New York at taxpayer's expense. Agents advised but did not directly order them to stay out of the public eye. Public interest in the English couple had risen to fever pitch across the globe after detailed news of their involvement in stopping the JFK attack had leaked, and now every show on TV and radio wanted a piece of them. Gerard and Alice were naturally excited in the days leading up to their first TV appearance. But they became utterly fed-up after they appeared on the fifth and sixth and seventh show. Without complaining too much, they had endured nights of having TV make-up applied to their faces by the people in each studio to make them presentable for television. However, when this treatment was added to the indignity of being dragged from one end of the studio to the other before being pushed out into the unforgiving glare of the T. V lights, it meant the magic and illusion of television lost its sparkle for both. They struggled to hide their boredom and just about managed to remain polite, even while the host of the eighth show in fourteen days insisted yet again that they repeat the story of the JFK airport saga for yet another breathless studio audience.

Washington D.C.

In contrast to their pretense of being excited and eager during their time in numerous television studios, the Nolans did not have to pretend to be interested while attending an event in Washington D.C. on a chilly morning two weeks after their multiple TV appearances had concluded. Standing on the front lawn of the White House, they answered question from reporters. US President Edwin Stamp, with his talent for taking personal credit for everything positive that happened, announced to the world that he had "a big, a really, really big surprise, the best surprise, for the heroes, for our best friends from Britain, these great English folks, Gerry... Gerard and uh, Alice."

The airline owners had gotten together and agreed a reward for the Nolans. The President, by pulling rank on the senior executives of the U.S. airline companies, got to make the presentation on the airline's behalf. He handed over to the Nolans a specially commissioned redwood sculpture of the American eagle. The impressive bird stood on a stout tree branch, razor sharp talons gripping the wood, with wings outstretched and shining, black eyes scanning its environment for prey.

The next gift, again presented by the President, was a check for twenty-five million dollars.

After more photos were taken, the VIP group returned to the White House for a lavish lunch. Edwin Stamp and his wife both noticed Gerard Nolan didn't seem to be very affectionate or even close to his wife from what they saw in the few hours the Nolans visited them in Washington. They sat slightly apart at lunch and while President Stamp and his wife held hands while walking the grounds of the White House earlier that day, the Nolans seemed content to walk their own paths. Alice spent time chatting to her Secret Service escort, while Gerard Nolan was happy to walk in solitary silence taking in the sights and sounds of the famous residence. Occasionally, he asked a question about a statue or painting but otherwise, seemingly lost in his own thoughts. The English were supposedly trained from childhood not to show emotion Stamp had read, and although it seemed like a goddam weird way to be, he guessed Gerard Nolan had earned a bit of leeway on the whole privacy front. Anyway, it probably wasn't anybody's business but the Nolan's themselves. Each marriage has its own ways, traditions, and secrets, and it naturally seemed strange to outsiders, looking in.

early December.
New York

Three weeks later, the whirlwind of publicity surrounding the Nolans had cooled down. It was clear to see a different news story was holding the headlines now. In that day's newspaper, it had been revealed that a major Hollywood movie industry figure had been publicly accused of indecent assault of an employee of the film studio. In the days following the initial allegations, other women had since come forward to say he also had abused them. Within days of that story breaking, people's focus was on the celebrity scandal.

The Nolans woke up early in their New York hotel on the first day on which they weren't headline news and realized they had their own lives back. The reward money was safely in their bank back home in the UK and by special arrangement between the US and the UK; the money would be tax free. They discussed it over breakfast and agreed it was time to go. They packed up their belongings in the hotel room, standing side by side, neither saying much to the other, lost in their own thoughts. They were now wealthy to the point that neither would ever want for anything material again. The FBI had warned them they might now be targets of attack themselves because of having stopped the terrorist attacks at JFK. So foreign travel was probably a bad idea for the foreseeable future. Nevertheless, they were determined to return to the UK and at least attempt to live some semblance of a normal life. There were numerous phone calls and emails between the US federal agencies and their British counterparts in relation to the impending departure from the US and the arrival into the UK of this very recognizable couple.

The agents in America were aware they could not prevent the Nolans from leaving America. Federal agents felt Gerard Nolan was not convinced there was any threat to him or his wife. He did not understand quite why the American agents were worried about the couple venturing out on their own. The US agents were concerned there might not be sufficient protection afforded them by the security services in Britain. The US federal agencies had been in regular contact with their British colleagues, who had promised to sit down with the Nolans once they landed back in the UK. At that meeting, British agents would advise the Nolans of the measures the couple needed to take in their home and in their daily lives to protect themselves. If the Nolans did not take the warnings seriously, there wasn't a lot anybody could do to force them to accept police protection. Particularly when nobody even knew for sure if there was a threat or from where any potential threat might come. It was assumed there was a terrorist group or individual out in the world feeling angry at the thwarting of their attack on JFK Airport. It was further assumed that Gerard Nolan would be the specific target of a revenge attack. Gerard Nolan himself was either oblivious or unworried at the prospect of being attacked, and law enforcement agents from either side of the Atlantic Ocean couldn't convince him otherwise.

Due to the outpouring of affection and gratitude from the public toward the Nolans, a storage room in the White House basement was almost filled with gifts, soft toys and cards sent by grateful Americans. Alice Nolan asked the US First Lady if she would identify some charities that would accept the hundreds of scented candles, pens, and plush toys. Maybe the charities could sell the items to raise some funds. Alice had separately arranged with Secret Service agents in the White House to have the sacks of cards shipped to a storage box in the UK. She intended to reply to any of them that had supplied a return address.

There were hundreds of letters and cards from the passengers that had been saved by Gerard's actions that day. The full count of potential passengers showed that over three thousand people would have been killed just on the planes alone. Estimates of total loss of life ranged from fifteen to thirty thousand if the nineteen planes had come down in cities or large towns. All those people were alive today because Gerard liked to watch people when he got bored. His habit of counting tiles had helped him to be in the right place at the right moment to witness a covert exchange of an object between two men. People said obsessive compulsive behavior was a sign of mental illness, but in this case, it had saved a lot of people from certain death.

Gerard and Alice had an appointment at The White House the next day to say goodbye to President Stamp and his wife Marilyn. The photographers were out in force, but this time there were just a few reporters, mostly from the magazines, asking gentle questions about the Nolans' plans for when they got back to England. It was all a lot more restrained than the first time they had faced the press on the lawn of the White House, and it was another sign that the world was moving on from the aborted attack on JFK and by extension, from the Nolans as celebrities. There were more exciting current events to provide headlines now. And the Nolans were content to let the change happen. They had both enjoyed their time in the spotlight as celebrities and now it was just about ending.

2018 Christmas week.
London, England.

In advance of their return to England, the Nolans had reserved a suite in the Dorchester hotel in London. After checking in, they had taken a short nap to shake off the tiredness from traveling. They had then spent the remainder of their first day back in their own country, taking hot baths, ordering unwanted snacks from room service, and walking aimlessly around the spacious hotel room. They understood they were hiding from the British media and they both knew they would have to emerge sooner or later. They had heard a showbiz pundit on the morning radio news telling the nation that the Nolans had quietly returned to the UK. The rumor mill now seemed to have them appearing, by some magical process, on multiple different TV and radio shows simultaneously. Supposedly, they would be making a public appearance in London before going on to meet members of the Royal family for tea at the Palace. None of this was even remotely true, but it did demonstrate how big the appetite for an appearance by the Nolans in their own country was. The British media had been present in the US at just about every outing by the Nolans and had reported back faithfully to their British viewers and readers on any developments. It now seemed that those same media outlets wanted to repeat all of it on British soil.

The next morning, before any reporters could discover where they were staying, Gerard and

Alice went to the bank in which they had held accounts for a few years. They had made an

appointment by phone the previous day and upon arrival, the bank manager ushered them into his office, got them both seated and asked what he could do for them today. Gerard was relieved the banker had at least refrained from asking for a selfie with the heroes of the hour. They told him what they wanted to do; he asked some banker questions, and all was done as requested. They both signed the necessary documents and left as quickly as they could, in the cab they had left waiting outside with the promise of a twenty-pound tip if he stayed until they returned. The cab was still parked where they had left him, right outside the bank. Twenty-pound tippers were not an everyday occurrence and were not to be annoyed by making them walk too far from their appointment back to the car. The cabbie barely glanced at them during the trip; he was paying close attention to commentary on a cricket match on a dashboard-mounted smartphone and looked only occasionally at the road, and even less at the passengers in the back seat. He wasn't so distracted that he forgot about accepting the fare, plus the promised twenty quid tip. The instant the Nolans entered the hotel lobby and the hotel manager approached swiftly. He had a sheaf of messages from what appeared to be every newspaper and all the TV chat shows. There were also messages from a couple of celebrity lawyers that were offering to represent the Nolans in the UK. Gerard looked at Alice. They both rolled their eyes at the same time and then both burst out laughing. It seemed their secret location was no longer a secret. It was time to face the public.

It had been as if they felt they had done something wrong, the way they had been avoiding public attention in their own country. That would cease right now. They were bona fide heroes, and they would start acting like it. They phoned the showbiz lawyer, whose card was on top of the pile, and made an appointment. The difference now was that the highly paid representative of the stars would be coming to their hotel room to talk. They no longer had to go anywhere unless they chose to.

In addition to making plans to meet the press and the public, more private living arrangements were required. The Dorchester Hotel was up there with the very best, but it had now served its purpose as a hiding place. The Nolans decided to remain there for the holiday period, they would enjoy Christmas at the Hotel. Real changes in circumstances would be made in the New Year.

Queens, New York.
January 2019

Several days after the Nolans had visited with their friendly bank manager, Port Authority police officer John Corcoran was at home thousands of miles away in Queens. The doorbell interrupted his breakfast and when he opened his front door; the mailman informed John he had to sign for a letter as somebody had sent it by tracked mail from outside the US. John signed for the letter, thanked the mailman and closed the front door. He reflected sadly that until recently he would have been warned of a visitor's approach by the barking and growling of Roger, his Irish setter. John had gotten him as a puppy years ago from a friend and had raised and trained the gentle natured dog. The only thing he could never discipline Roger out of was his habit of going berserk at the mailman.

In recent years, the dog had slowed down and had become a little less hostile at the rattle of the mailbox outside. Roger had finally gotten too old and sick and was in pain just moving around. The compassionate thing to do was clear to see, but John had been putting off the dreaded trip to the vets to have his pal put to sleep. John had gotten as far as gathering a couple of leaflets from local vets to try to choose a vet that looked friendly and caring. The pamphlets advertising vets' services had been on his kitchen table for a couple of weeks, silently nagging at him to do the right thing. Meanwhile, Roger got older and took longer and longer to raise himself from his basket in the sunny spot on the kitchen floor each morning when John came down for breakfast. Now, though, there were no longer any pamphlets from the vet's practices. Roger had died in his sleep one night with no assistance from a vet's drug. John came down one morning and there was zero reaction from Roger to his owner's presence in the kitchen. John, fearing the worst but not yet willing to touch the dog to get confirmation, went outside and, leaving the front door open, he rattled the slot on his mailbox. He rattled it again. There was no sound or movement from inside the house, and John knew his old pal had finally passed away. Roger had never been able to stop himself from reacting to the letterbox.

John returned to the kitchen table with the letter from overseas. He managed to avoid smearing marmalade on the letter when he opened it while also trying to continue eating breakfast. The heading said it was from a bank in the UK and his immediate reaction was to throw it in the small bin that stood in the corner of his small kitchen. He assumed the letter was a scam, as he had never done any banking business in the UK. Then, realizing the letter had come by signed mail, he figured he might at least check it out first. He called the number provided on the letter and found himself talking to an English accented gentleman.

The banker, George by name, told John that a substantial sum had been left with the bank for transfer to the account of John Corcoran. They only needed his bank details, and the money would be sent immediately. John, recalling his earlier suspicion that the letter was a scam, told George he would check with his own bank and then would get back to George with details of his account.

Following the phone call, John was in the shower trying to remember if he had wealthy relatives in Europe that might suddenly have remembered their uncle/nephew or cousin in America. Maybe an old friend of his Father had died and bequeathed a few thousand dollars to him. His phone rang while he was in the shower and he stumbled out into the hall, dripping water. He answered the phone to hear a voice say his name. The voice had an English accent like the man from the bank, but this voice seemed familiar. 'Officer John Corcoran? Long time no speak, eh? It's Gerard Nolan here. How are you John?

John was surprised to hear this man on the phone, as he had assumed the Nolans had forgotten

all about him the instant he was no longer needed as their protection officer in New York. John

had remained by the Nolans' side from the moment Rachel Connor from Homeland Security

Agent had instructed him to protect them as witnesses. Then the usual alphabet soup of Federal

Agencies had arrived in force at the airport. The feds had immediately gotten busy taking over

the operation from the Port Authority PD and the TSA. US marshals had spirited the Nolans

away to protective custody to ensure they were kept safe until all suspects were apprehended.

John had heard through unofficial channels the protective custody arrangements had only lasted

a few hours. That as soon as the truth of the attack on JFK was discovered, and it was realized

that there weren't several actual terrorists running around New York, the Nolans had been

released from the custody of the marshals and left to their own devices, albeit in the luxury of a

Four Seasons hotel.

After the Nolans had departed with their Marshal escort, John Corcoran was left standing alone in the security office because the agents had gone downstairs to be part of the arrest of the suspected terrorists. After a few minutes alone, he simply left to re-join his police unit. His colleagues in the police department spent a few minutes clapping him on the back and congratulating him on his good work and then normal routine resumed. John didn't admit to colleagues that it was Gerard Nolan who had been the man with all the right ideas, that it was Nolan who was calm in the face of an impending terrorist attack.

John tried not to feel jealous or left out while he watched on TV as the Nolans were feted on the shows and while they went hobnobbing with the President of the US and the White House crowd. John reminded himself he had just been a cop doing his job, and he still had that job to do. Time passed and Roger the dog died, and other things happened as things always do, and John had gotten on with his life and his job.

Months later and all the fuss had died down and mostly John had forgotten how he had been at the center of a major incident. Now here was Gerard Nolan, calling personally to let him know that John would be receiving a letter from an English bank if he hadn't already received it. It was in relation to John's share of the reward money which had been given to thank them for stopping the attack at JFK. Gerard apologized for not being in touch earlier, but time had just flown by, and everything had been so crazy with all the television shows etc. John told Gerard not to worry about it; he was just doing his job. That English accent, coming through a transatlantic phone cable, seemed curiously flat in John's ear when it said, 'it's your share of the reward, you deserve it John; you did far more than just your job. I couldn't have done any of it without you. John. Anyway, I've sent you five million dollars. Thanks again John'.

Police officer John Corcoran, very soon to be retired due to the unexpected lodgment to his bank account, almost fell over in the hallway at hearing the amount. He tried a halfhearted refusal of the money that sounded false and forced even to his own ears, but Nolan was adamant that John was to accept it in its entirety. He and Gerard exchanged further pleasantries and promises to keep in touch, and then hung up. Later that day, having calmed down and thought calmly about his new situation, John decided he agreed with Gerard Nolan. He did deserve the money. Out of his head went any thoughts of a career in administration in the police force or the fire service and instead John started thinking he needed a bigger house and a new car. He would buy a house that came with a bit of land around it out in a rural area. He had a sudden longing to visit the dog pound and simply collect every rescue dog in the place. Since Roger the Irish setter had died, John had felt a need for some company, especially in the evenings. A few dogs would be a fine addition to his new garden. He did deserve it; he was quickly coming around to believing that.

After the JFK attack.
America.
2019.

In the aftermath of the thwarted attacks in JFK airport, US President Edwin Stamp made
allegations and threats. He tried to get the US Air Force to drop bombs on Iran, Russia and,
bizarrely, Afghanistan and Iraq. At the suggestion of bombing Afghanistan and Iraq, the Joint
Chiefs informed him they would rather prefer to get American troops and personnel out before
`bombing those shitholes back to the stone age`.

They simply ignored his order to attack Iran and Russia. It would be illegal and stupid, so they felt safe enough in not doing it. Stamp went on talk shows and on radio shows where he blamed everybody from Syrian rebels to the Iranian President. In his paranoia, he included the Russians in a vague group of nations who, being jealous of American brilliance and freedom, had conspired to damage the greatest US city and murder American citizens. He blamed former President Barack Obama for letting in too many illegal immigrants and he blamed the Democrats for being soft on crime. Without exception, the accused persons, nations, and institutions maintained a dignified silence as the ranting continued on Twitter and in rambling, unscripted press briefings at the White House. It was generally felt that to even retort to anything said by this President was to invite more crazy insults and angry accusations. Let him blow off steam and he might soon shut up.

All the blustering was described by somebody as being like the final sting of a dying wasp. It was widely assumed that President

Edwin Stamp would not be in the big chair for much longer. He had misused the Office of the President of the United States to enrich various family members and to boost profits in his numerous companies and businesses, most of which had been bordering on failures before Stamp got elected. He had used the Secret Service to investigate some of his business rivals by starting rumors of false billing while these companies were working on federal government contracts. When he got the reports from those investigations, he then leaked any financial problems being suffered by those businesses to journalists he knew wouldn't inquire too deeply into the truth of the leaks. Even the private marital difficulties of the most senior people in his competitors were leaked to his favorite news outlets in exchange for favorable reporting of Stamps Presidency. His adult children made commercial deals for their fashion products, and they boosted business in their consultancy services using the Presidential Seal to attract and persuade high net worth individuals to invest in the ventures.

In at least two cases under investigation by two separate States Attorneys, a major investor in the companies owned by Stamps kids was found to be an Eastern European trafficker of children and women to the sex trade in America. Another man that had put large sums of cash into the warehousing and logistics company owned by President Stamps' son-in-law was an illegal weapons dealer known to have sold guns to insurgent groups in Syria, Iraq, and Somalia. Guns supplied by this man were suspected to have been used to kill American and British soldiers.

In his presidential election campaign, Edwin Stamp had repeatedly used the slogan, 'we are going to drain the swamp' in a reference to alleged corruption and cronyism in Washington DC. DC itself is incorrectly thought to have been built on reclaimed swampland. From the day Stamp seated himself behind the desk in the Oval Office, he constantly had his eye on deals that only served to enrich his own family and friends. He had created his own swamp of corruption and nepotism and it was believed the murky waters would very soon rise and overwhelm the entire Stamp Presidency, along with his family's businesses. It seemed only a matter of time before impeachment proceedings and criminal investigations, dragging on now for almost two years, caught up with him and his cronies. There was simply too much wrongdoing and unethical behavior for people to ignore it any longer.

Near the end of his first term in office, Stamp was working hard preparing for the presidential elections, fighting to win a second term. The JFK attack had occurred when Stamp had been in office for two years, a full twelve months before the current election campaign began. Stamp might have benefitted electorally from being President on the day of the attack as people might have given him credit for his handling of the crisis. Unfortunately, Edwin Stamp, having been in office for two years at that point, was well and truly on the way to being dumped by voters. That was if he wasn't first impeached by prosecutors.

But just when most observers had become convinced this inept President was finished in office, everything abruptly changed. The supposedly lame-duck President, considered by most commentators to be the worst President in living memory, somehow won a second term and remained in the oval office.

Just when all seemed lost in the polls, the President received a massive boost during the election campaign that swung more than enough votes in his favor. His instinctive response to a police brutality and murder case brought a massive surge in popularity from the black community. It happened like this.

A major criminal case against three Los Angeles police officers that were accused of murdering two black teenagers was before the courts. The officers were white and two of them were further accused of threatening the teenagers' friends and neighbors at gunpoint at the scene of the shooting to frighten potential witnesses away from the crime scene. The suspicion was so the officers could place a gun on the person of one of the victims so the cops could claim self-defense as the reason for shooting civilians. The incident had taken place in gang dominated area in the Crenshaw district. The area was almost always in a state of tension due to crime levels being high. And there was very little action by city authorities or by the federal government to improve the situation.

White cops throwing their weight around were mostly ignored by the street kids as just more

background noise. White cops shooting young Black males to death right there in the

neighborhood was another thing altogether. The place was about to explode. The case was a

tipping point in race relations in the city, even more so than the Rodney King incident or any of

the numerous incidents of police brutality. This was simply one incident too far and people had

enough. The black community was poised to go on the rampage if the charges filed by

prosecutors were anything less than first-degree murder against the officers that had pulled the

trigger. There were multiple calls for a series of strikes in all industries. Community activists were

all over social media and on the streets, encouraging people to commit acts of civil disobedience.

People were warned to make sure to keep any such acts completely peaceful and non-violent.

The black community reached out to the Latino and Asian communities, asking them to show

solidarity by agreeing upon a mutually agreed day where all businesses owned by people from minority communities would close. Street protests and marches began in cities, towns, and

housing areas all over America. As tension rose, more and more white people began joining the

protests to show support for their Black neighbors. There were mass walk-outs from commercial

premises, from schools and finally from Federal buildings as government employees joined the

marches, demanding real police reform.

Before the case could even be listed in court and before the situation could degenerate into actual violence on the streets, President Stamp came sweeping up Crenshaw Boulevard in the usual presidential cavalcade. When the large black SUVs full of armed Secret Service agents stopped outside Crenshaw High School, locals thought it was a raid of some sort. When the massive, highly recognizable figure of President Edwin Stamp clambered out of the third vehicle in the parked line of SUVs, locals thought it was a hallucination. None of them could recall a sitting President visiting this part of town before. Not a white President anyway.

White House staff had called ahead and arranged for President Stamp to meet with black community leaders outside the high school. When local representatives arrived, there was already a sizeable crowd of black, Latino, and Asian men and women of all ages. They simply stood and stared at the Secret Service agents, who in turn stood at parade rest, and stared right back.

The families of the two murdered young men were brought to the gathering in minivans. They got there just as their community representatives pulled up in their own cars. Secret Service tried to get agents to stand between the locals and the President to protect their boss, but Stamp ordered the agents to stand aside. Stamp stepped into the gap and, spreading his arms, gathered the two grieving mothers into his embrace. Concluding the hug, he then turned to the fathers of the murdered men and offered his hand to them. Both men stepped forward without hesitation and shook hands with him. Secret Service agents breathed sighs of relief and, just like that, the crowd relaxed, and conversations began.

During an exhausting period of eight hours, part of which he spent in church praying alongside the family and friends of the murdered boys, President Stamp transformed his Presidency from dead in the water, to fighting fit. Most of that fateful day was spent walking and talking with black community leaders in open dialogue on the streets. Presidential advisers, when earlier asked about the feasibility of Stamp doing this walk about, warned that Stamp would be shot if he went out on these streets. The Secret Service tried to refuse to take responsibility for safety, and President Stamps' reply was that he was more afraid of losing the election than losing his life.

President Stamp now stood on the street alongside leaders of the black community to address the large crowd that gathered swiftly as word spread that the President was in the neighborhood. Others had been following the events of the day from their apartment windows and from building doorways. The President was unaware that the community leaders standing beside him had spent tense minutes pleading with the more reactionary members of the neighborhood, not to attack or verbally abuse the President. At the point where the meeting on the street began, the local representatives still weren't completely sure there wouldn't be a violent incident right there.

President Stamp asked the crowd to accept his apology for what his police officers had done. He told them he felt ashamed to be President of America while these things were still happening in this great nation, in the twenty-first century. It was not going to be allowed to continue any longer. Big changes were going to be made right away.

He produced a sheet of paper from his jacket pocket and handing it over to a senior member of the community delegation. He announced it to be a signed Presidential order mandating immediate reform of all police departments across the nation. Any police department that failed to agree to all or even any of the reforms would be excluded from Federal funding with immediate effect and federal agents would be sent to take over the department. Officers would from now on have to wear an active body camera and it would be made a criminal offence to either turn off the camera or to go out on patrol without a functioning camera unit. All officers would be required to undergo compulsory retraining courses at the Federal Law Enforcement Training Center to teach them how to interact respectfully and correctly with members of the public, regardless of the person's color or religious beliefs. There would be new, harsher automatic penalties for any officer found to be mistreating people of any color while arresting or questioning them. Stop and search activity carried out by white patrol officers of black males was hereby banned.

The official document from which Stamp had copied these reforms had been contained in a Police reform paper under consideration by the Obama administration years before. It had not been implemented at the time and was forgotten by Democrats after they lost the election to Stamp. White House Chief of Staff Dwayne Fort had seen it mentioned in an internal memo left on a computer after Stamp had won the first election nearly five years ago. Obamas people had by then left their offices in the White House and some had not fully cleared their computers as instructed. Fort had searched the filing system for the actual paper, eventually finding it in the archives room.

Dwayne Fort had brought it to a meeting in the Oval Office at which the President and some of his government cabinet were present. Fort had read out the list of reforms as a joke, pretending he genuinely wanted President Stamp to enforce the changes in America's police forces. They had all enjoyed a good laugh over some of the items on the list. The list had been left on the

President's table among the half empty coffee cups and plates of sandwiches once the meeting

had ended. Dwayne Fort forgot all about it afterward. If he thought about the list at all, he

simply assumed it went into the secure paper shredder along with any other scribblings and

doodles that such meetings inevitably produced.

But now, months later, here was President Stamp handing over that same list of liberal reforms to black leaders to appease them, and to show them that their President was standing with them currently. Dwayne Fort had been in Washington, DC, politics for a long time in various roles. He had seen and been involved in some underhanded political maneuvers and had witnessed some of the most cunning operators in action during his long service. This was a new level of sneaky right here, though. Edwin Stamp, or somebody close to him, had clearly seen a future opportunity in the oval office that day and had picked up the reform bill from the table and kept it. That hoped-for opportunity had now presented itself in a situation that was perfect for President Stamp. To excuse the very liberal tone of the Police reform bill he had just announced, Stamp would claim he was being forced to act decisively due to the persistently racist actions of certain police officers. He had to save the city of Los Angeles from the destruction about to be brought down upon it by understandably angry black people. The Police Unions would have no choice but to accept the reforms, or they would stand accused of supporting racist, murdering officers.

Stamp's large contingent of white male supporters consisted mainly of gun carrying, truck driving, freedom lovers, and they hated the police almost as much as they hated black people. So there probably wouldn't be much of a backlash from them. His white

Christian voter base would have to accept this novel situation as the direct result of police officers ignoring the clear signs of cultural change that had been showing for years. There were only so many police-involved murders that the public could ignore before decent people demanded change.

The black community was astonished at the level of reform contained in the documents. And they were impressed that this white President had been willing to make a personal visit to appeal to them. Instead of going on television as previous Presidents might have done, he had come down to the street and walked with them, asking questions about how bad things were in the housing projects and about what was needed to improve things.

The President suggested getting the Vice-President to set up a task force with a view of trying to get a grip on the unemployment and crime that plagued these poverty-stricken areas. He asked the community leaders to forward a few names from their own neighborhoods that could be part of a committee to bring local knowledge to the task force. There would be Federal money and resources brought to bear on the issues. Vice-President Lance Worth would hate having to sit with black civilians and talk to criminals and unemployed types, but Stamp couldn't care less what Worth liked or disliked. He had been chosen as Stamps running mate mostly due to his high standing with White Christian voters, those who held permanent positions on the moral high ground. Stamp had too many divorces and scandals in his life for the evangelicals to accept him easily. Lance Worth, with his church deacon hairstyle and perfectly respectable lifestyle, smoothed those troubled waters nicely. He sure was a pain in the ass to have around, though. Which was why Stamp had zero hesitation giving Worth all the crappy assignments. Any time the Vice President complained at yet another posting to another committee or task force, Stamp invariably replied, "you have to ask, what would Jesus do?".

Presidential approval ratings shot up in the voter polls following his day out in South LA and he rose even higher in the estimation of black communities nationwide later that week when he made a controversial comment on television. After he was asked a direct question by a TV reporter about the criminal charges facing the three police officers involved in the killing of the black men, The President stated on camera that he believed the three police officers had indeed committed the crime of which they stood accused. He said he hoped the judge and prosecutors would have great success in the trial and he prayed the jury would do their duty and that the officers would be punished to the full extent of the law.

There followed an immediate backlash from members of the judiciary and from legally astute commentators and television pundits. They said the President was interfering in an ongoing court case; he was placing undue pressure on a jury that had not even been sworn in at that point. Police Union representatives, already beside themselves with anger and indignation over President Stamps Police reform bill, were invited on to news programs and talk shows to complain about the comments made by the President. By stating that these police officers were guilty of murder even before any court had reached a verdict, Stamp had put that guilt on all police officers. The representatives said the President had disrespected all their members. They demanded the President withdraw his comments and apologize. They threatened to call for a vote on strike action by all police officers that they swore would cripple the nation, even more than the protests and store closures brought about by black activists, had done earlier.

Their combative attitude backfired on the police union reps spectacularly just a few hours later. The President was asked later that day at a news briefing if he had lost respect for all police officers like the union reps were accusing. He glared directly at the camera and asked, `are these union reps suggesting I should respect cops that kill unarmed teenagers on the street? I respect all decent law-abiding citizens, and I have the greatest respect and admiration for hardworking, honest police officers. However, if you break the law, if you kill unarmed kids, as these three officers clearly did, I have nothing but contempt for you. And I've nothing but contempt for the people that might defend those illegal actions`.

On the question of strike action by police officers, the President told the reporters that if the police unions organized industrial action in police departments, he would bring in the National Guard or the FBI or the US Marine Corps or whatever was necessary to perform patrol duties on American streets. He moved away from the microphone, and then turning back with a nasty grin on his face, he concluded the press conference by saying, `at least with the National Guard on the streets instead of racist cops, there will be less black folk getting harassed, hurt, and killed`.

These were the most coherent and presidential statements anyone heard being uttered by this President since he had been elected. It was unconstitutional and quite possibly illegal for him to have made the comments in public, but this President had never balked at ignoring constitutional restraints before. The black, Hispanic, and ethnic minority community leaders across America thanked him publicly for his comments and for his support. Those communities thanked him again the following November, by voting for him in their millions.

The President's white Christian voter base was said to be the most fervently racist people in America. They now found themselves at Edwin Stamp rallies singing and cheering alongside people of color that were holding aloft, #BlackLivesMatter placards. To support Stamp meant being in favor of harsh penalties for racist cops, and this caused a debate among certain right-wing groups as to how to marry the two viewpoints. A lot of them were not sure if they should be supporting a President that had gone after white cops for killing black people. But they also wanted to support a President that intended to Make America Great Again. They identified as Americans, so this slogan made them feel like they could be great too. In the end, they decided to ignore the conundrum and simply showed up in huge numbers to help get their President across the finish line with a comfortable winning margin.

Local election candidates from ethnic minority communities found their own campaign meetings drastically reduced in attendance figures. Their supporters were now entirely made up of only their most loyal friends and family. Their regular crowds of minority voters were now at Stamp rallies elsewhere. The candidates suspected that even the dwindling group of supportive relatives that remained probably also wished to be at a Stamp rally, but family ties bound them to show support to their relatives.

Political confusion reigned supreme, and the media loved it even while not being able to understand exactly how the political landscape had been so completely transformed.

In the first election campaign four years earlier, Edwin Stamp had proven himself incredibly difficult to beat in an election. Once he had won the election and was President, he showed it to be near impossible to pin criminal charges on him, never mind getting him into an impeachment.

He was now showing the world a different side to his nature. In the eighties and nineties, before Stamp had entered politics, he had a reputation for being vicious in property deals and in business negotiations. He kept opponents off balance by making personal comments about them and their families. He regularly hired private investigators to dig up any sleaze or financial issues on the part of someone with whom he was in competition on a land purchase or other deal. Then he would threaten to reveal the information to whoever would result in the worst damage.

He had used similar tactics in the first election campaign to bully his way to the top of the Republican party's list of presidential nominees. Once there, he bullied party donors to give bigger and bigger sums of money to his campaign. There were suspicions among Republican party managers that a lot of the contributions had gone into Stamps personal account, never to be seen again. Now that he had been forced to battle for re-election, those street fighting instincts had surfaced once again. The big issue of the day was the three police officers and Stamp had gone unhesitatingly into that melee, fists and feet flying. And once again, it was exactly what the American people wanted to see from their political leaders.

Senior Democrat party members were calling for a Congressional Ethics investigation into

President Stamp's comments about the police officers. Unfortunately for those hoping to nail

the man to a wall, there were already too many inquiries, Senate hearings and Grand Jury

investigations into the various allegations made against Stamp and his family during his first four

years in office. These latest accusations simply got swallowed up in the noise. Millions of words

had been written following the first election he had won four years ago about how Edwin Stamp

had torn up the handbook on how to run for President and how he had succeeded regardless of

the fact he had zero political experience. This latest episode only proved how much of a survivor

he truly was. He won the election and swept back into office. His supporters were overjoyed. His

detractors feared he would be even more insufferable than before.

Four months after the presidential elections, in a Los Angeles courtroom, all three police officers were found guilty and were each sentenced to twenty-five years in prison. The President immediately went on Twitter, where he thanked the judge and jury for their common sense and decency. He said he had held full confidence in them all along, he had simply felt they might have needed a little Presidential nudge. As was by now customary, the Presidential tweet contained more than a few thumbs-up emojis, smiley faces and American flags.

All the public goodwill towards their President was in the past, he had run out of political credit with the American people. He was now over a year into his second term and support for the Stamp Presidency was sinking fast. Stamp himself was once again under the spotlight of suspicion and accusation over his family businesses and his personal life. A lot of American voters were now regretting their decision to vote him back into office.

The aftermath of JFK attack.
Zero leads.

Months had passed since the failed attack at JFK airport. To this day, no organization had claimed responsibility for the attempted bombing of nineteen planes. Monitoring by the NSA failed to detect any online chatter among the usual groups, with not even a hint of the source of the attack. The Secret Service and every federal agency had spent their entire annual budgets in a matter of months on all the overtime that had been worked by scores of agents. Hundreds of small towns across America had found their once sleepy streets swarming with investigators sent from FBI field offices. With dozens of agents trawling through the records held on local militia groups or on anybody that had ever expressed anti-Government sentiment, quite a few people with shady pasts abruptly quit their jobs and headed for the hills. Old hunting cabins in un-mapped locations out in the dense woods, on Native American Reservation land, on unincorporated land or indeed anywhere the Feds could not legally or easily intrude became very desirable places to spend a week or two to avoid the awkward questions being asked by bored agents.

White supremacist Americans had heard about the Arab robed man involved at JFK, so the target for their hate was anybody that looked 'foreign'. With so-called ordinary Americans being hounded and questioned by the Federal agencies, the white power thugs present in many towns passed on the harassment to anyone that was not white and clean-shaven. Any male that looked even remotely Middle Eastern was a target for abuse and violence. Mosques and Islamic schools were daubed with graffiti. Muslim men and women were chased and verbally abused with angry locals demanding they get out, calling them terrorists, and telling them America is Christian and white. In the absence of real information, America's white extremists found it a simple matter to foment trouble for the Asian and Middle Eastern communities. Normally moderate Americans became just a bit more hardline in their outlook towards Arabic and Asian minorities. Membership applications for supremacist groups increased overnight.

The Federal government paid for ad space and got Hollywood actors to air plaintive appeals on TV and in newspapers trying to convince America that it had not been proven that anyone of Middle Eastern or Arabic or Asian ethnicity was responsible for the JFK attack. They repeated earlier appeals for any information as to the identity of those responsible. They got zero useful information.

Months had passed and not a single solid lead or clue was found as to who the sponsor and organizer had been. International law enforcement and anti-terrorist police units had tried to assist its American counterparts by picking up hundreds of suspected extremists in cities and towns across Europe and Asia for questioning. In all the transcripts of interviews, in thousands of minutes of voice recordings from aggressive questioning of bearded and robed men, there had been nothing of any worth to investigators. The men being questioned had refused to answer the questions in any meaningful way. Many of them simply sang songs and recited poetry in Arabic to avoid speaking to the authorities. Across Europe and the world, there was little or no cooperation with authorities, even in cases where there was no risk to the prisoners of incriminating themselves. It was as if there was a worldwide agreement among radical religious groups and militant political activists not to allow themselves to be dragged into any possible connection to whoever had attacked the American airport.

Was that person so scary or so powerful that they had frightened every one of the usual suspects

into keeping silent? Or had the JFK operation been planned and nearly executed by a group that had maintained the tightest operational security that investigators had ever seen? It was unheard

of for there not to be some level of discussion or at least rumor and gossip among radical

operatives in online chatrooms about an operation as massive as the JFK incident.

British police were an integral part of the international effort to track down the perpetrators of the New York attack. The UK, along with other key nations that held close ties with the US, had received detailed questionnaires compiled by specialist agents from the C.I.A. and the F.B.I. These questions were designed to be identical in every country, even after translation into the local language. The idea was that the completed question forms, when returned to the US for processing, would highlight possible connections between suspects in different countries or places.

For example, a detainee in custody in Paris or London or Rome might admit during interrogation that he had met a certain man in a refugee camp in Gaza a couple of years ago. The detainee would admit that this man was known to be prominent in certain radical circles. He had one blue eye and one brown eye, or it might be that this man was missing part of his left ear. This man, distinctly marked or scarred, was known to have contact with Hezbollah commanders, or perhaps it was that he knew how to contact ISIS recruiters in Syria. If a man wanted to join a fighting group in one of the many areas of conflict, this man might make introductions if he felt you were worthy of his time.

Later, in a different interrogation, another detainee in a different country might also mention

meeting a man with the same description with the odd colored eyes or the same damaged ear.

When those two descriptions were fed into the data base and the matching facts were noted, a network of possible contacts of this man with the odd eyes would emerge. The significant man would be given a codename and then added to a capture list for circulation to CIA and Military Intelligence bases in Syria, Iraq, and Afghanistan.

The process of collating linked information to make connections and to gather all the separate parts of a network had been in use for years, but it became even easier with the world-wide-web and the global inter-connectedness that came from everybody wanting instant messaging capabilities. It was the real-world embodiment of the legislation in the American Patriot Act in that the replies to questions asked of one person might link that person to other, seemingly unconnected persons. Then the linked persons would be brought in for questioning simply because they were connected to the original suspect. In investigations where civilians were involved, whole networks of individuals that shared an interest, for example, a book club or a niche hobby group, might find themselves the subject of intense investigation simply due to a computer algorithm picking up keywords in their emails or text messages.

In the case of the international hunt for the JFK attackers, the investigations resulting from the questionnaires would be carried out by US federal agencies even when the subject of the inquiry was not ordinarily resident in the US. Library records, home and business email, bank accounts, internet search history and travel records would all form part of the inquiries. Each detail and link were followed to its conclusion. In some cases, people found to be innocent were never cleared from the system and found themselves, years later, being stopped at international airports because their name showed on a no-fly list. In the case of the attack at JFK airport, the saturation of civilian life by this law enforcement activity resulted in almost zero reward to investigators. For months, no credible information was gleaned from any source anywhere in the world.

Birmingham, England.

But then, there was one break in the wall of silence. In a police interview room in Birmingham,

England, there was a single spark of human-to-human communication in all that information

darkness. An English detective had gotten a suspect to talk freely, by the simple method of just

chatting to the prisoner. Instantly, American agents were rushing to that city, eager to fan the

spark into flame.

Birmingham, England.

In the months prior to finding himself in an interview room with Ibrahim Mahmoud, Nicholas King had been promoted from Police Constable to Detective Constable. He was still full of excitement at being involved in real questioning sessions and was almost childishly eager to show his skills. He had spent three years on foot and vehicle patrol in the estates around the area and was well versed in the history of the more notorious local characters. He met and befriended those that half-seriously claimed to be descended from criminal gangs such as the infamous Sabini gang, the Peaky Blinders and half a dozen other such outfits.

The local history of illegal enterprise was one that was repeated in most major population centers in the UK. In the years following World War One, Birmingham crime gangs thrived for many of the same reasons as those in places like Liverpool and Manchester. Successive British governments doing very little to help lift people out of poverty, and a badly funded police force that was happy to be paid by criminals to look the other way. The network of canals and rivers used for nationwide transport of goods was perfectly suited to being taken under the control of ruthless gangs of river gypsies. Unofficial toll collection and illegal protection rackets charged on the passage of commercial freight were major sources of income for many criminal gangs.

One incident had helped bring Nicholas to the attention of his senior officers. On a hot day the previous Summer, Nicholas had gone after a handbag snatcher, and had chased the guy through the surrounds of a flats complex. Nicholas had lost his uniform helmet in the chase, which ended with the mugger being knocked to the ground by three teenager who kept him grounded, until Nicholas arrived on the scene, gasping for breath, to make the arrest.

Nicholas thanked the laughing teenagers and marched the mugger into the station to book him in for the crime. He then reported that he had lost his police helmet. The smirking desk officer reached under the counter and handed over a scuffed and dusty police helmet. Two twelve-year-old boys, seeing Nicholas's name written inside the rim, had delivered the helmet on their bicycles just a few minutes before Nicholas had arrived back. For weeks afterward, as Nicholas was leaving to go on patrol or to go home after his shift, officers in the building would shout, ` got your helmet? `

But it was not lost on his superiors that kids from one of the toughest estates had known and liked Nicholas enough to return his helmet instead of using it as a toilet, as would be the case usually. Community rapport was always very popular with the politically minded commanding officers.

King was granted his desired move to the detective unit. He asked to be placed into the serious crimes division, to learn about the investigation of murders. Previously, as a uniformed officer, Nicholas had been first on scene at several gunshot murders and knife crimes. Often the result of a feud between competing drug gangs, the victims were killed and dumped in and around the canals and fields in the area. Nicholas would get a call from a local resident out walking their dog and had come across the pitiful remains of some poor drug addict that had gotten into debt with a dealer. Or a gang's drugs storage facility would get raided by the police, and there would be a spate of killings, as the gang purged their ranks of members, they suspected of being a police informant.

At his first crime scene as a detective, he was already a seasoned veteran of such settings and no longer felt an urge to vomit all over the place on seeing a gunshot wound up close. As the inexperienced investigator, he got paired with a veteran detective that had transferred in from another district. Mike Farrell, Nicholas' new mentor and supervisor, had been a detective for twelve years in Manchester. Mike had recently gotten divorced, and the main driver of the split was his wife finding a new man that wasn't a police detective and was therefore actually present in her life.

Mike's daughter Linda, while avoiding taking sides in the bitter rows that followed her parents' divorce, had offered her father a room in her home in Bickenhill in Birmingham. She and her husband owned and operated successful restaurants located in Birmingham airport and in the National Exhibition Center. They had bought a large house in the suburbs with the idea that it would be good for entertaining. They were too busy in the restaurants to host a dinner party in their home, but it remained an option. So, they had more than enough spare rooms to allow Linda's father to come live with them. So, Mike put in a request to transfer from Manchester to Birmingham.

Once settled in Birmingham, he got teamed with the rookie detective Nicholas King. He might have been inexperienced as a detective, but Nicholas King proved to be a solid resource about the local crime scene. Mike Farrell was able to take advantage of Nicholas' local knowledge and Nicholas picked up a lot of the methods and shortcuts used by the experienced detective. Mike Farrell was a good instructor, but he was somewhat jaded as a police officer. He tended to leave a lot of the tedium of police work to his eager colleague, justifying it as good training for the new detective working alongside him. Nicholas King enjoyed the freedom it gave him.

When the attacks on JFK in New York took place, it became a matter of all hands-on deck in every police force in the western world. Detectives were told to prioritize any leads on the JFK attack over any non-urgent investigation. Detectives were to familiarize themselves with the incident in the US. They were to read and learn the questions contained in the files sent by the American agents. All detective rosters now included a couple of shifts each week in which each detective team was assigned to questioning incoming suspects for questioning. These interrogation sessions became the one part of their job, more than any other aspect, that all cops dreaded due to its mind-numbing monotony. The same questions, asked in the same way of almost identical people every time. And the suspects answered with denials, verbal abuse, grunts or with a silence that could not be pierced. And the cops got no information. And none. And still, none.

Then one day, uniformed officers, while working from a list of addresses doing routine door-to-door enquiries, asking as to the location of the named tenant at each address, encountered Ibrahim Mahmoud. And from Ibrahim, came a break in the monotony, in the silence of the questioning of suspects.

Nicholas King and Mike Farrell were the detectives on duty when Ibrahim Mahmoud was brought in. Mike was the senior detective in the partnership, and as such, he had the authority to decide it was beneath his dignity to be reading prepared questions and jotting down the prisoners' replies. He handed over seniority to Nicholas and told him to enjoy being the lead investigator in the interrogation of poor, uneducated Ibrahim Mahmoud.

When Ibrahim was led into the interview room by the custody officer, Mike was playing games on his phone with an earphone stuck in one ear. Nicholas King, by contrast, was sitting up straight in his chair, shuffling papers and folders around the interview desk and doing his best to look as if he belonged there.

Ibrahim, with a custody officer holding his arm, was helped to the seat directly facing Nicholas King. Detective King glanced across at the prisoner, shuffled his papers one final time, cleared his throat, and began asking the questions as he had been instructed.

After listening to Nicholas asking the first few questions from the long list, Mike Farrell felt Nicholas King was too nice, too friendly to be an effective interrogator. He was showing far too much sympathy for Ibrahim's situation, and to his complaints of being roughly handled by police officers. Because Mike did not believe that English police detectives should be wasting their time doing this menial administrative task on behalf of the US government, he was not especially willing to get involved, so he let Nicholas work his way through the list. The inattention from Mike allowed Ibrahim to interact directly with Nicholas and soon a friendship of sorts was developing between the younger men in the interview room.

Ibrahim had been dealing with authority figures for years, usually armed Yemeni military or police that automatically assumed that because he was from the camps out in the bad lands, then it followed, he was a criminal. He learned to appear more vulnerable than he was, and he became quite adept at appealing to government officials to gain some benefit for him and his mother.

Nicholas King was conditioned by long exposure to the street kids and the poor families in the council estates he patrolled as a young, impressionable police officer. He suffered from an overabundance of generosity of spirit when he came across a charity case. He had given his own money to people that came to him with hard luck stories on the streets, and he found it difficult to refuse help to anybody that asked him. Ibrahim recognized this softness in Nicholas King and appealed to it. A lot of what came later, both good and bad, followed from that.

When uniformed Police officers in Birmingham brought young Ibrahim Mahmoud into the station for processing, it was because he had allegedly attacked police officers with a kitchen knife. Unlike other men questioned in countless other police stations in dozens of other countries, Ibrahim did not attempt to remain silent. He did not sing protest songs or shout abuse at interrogators. Nor did he ask for a solicitor to be present. To the delight of detectives, they quickly discovered that this young man was more than happy to talk to them. He saw nothing wrong in the things he and his family and his friends had done and been involved with in his home in Yemen in the years before he had come to Britain. When he first started talking, there were two detectives, bored to tears, listening to the verbal ramblings of this immature man with a poor command of English and a heavy accent that was almost funny to listen to. He sounded like somebody doing a bad impression of a Middle Eastern person speaking English due to having learned English from watching old Hammer House horror movies and Carry-on comedies.

After Ibrahim had been talking for a while, police officers finally realized what he knew and to whom he was related. There were a lot more people listening to him. It had taken some time to reach the point where officers were taking him seriously, but eventually, they all stopped laughing at his accent. They were too busy trying to figure out just how close this young man would bring them to catching the person responsible for the JFK attack?

Until Ibrahim began talking about his family, there were no other lines of enquiry. Ibrahim Mahmoud became the star attraction and the center of the universe for two governments. For a man like him, desperate to make a success of his life, starved of the praise and attention he felt himself entitled, his time in the spotlight was not something to be gotten through quickly. Ibrahim realized very quickly that these cops saw value in his contribution. They were treating him like an honored guest, and he intended to stretch it out for as long as he could. He was already thinking of the things he might gain for his mother and himself.

Nicholas and Mike had read the arrest report for Ibrahim Mahmoud and knew that Ibrahim had been living in a council owned flat, along with his mother. On council rent records, the flat was listed as being rented by one Maamar Hamidou. Every one of the detectives was aware of Maamar and his relevance to a hunt for terrorists. Although he had not been seen in the UK for years, Maamar was still most definitely a person of interest for several reasons.

Officers cared little for Maamar's nephew Ibrahim, as he was not thought to have a connection to any radical group. He had never been recorded as involved with the activities of his terrorist uncle.

There was no point in trying to prosecute Ibrahim for resisting arrest. He had never intended to hurt the officers at the flat. That was just him trying to show the world he was a tough guy. If charged and convicted, he wouldn't last a week in prison. They would let the young man talk for a while and then they would send him home to his mother with a warning to behave himself.

The search for Maamar Hamidou.
Yemen.

In the search for suspects for the JFK attacks, Maamars flat in Birmingham had been on a list of addresses to be checked by local police. There was the slight hope that Maamar might have returned there, and officers were told to see if any of Maamars terrorist comrades might be hiding there. The most current information on Maamar was that he had fled from Britain several years previously. He was assumed to have gone back to his Middle Eastern homeland of Yemen. He was known to have a sister living in Yemen, and as soon as that fact became known, British intelligence put some casual surveillance on the village where Emani and her son were living. The watching was done by a local truck driver who worked as a CIA asset but was also used by other agencies.

The asset had relatives nearby and regularly stayed in the area while waiting for new trucking jobs to come up. He was able to keep watch on the house and village where Emani and Ibrahim lived, to see if Maamar might visit. No such visit had been observed, however, and the intelligence asset was transferred to other assignments.

The intelligence analysts made a note on the Maamar file to have somebody return to check the area, and to ask around about Emani at that time, but mostly she was forgotten, while her son barely registered as a presence at all.

If Ibrahim had known how little the CIA analyst that compiled the report thought of him, he would have shrugged and mentally added her to the long list of people that had ignored or belittled him since childhood. He was constantly being ignored and even as a child; he hated feeling like a nobody.

The government in Yemen held a file on Maamar Hamidou and were, of course, aware that his sister and nephew were living in

Yemen. But Ibrahim had never shown even a slight interest in following his uncle into fighting against the Western world and its allies. The Yemeni government had not bothered keeping Ibrahim under serious watch. A single folder buried inside the lengthy file on Maamar contained as a side note, a school report on his nephew Ibrahim from twelve years previously. The school was administered by a French NGO and had set up large canvas tents on the side of the main road which led Westward to Sanaa, the disputed capital city.

Ibrahim had attended class a few times, but the kids in his village were mostly of Houthi parents, so going to a school with such strong Western influence was never going to be permitted for very long, even in such a remote village. The men were never too strict in their observance of National laws and basically made their own rules for living. Due to Ibrahim's father no longer being in his life, the fathers of Ibrahim's friends saw it as their duty to provide masculine, moral guidance to Emani, Ibrahim's mother. She was told in no uncertain terms Ibrahim could no longer attend the school. When she tried to argue that her son needed an education, the men told her it was no longer possible because the school was now closed.

She discovered the truth of this when she walked to market two days later. There remained only a few bare patches in the field where numerous tents and supply pallets had stood the previous day. Nobody would answer her questions as to where the French educators had gone. All that remained of Ibrahim's school attendance was the single report in which Ibrahim was described as, ` of average intelligence but lacks enthusiasm for learning. Ibrahim tends to indulge in flights of fancy. He is telling tales of intrigue involving an uncle and his freedom fighter friends.

Birmingham, England.

In a police station in Birmingham, having endured a few minutes of listening to Ibrahim alternating between complaining and bragging, something Ibrahim said clicked in the mind of one of the cops sitting opposite. Detective Nicholas King sat up straight and asked Ibrahim to repeat his last sentence. When King was sure he understood what Ibrahim was saying, he asked Ibrahim a seemingly casual question. As sometimes happens during investigations, the reply from Ibrahim opened a whole world of possibilities.

Ibrahim, talking of his earlier life in Yemen, had mentioned he and his mother had a visit from Ibrahim's uncle to their home in Yemen. Nicholas King was aware from the family file that Ibrahim and his Mother Emani had very few relatives and reportedly none at all still living in Yemen.

So, Nicholas took a shot in the dark and asked Ibrahim, `when did your uncle Maamar visit? Was it when he escaped from prison in the West? `

Ibrahim looked at Detective King leaning forward eagerly as he asked about Uncle Maamar, and Ibrahim smiled. He had finally found something that interested the bored police officer.

Talking about Uncle Maamar happened to be Ibrahim's favorite subject, too.

Nicholas glanced at his colleague beside him and mouthed to his colleague to keep Ibrahim talking. Nicholas stood up and walked to the water cooler in the corner of the room with the pretense of getting some water. While standing there, he sent a text message to his senior officer upstairs to warn him they had a potentially important source of information. There would be hope that because of the insurgent groups that Maamar was known to run with, Maamar might prove to be a source of information about whoever organized the JFK attack.

96

The text message sent by Nicholas King contained the initials JFK. This was the agreed signal that said they might have somebody with information about the attack at JFK. This told the D.I. he now needed to inform their contact in the US Embassy in London.

The detective inspector read the text, considered his options, and then walked into his commander's office without knocking. The older man hung up on a phone call and looked at his inspector with a raised eyebrow. The D.I. told him they had a live catch in the station, possibly a source in the JFK operation. A person that warranted closer scrutiny by the Americans.

The commander picked up the phone and made a call. He trusted the detectives in his station house and knew better than to question whether they were correct or not. American intelligence analysts would be in Birmingham in a short time. They would be the ones to determine if Ibrahim was useful or if he was simply another braggart with nothing better to do than spin tall tales. Either way, that young man's life was about to be utterly transformed. For better or for worse, Ibrahim would soon cease to be the responsibility of the English police. He was about to become the property of the United States of America. They were not known for sharing their toys with their friends, not even their special friends. And they did not enjoy a reputation for being gentle with those toys.

The conversation in the phone call from the police commander to his contact in the US embassy was brief, but it resulted in the official levels of interest in Ibrahim Mahmoud suddenly spiking to new heights in several offices in the UK and abroad.

Immediately after that phone call, three men and two women, field agents of the Central Intelligence Agency, departed from the Embassy in London and arrived at the Birmingham police station in a Range Rover.

There were quick response teams like these, all over the UK, and in locations across Europe and around the world. They all had the same objective, which was to track down and apprehend the person or people responsible for the failed assault on nineteen aircraft in JFK airport. In line with the remits of the various agencies involved, the agents reported back to their section chiefs any developments as they might occur. Reports to date had been thin and sparse, with nothing of value or interest. Now, though, Ibrahim Mahmoud was in the net, and he would be lucky to survive through the process of information extraction, which was about to be unleashed upon him and his family.

The agents finally had something positive to report. They would squeeze the young man from Yemen and try to turn this news into very good news. Everybody wanted to make the President happy. A happy President tended not to fire people from their federal government jobs. Also, when the POTUS was happy, he tended not to order military chiefs to bomb foreign nations on a whim. This made everybody's job a bit easier. It certainly made the lives of the people in foreign nations, that might otherwise be targets of those missiles, a lot more comfortable.

The five-person team in London was briefed by their CIA supervisor as to the situation in Birmingham. The briefing took place while they ascended in the elevator to the roof of the building, each agent carrying a single piece of hand luggage. Waiting for them on the windswept roof was a Black Hawk helicopter, its blades already spinning up towards full throttle.

On the fuselage of the big helicopter were three patched areas near the crew door. These were the result of repairs carried out after the craft got hit by Kalashnikov rounds in a town square in Lebanon while lifting a CIA asset and her handler out in a hurry four months previously. The helicopter had a lot of hard miles on its clock. Current station, Birmingham, England, was like a retirement home for the craft.

The chief pilot on board was named Kayn Lansky, and he was the youngest son of a Vietnam war era helicopter pilot. His father was dead now, but a year before he died, Kayn had brought the old man up in a Blackhawk. The look of surprised delight on his father's face at the power and speed of this newer generation of military choppers was something that Kayn now wished he had captured on camera. His father had flown Bell AH1 attack helicopters as escort to transport helicopters in Vietnam and he had passed on his love of the aircraft to his sons. A treasured Lansky family possession was a restored and fully operational Bell AH1 'Huey Cobra' and Kayn had learned his chopper skills as a twelve-year-old. He flew with his father in the tandem seat in case adult intervention became necessary. The tandem controls had never once been needed; Kayn proved to be a natural pilot.

The CIA agents, accustomed to being lifted off rooftops in such dramatic fashion, wasted no time in clambering aboard and strapping themselves into the seats. A road distance of over one hundred miles above London traffic, and into Birmingham, seemed very short when you were flying at Black Hawk speeds and very soon the five agents were climbing out again, ducking dramatically but unnecessarily under the spinning blades, and running to the waiting cars that would transport them to the police station in Birmingham town center.

If the journey had been of a longer duration, the agents might have been treated to the story of how Kayn's father got a ride in a Blackhawk. Three of the CIA operatives had heard it twice on previous trips with Kayn. It was the price one paid for being transported by the very best helicopter pilot in the employ of the CIA. Kayn, for his part, never saw his passengers' faces, and was telling the story over the internal intercom system through which his passengers had to listen to it on their headsets. Kayn wasn't aware of those times when he was carrying a passenger for a second time. He told the helicopter story to everyone that got airborne for journeys of more than an hour, just to be talking.

Before seeing Ibrahim in the flesh in the Birmingham police station, the American agents had left the helicopter on the rooftop helipad, jogged down the stairs and climbed into the waiting Land Rover, sent by colleagues in the British Security services. A short drive through the streets of Birmingham soon had them swinging in through a quiet suburban area past a small shopping center. The route to the station made a couple of the agents think the driver had made a mistake. It looked like they were heading to a person's home, instead of to a Police station. Then they turned a corner, passing yet more homes, and the car bounced up onto a pavement and came to a smooth stop in a narrow lane between single-story buildings. Seeing the police sign on the wall outside, they wasted no time departing the vehicle and quickly walked in through the rear entrance of West Midlands Police Station, Birmingham.

There they found the Police Commander himself waiting for them in the corridor. He escorted them through the building without requiring them to register their presence in the visitor's logbook. He did not want any record of these visitors in his police station. The commander was already thinking ahead to the unsettling possibility that Ibrahim Mahmoud might get turned into a non-person. One that required removal in a blacked-out van from where Ibrahim would end up in an unlisted location in the Czech Republic or possibly even Guantanamo Bay in Cuba if the Americans deemed him to be of sufficient risk to their National Security. That was for later, though. Right now, Ibrahim was everybody's favorite person and would be treated very nicely indeed.

Until he wasn't, anymore.

The Commander asked the Americans to follow him to a spacious office adjacent to the interview room. Already in the room were the Detective Inspector and two secretaries from the Foreign

Office. The D.I. quickly briefed the newly arrived American specialists on the situation in the interrogation room. He made sure to give plenty of credit to his officers, first to the uniformed branch for bringing Ibrahim in, and then to his detectives for getting Ibrahim to talk so openly without the need for any so-called 'enhanced interrogation' techniques.

The CIA agents gratefully accepted large mugs of strong coffee and settled down to watch the camera feed on the large screen. They could also listen to the dialogue being transmitted from the interview room. The two foreign office stenographers made sure the American agents were supplied with typed transcripts of everything said so far. Three of the agents sat back and began reading the typed notes while the remaining two agents sat upright listening and watching the camera screens in real-time. When the three agents finished reading the notes, they handed the folders over to the two agents and they switched roles. It meant all five agents were fully conversant with all aspects of the interview up to the minute.

On the screen in full color, and coming through the speakers in clear audio, Ibrahim had been spinning more tales of daring adventures he and his uncle had been on together in their homeland, Yemen. Now, at Nicholas King's prompting, Ibrahim had reverted to telling his life story, throwing in plenty of self-pity about how impoverished he and his family were, and how strong his mother had been raising a child on her own since her husband left.

Detective King had been made aware of the American visitors watching from the room next door and, for their benefit, he worked to get Ibrahim to go back to that part of his tale where he was still living in Yemen with his mother. When Ibrahim got to the part in his story where he casually revealed his having lived and travelled with Maamar Hamidou in Yemen, there were sharp intakes of breath from the American agents in the monitoring room. This was indeed news worth travelling to Birmingham for.

Ibrahim's value as a potential source of intelligence had just been confirmed to the satisfaction of the agents from the US.

The English cops knew it was now only a matter of time before these agents decided they needed to take Ibrahim to a place where the laws of the land did not apply. Yes, he was talking freely, and he seemed to be cooperating. But how much was he not telling them? The CIA operatives knew these terrorist kids were highly trained in disinformation and counterintelligence.

If the Americans had any say in what happened to Ibrahim, they would subject Ibrahim to a couple of days in a brightly lit room with any attempt at sleeping constantly and randomly, interrupted by bursts of screaming and loud rock music. That would be followed by a few hours locked in a dark box with the room temperature lowered to the chill used for raw meat transportation. A subject enduring that level of tiredness and stress added to the fear of being frozen to death would encourage conversation with a lot more detail. The Brits tended to frown upon that sort of behavior these days, even though a lot of it had been perfected by their own Special forces guys years ago. They were just too civilized now. They prosecuted terror suspects through their courts and tried to change them through prison rehabilitation. Everyone knew prison was simply a staging point to the next phase for most of these insurgents. These men used prison time to rest and recover, to network with men that shared the same interests as themselves. Which in most cases simply meant both men wanted to wreck everything in the decadent West. Prison wasn't the answer. Pain and fear were required to break these men.

The story that Ibrahim told was that he had not always lived in Britain. He had only moved there since fleeing his Yemen homeland a few years previously. The way Ibrahim told it, his Uncle Maamar was a great man, an honorable warrior, and a good person. The word terrorist was never mentioned, not by Ibrahim and certainly not by the English officers. The cops weren't naïve about Maamar, it was just that they were determined to keep Ibrahim talking away. Them calling his beloved Uncle a terrorist would not be conducive to keeping the conversation flowing. At this point, the officers assumed that Ibrahim only knew his uncle from being told about him by his mother, who was Maamars younger sister. They had no information at that stage that the two men had ever actually met. The direction of the questioning changed once Ibrahim revealed his closeness to Maamar.

It was well documented that Maamar Hamidou was involved with some genuinely nasty people. He was allied with the top suspects in several gun and grenade attacks on some exclusive and very expensive beach resorts frequented by American and Saudi oil executives and government officials. Capturing Maamar would be great on its own, but it should also lead to bigger catches. Once you had a few of these people in custody, you could apply serious pressure and sometimes get them to reveal names of whatever suited sponsors they might have met with. In this way, entire extremist networks could be broken up and another part of the world would be made a little safer. Safer at least from a Westerners perspective.

Of course, Maamar and his associates had a different view of the whole situation. The only interest Maamar had in anything to do with westerners was in whether he could shoot it or blow it up.

Ibrahim was proud of his Uncle Maamar and of the group he was part of in Yemen, and he had no hesitation in telling these detectives what they wanted to hear. They were very interested in the men Maamar met with in the mountains. Did Ibrahim recall any names from when he was camping up there with Maamar? The cops asked all sorts of questions about the type of weapons and equipment used by the groups in these camps. Was the equipment new or old? Was it ex-military gear or civilian camping stuff? Were they all Yemeni men or were there other nationalities mingling with them? The officers wanted to know if he had ever spoken to or seen any European or American men in the camps? Was Maamar in a position of command in the group, or was he simply another fighter in the ranks? Ibrahim was delighted to find these foreign policemen so knowledgeable about his Uncle Maamar. It meant that news of his heroic struggle had travelled thousands of miles, from his homeland all the way to England. Maamar would be proud. It was important to Ibrahim that the legend of Yemeni warriors, like his uncle, was told around the world.

Ibrahim wasn't to know, but the two detectives asking him questions were receiving silent messages on their laptop screen from the CIA specialists next door. These messages contained the questions that the US agents most needed answers to. The group that had flown in by helicopter from London were furious with the slow, gentle pace at which Nicholas King was conducting the interview with the laid-back Ibrahim. The agents were desperate to get in there with Ibrahim and drag the information from him by force as quickly as possible. Unfortunately for them, but luckily for Ibrahim, the agents were under strict orders from their ambassador in London, who in turn was passing the order on from the President's advisers in Washington, DC. All US operatives were to stay out of the sight and hearing of Ibrahim. He was currently talking freely and had already given them plenty to work with. The expert opinion was that he might suddenly lose the power of speech if he heard American accents. Yemeni kids were taught from birth to despise America. A lot of white American kids felt the same about the people of Yemen. A large percentage of either group of youngsters would fail to find the other country on a map without assistance.

From Ibrahim's point of view, he didn't really care what nationality his hosts were. They were mainly white men, and he couldn't fully tell the difference between American and English accents. It was rare indeed that he found himself the center of attention with all these important people hanging on his every word.

Ibrahim had always held a strong dislike of being treated as a nobody, but these well-dressed officers were speaking to him as if he was their equal. They were even filming him with their fancy camera!

Being treated as a person of importance reminded Ibrahim of the nice French teachers when he was a child in their school. They regularly made little videos of the children working at their school desks. The head teacher told the children that the President of France wanted to see how much progress the kids were making. The teachers told the kids that this President was a very important man in Europe, and that he wanted to give a better life to children in places like Yemen. Ibrahim wasn't sure why the school had been sent away by the men in his village. As usual, when he asked his mother about things that were difficult to understand, she told him he would need to grow up a lot before he would be able to figure out why the world was so complicated. He began to understand she gave this answer when she herself didn't understand. He had overheard his mother arguing with two of their neighbors about the school. It seemed the men had threatened the schoolteachers and told them to pack up and leave, that their kind of teaching was not welcome in Yemen.

Ibrahim quickly realized that he liked the feeling of power all this official attention gave him, and he certainly wanted that feeling to continue. For that reason, it took him quite a long time to reveal to detectives that Maamar Hamidou, along with his closest comrades, had almost certainly been killed in Saudi Arabia three years ago. Ibrahim did not want to return to being ignored, which would be the case if he had nothing of interest for these people. Also, he did not want to disappoint the nice police officers by ending the story on such a sad note. They seemed so very interested in his stories about his warrior uncle's heroic exploits.

That, of course, was something they held in common with Ibrahim. He idolized his uncle and was eager to keep alive the legend of the great man.

Anyway, Ibrahim reasoned that it hadn't been confirmed that Maamar was dead, so he wasn't really lying to the police. Ibrahim remembered the day he tried to discuss his uncle Maamar with his mother. It was soon after they got to England and had moved into the family flat. Ibrahim had found an old letter about new rent rates from the city council, addressed to Uncle Maamar at the flat. He showed it to his mother and asked if she thought Maamar was ok. Did she know if he had been killed in the operation he had been on, just before Ibrahim and Emani fled from Yemen? She had slapped his face and told him to shut up. Then she hugged him. She refused to entertain the possibility that her brother had not survived that mission. So, Ibrahim really didn't have a definitive answer one way or the other.

Far better to keep telling the police what they wanted to hear. Better to believe that Maamar had survived the attack and was in hiding in Yemen.

That way, everyone could be happy.

In the interviews, Ibrahim revealed his personal contact with Maamar in Yemen, and within hours, US intelligence satellites had been re-tasked to cover the region surrounding the village Ibrahim was known to have lived. They lived in what was originally a refugee camp for persons that were displaced from their villages during a war with Saudi Arabia years before. Such camps became de facto permanent settlements over time, due to their longevity. The camp in which Ibrahim lived was located on the main route North to Sanaa, the capital. Agents were able to use Ibrahim's village as a starting point for their satellite mapping.

From pointed questions asked by Nicholas King, agents had determined approximately where Ibrahim and his uncle had gone to join the meetings in the mountains. Special emphasis was placed by spy satellites and camera drones on areas in and around the mountains to the West. Ibrahim said he and Maamar had driven toward the setting sun when going to visit the mountain hideouts. They had camped with a large group of armed men on different occasions, and Ibrahim had mentioned hearing voices using Saudi slang words and with Saudi accents in the group around the fire. Shia Houthi groups with men such as Maamar among their numbers had been waging guerilla war against Saudi assets and Yemeni government targets for years. The men using Saudi slang would probably have been living and working in Saudi Arabia for months prior to carrying out attacks in the Kingdom. They would have learned the slang from their Saudi work colleagues. This was another indicator for the American agents that Maamar would be worth grabbing for interrogation as soon as possible. The Arab robed man caught in JFK airport was thought to be of Saudi origin, though he had yet to be identified. No nation had stepped forward to claim him as a citizen and he remained in custody, still without charge.

Being able to locate these groups' meeting places might allow the Americans to place listening devices in the surrounding environment to eavesdrop on future meetings of insurgent groups.

YEMEN.

Yemen had suffered through centuries of conflict with people of similar political doctrines and faiths fighting alongside each other against opposing forces in long wars and short conflicts. The participants on either side of each conflict were interchangeable, depending on the current political climate on the Arabian Peninsula. The only consistency was that Yemen itself remained central to the plans of a lot of outside interests. It had always been at the crossroads of profitable trade routes across Asia and Africa. That situation had not been simplified in the modern era. There were wars between North and South Yemen, conflicts between various factions in either region of Yemen, there had been invasions and attacks by foreign nations and threaded through the modern-day fighting was the fanatical presence of ISIS and Al-Qaeda, both of which drew support from Saudi Arabia and from American operatives striving to further their own national interests. These foreign agitators were none too choosy as to who they used to carry on their agenda. In the present time, even long experienced CIA analysts stumbled through briefings when asked to explain whatever was the latest conflict. There were simply too many shifting loyalties and alliances to keep track of effectively.

Middle East.

C.I.A. analysts, working on middle eastern operations, had ambitions of being instrumental in capturing an active cell of terrorists involving high level Saudi government involvement. Bin Laden was the family name the analysts invariably thought of as being the sponsors of such groups, but there were offshoots of the Saudi ruling family of Ibn Saud with their own agendas. These splinter groups were clearly prepared to funnel money and support to radical groups like the group in which Maamar Hamidou had been involved. To be able to prove such a connection would be of huge value to the agency. They had been warning their own government about the risks to the US of high-level Saudi collusion with radical groups that were operating out of the lawless badlands of Yemen for years.

An operational success was badly needed by the CIA. One resulting in the capture of a few Saudi Arabian royal family members or government figures actively meeting with confirmed insurgents such as Maamar Hamidou would force the US government to condemn the Saudis, at least publicly. And that might bring about a substantial change in Saudi-US relations. It would certainly loosen the political restraints imposed on CIA operations in the region and allow the CIA field agents to do their jobs properly.

The Israeli National intelligence agency, along with an allied group inside the CIA, was itching to take a crack at junior members of the Saudi royal family. The intelligence operatives were operating under a strict hands-off rule handed down by the American White House and the Israeli Knesset years ago.

If they got the green light to begin operations against terrorist sponsors operating inside allies of the US, it wouldn't take long to compile a dossier of names in the Royal family in the Kingdom. That list could be passed to certain members of the US Congress who would use it to force action from their political bosses that sat on powerful legislative committees. There were plenty of senators and congress people that did not agree with the American stance on The Middle East. They agreed with the assessments of CIA operatives in the region that America should drag itself out of Arab affairs and let the Arab people of each nation govern themselves for better or for worse.

America was not as dependent upon Saudi oil as it once had been, and now was the time to cut ties.

Ibrahim Mahmoud, with his family ties to Maamar and his insurgent comrades, was only a little fish, but the sharks circling him were getting bigger and more ruthless by the minute. What started with a young man in a police station in Birmingham, England, was becoming properly international, as more intelligence agency personnel got into it.

Middle Eastern region.

Successive US Presidents had refused to act, either militarily or politically, on the ground against radical groups, using the excuse that they needed to protect American commercial interests in the region. Which really meant they wanted to remain good friends with Saudi Arabia. America and the Saudi royal family had been close pals since the days of King Saud being courted, and befriended, by American executives of the oil companies, before and after World War two. Such relationships resulted in the formation of oil companies such as Aramco, partnerships that were to become massively profitable for both sides.

Relations between America and Saudi Arabia soured somewhat over the years due to the Israeli situation, but the two countries remained friendly enough. However, there were factions within the Saudi government, and in the royal family, that did not want to be on any sort of terms with the Americans.

The Arab world felt they had learned everything America had to teach, and most of it was anathema to Arab culture and tradition. The enormous wealth generated by oil extraction was certainly useful when it came to exerting influence in the political power centers of the world, but the stink of corruption and western decadence that came with such affluence was not welcomed by all. Behind the scenes, some were working to force America out of Arab nations and to persuade them to leave Arab affairs to Arabs. Groups like the wealthy coterie that funded and supported Maamar, and his friends were an integral part of that effort.

CIA efforts to capture influential figures like Maamar were aimed towards getting someone to go on record with the name of a Saudi government official that had attended meetings or handed over funding to a terrorist group. Ibrahim had given investigators a possible entry into the world of middle eastern terror group operations. The agents in England would now proceed to squeeze every bit of information from him.

MAAMAR

Several years previously, while Emani and her son Ibrahim were still living in Yemen, unbeknownst to them, Maamar was already an accomplished bomb maker and multiple killer. He had been operating in Western Europe as a lone contractor, planning operations against western targets with whichever group of terrorists was currently active. Unfortunately for Maamar, the ultra-radical group he was working with in Britain had been infiltrated by no less than two SO15 agents. The agents were so deeply undercover in the terrorist group that neither agent was aware of the other. SO15 senior command, acting upon information from one of their agents, raided the storage unit in which Maamar was busily mixing chemicals in preparation for making a massive bomb. He was caught in possession of a large quantity of modified chemical fertilizer. Being nowhere near a farm where he might use such a product and not having a garden where one might reasonably expect to use fertilizer, Maamar had gone to Belmarsh Prison for an enforced holiday at British taxpayer's expense.

He was granted temporary release from prison after three years for the funeral of the older sister of his UK based wife. The head of a mosque, at which Maamar prayed, went so far as to vouch for him for the two-day release from prison. The Imam had written personally to the prison authorities and offered his own home as a temporary residence for Maamar while he was outside prison. Prison chiefs compromised and allowed a one-day release on the condition that two prison officers accompanied the prisoner to the funeral. On the day of the funeral, Maamar went to visit the home of his wife's family. The two prison officers escorting him were prevented from entering the family home of the deceased. The guards had tried to walk into the home alongside Maamar and were blocked by the physical presence of approximately a dozen large males who stood shoulder-to-shoulder across the front garden and entrance to the home.

Attempts by one officer to venture around to the rear of the property to ascertain if an escape was being attempted resulted in that officer receiving multiple dog bites inflicted by the three mongrel dogs running untethered in the rear garden. The prison guard, in considerable pain and frightened he might have rabies, flagged down a passing taxi and got himself to hospital emergency department for treatment. He completely forgot to inform his colleague that had been left standing on the pavement at the front of the house.

By the time the funeral service started, Maamar had gone from the area and was being driven to Dover. From there, he had departed the UK and disappeared into the melting pot of a damaged Western Asian region. He had gone home.

Later that day, on foot of a report by the two prison guards, a dog warden accompanied by armed police officers, arrived at the address to take the vicious dogs into custody. The warden and his police escort were given full access to the garden by the tenants of the house from where Maamar had escaped. There were no longer any dogs in the garden. The Arab men in the garden smiled as they watched the dog warden and his escort, depart empty handed.

Yemen.

Yemen was on the periphery of a slowly cooling war zone. A region from which foreign armed forces had since departed, but in which there was now yet another war being fought. There was minimal civil administration in the region from which Maamar and his family originated. So, there was little chance of authorities ever finding the man in such a place. His profile was added to the capture lists and US operatives on the ground in Saudi Arabia and in Yemen were asked to keep an eye out for him. His picture and description were posted in public places with an offer of a reward for information. Every time the reward was advertised, there was an increase in sightings of him and others on the wanted list. After a week, the sightings stopped until the reward got re-posted again.

There was no chance of anyone with real information coming forward. They might claim the reward, but they would be killed before they could enjoy the money. To collect the reward, they had to enter the US compound and be logged in as a visitor. This meant standing in full view of the street while the US military ran background checks, etc. If you were Yemeni, and were seen visiting the US base, there would be questions asked by local militia. They would want to know the reason for your visit to the home base of the American devils. Then they would shoot you to deter others from dealing with the enemy. You can't spend reward money if you're dead.

Birmingham, England.

In Maamars absence, members of his wife's family living in Britain, had kept Maamars council flat in the family by paying the rent and claiming it was still needed by his wife, who had done nothing wrong. The family members cleaned it and slept in it on occasion so the neighbors would think somebody lived in it full time. Otherwise, some neighbor might report the property to the council as being vacant.

Ibrahim and his Mother Emani fled from Yemen to the UK, with Maamars UK address in hand. Maamar had arranged to get them both away from Yemen. His insurgent activities had made it too dangerous for them to stay in their homeland. He would not be around to offer any protection, so it was better that they got away. He felt there would be reprisals from the authorities against his sister and her son now that he was known to the Americans.

Upon arrival at the flat in Birmingham, mother and son were handed the keys by Maamars aunt on his wife's side of the family. They were told it was now their home and their responsibility. Emani was quickly told how to apply for social welfare, and it was explained to her how to operate the various labor-saving devices in the flat. She had very little experience of reliable electricity and none of electric cookers and such things.

Emani was Maamars sister, and she missed him a lot. She did not know or love the family he had married into and would not miss them if they did not visit. They showed no interest in Maamars nephew, Ibrahim. Emani had lived her entire life without family nearby and would be content to continue in that way.

Emani settled into life in Birmingham with her son Ibrahim. She tried not to think of what might have happened to her brother Maamar back in Yemen three years before. He was ever the fighter and had protected her when they were kids in the refugee camps, in the uncharted lands between Saudi Arabia and Yemen. He protected her and she helped him as much as she could. She loved him and looked up to him. Now he was more than likely gone forever.

She had to try to keep her son away from the people that had recruited Maamar to the cause that had probably killed him. She hoped Maamar had been correct in thinking that by running away to Britain, that they would be safe. It had now been three years since Maamar had persuaded her to flee their homeland and travel to Britain. Since then, she had lived an uneventful life in England for those three years and Emani had begun to believe things might get better for her son. Better than they had been for her and Maamar growing up.

Unfortunately, that quiet life, lived unnoticed by the police was about to crash head-on into an international hunt for a mysterious terrorist organizer.

Emani went out to buy groceries.

Police officers knocked on the door of the flat she shared with Ibrahim.

Ibrahim was home alone and reacted badly to the police at his door.

Three events, happening in sequence, brought an uneducated young immigrant to the attention of police. Ibrahim in police custody, became a person of interest because investigators thought he could lead them to his terrorist uncle. The uncle might have knowledge of other terrorists, higher up the food chain. Those people could lead to the person that attacked JFK airport.

Instead, eventually, they discovered Ibrahim had been in the personal company of the very man that planned and nearly executed the worst terrorist attack in human history.

Ibrahim had spent that day, like he did most days, surfing the internet. He was an avid watcher of YouTube conspiracy theory channels. He was unemployed, mostly friendless, and constantly angry at the world. He had studied the videos of bearded, wild-eyed men ranting and shouting. From around the world, there were shakily filmed scenes showing newly raised levels of harassment and abuse being directed at Muslim and Arabic men since the attack on the American airport.

Already filled with righteous indignation on behalf of himself and his perceived mistreatment by authority figures, he was becoming utterly incensed with fury at the injustice levelled at his fellow Muslims. So, when he opened the front door and saw the blue Police uniforms on the doorstep, he almost exploded with an incoherent rage.

Forgetting that the flat was in his Uncle Maamars name, and that Maamar was an escaped convict, Ibrahim heard the cops trying to explain the reason for their visit and he wrongly assumed it was racial profiling by the police, that he and his mother were being targeted due to their religion and appearance. Ibrahim spat at the police officers when they asked after his uncle, the runaway terrorist. He accused them of lying about their reason for coming to his home

The tense situation deteriorated even further when, while shouting angrily in Arabic, Maamar's angry nephew raised a large kitchen knife. Ibrahim had been cutting bread earlier and had left the knife on the counter for his Mother to clean later. The police report described the knife being wielded in, `a clearly threatening manner, we feared the encounter was turning into one of those lone wolf attacks. We took appropriate action to defend ourselves`.

One officer opened a retractable baton and swung it at Ibrahim's raised arm, knocking the knife harmlessly to one side. The instant the carving knife was lowered, two of the other cops, both big, rugby playing sides of British beef, threw themselves bodily on the skinny lad with a crash that shook the thin walls and floors of the shabby flat, jarring cheap ornaments and pictures off mismatched sideboards and shelves, where they smashed to pieces on the bare floor. The shock of the impact reverberated through the building. The elderly Azerbaijani gentleman living directly downstairs, he being a veteran of earthquakes in his homeland, rose from his armchair and stepped quickly into the meagre protection afforded by the doorframe between his kitchen and bedroom, and stood there patiently for exactly twenty minutes timed on his wristwatch, his hands braced against the door uprights. When no further tremors were forthcoming, he shrugged, and returned to watching the daytime television shows.

Meanwhile, upstairs, the pathetically aggressive nephew of an international fugitive had been plastic-cuffed on wrists and ankles. He was picked up by the policemen he had earlier attacked, and carrying him bodily out of the flat, they manhandled him down eight flights of concrete stairs, which stank of urine, neglect, and desperation. After being transported to the police station and left to ferment overnight in a small cell, Ibrahim did not smell much better.

The custody sergeant woke him at seven A.M. and offered breakfast, which Ibrahim refused with a sneer because he had seen the videos of police officers spitting on prisoners' food, or disguising Haram food as something permissible. The sergeant shrugged, took the tray away with him and signed the custody record with the note, "food served, food refused".

At nine am, Ibrahim was escorted to an interview room where Detective constable King and his colleague Mike Farrell awaited his arrival. It would be fair to say the two detectives were not all that excited to see this latest prisoner.

Ibrahim, in reply to Detective King's probing question about his family, replied that his Uncle Maamar had come unexpectedly to their home in Northern Yemen, four years ago. It was Ibrahim's first time to meet his mother's brother, although he had heard plenty of stories about the man. The instant Ibrahim revealed he had met Maamar in Yemen, the cops instantly showed an enthusiastic interest in Ibrahim's tales and stories. They clearly wanted to know about Uncle Maamar. From that point on, it was as if Ibrahim forgot he was in a police station. He simply began to talk. Nicholas King had only interrupted once, to send his text message to alert his superiors upstairs. Nicholas then returned to the table and simply let Ibrahim ramble on with his life story.

Ibrahim took them back in time, to Yemen, to a period a few years before. When he hadn't even met uncle Maamar yet.

Yemen, 2015

Ibrahim Mahmoud felt like a failure in life. He was suffering constant employment setbacks because of having Maamar Hamidou in his family. At this point, Ibrahim had not yet met his infamous Uncle Maamar. In the years when Maamar was terrorizing westerners in Europe and around the Middle East, Ibrahim was living quietly with his mother in their village in Yemen. His Mother unfailingly spoke of her brother as a good, decent man. She tried never to mention his bloody exploits, or that he was one of the more notorious terrorists in the world.

Unaware his uncle had plotted to murder Yemen soldiers and cops over the years, Ibrahim had tried to join the Yemen army to take advantage of the free education programs they offered. He was rejected twice with the official reason for the failure of his application being that he was undocumented since he was born in a camp on the border. He had no birth certificate or passport.

Now, without any formal education, he was reduced to taking casual positions with the oil companies to provide extra income for himself and his mother.

The jobs could be politely described as caretaker roles. It was cleaning scum off the water in the tanks used for cooling the drilling tools. He also had the task of washing various pieces of equipment when the night shift had ended and before the day shift came on site. In very hot weather, his hands got burned just lifting the hot steel components, because he kept forgetting to wrap cloths around them first. It was hard, dirty work, and he was paid very little. He constantly felt angry at his employers who refused to let him move to better positions in the company. Unbeknownst to Ibrahim, the manager in charge of his area knew all about Ibrahim's Uncle. The oil company did not want any members of that family getting too far into their business. They used him in the lowliest roles only.

The oil companies were in regular contact with the US State Department regarding possible threats against US interests. Part of this contact included the communication of any information about employees that might be deemed a threat to infrastructural security. Ibrahim was high on the threat list simply because his uncle might use him to gain access to a secure pipeline or to sensitive pumping machinery. Ibrahim was angry at his situation. Uncle Maamar remained a threat, and the intelligence agencies kept updating the oil companies. So, Ibrahim remained at the same low level in his menial job where he grew angrier every day.

Angry young men such as Ibrahim are easy prey for manipulative men to exploit for their own ends. One need only give them a target for their anger.

Birmingham, England.
2019.

In discovering, to his delight, that detectives were most enthusiastic about his uncle Maamar, Ibrahim focused on his recollection of his days and nights in Maamars company. He told the English cops all about the trips to the mountain camps, the nights spent sitting around fires while rough men smoked and told stories of their youth and of the battles they had fought. Ibrahim revealed a lot of important details that certainly helped the military people to narrow down their search areas while they looked for Maamar and his militant group comrades. But because he assumed these cops were interested in Maamar, Ibrahim failed to recount. until much later, the story of his own bizarre adventure in the company of Trevor Wilson in the Yemen desert.

The American agents in Birmingham were looking for Maamar to use him as a possible source of information, to assist in finding the person responsible for the JFK incident. But in focusing on Maamar, they failed to realise his naïve nephew was far more important.

It took some time before they recognized the error.

And Trevor Wilson used that time to advance his new plans ever closer to completion.

Yemen
2015.

One day, Ibrahim realized a simple fact about his employer. He realized they were American. American companies had bought their way into Ibrahim's homeland by investing in Yemen mining companies and by buying huge swathes of land at low prices. Now they were extracting oil and gas that rightfully belonged to the people of the country. And still they made him work at this shit job in which he earned barely enough to feed himself and his mother. His anger now had a target. His problems and failings were clearly being caused by American businesses exploiting him to maximize their profit.

He began talking to other young men that worked at jobs like his. And he found they too, were angry. Most of them wanted to act but were afraid of losing their job, so they tried to avoid talking to Ibrahim. He became known as a troublemaker. Other workers were told by their supervisors not to listen to his ranting.

Not everyone avoided him, though. An employee in the same company as Ibrahim, a younger man named Ahmed, sidled up to him while they were drinking cold water at the pump after work.

After engaging in small talk for a few moments, Ahmed told him there would be a meeting later that evening in a town situated just an hour's drive to the North of where they lived. Ahmed seemed confident that Ibrahim would be interested. Ibrahim asked what the meeting would be about, but his new friend just smiled and slyly touched the side of his nose. `You will find the answers when you come to the meeting, ` he was told. `It is a meeting of men like you and me, men that do not get the respect we deserve, men that are angry and might be ready to fight. Tonight, there will be an important guest talking to us. This man comes to us from the hated west, though he despises the west as much as we do, I think. I will come for you at eight in the evening and we can travel together.

Ibrahim went home to his mother, and they prepared dinner together. He did not mention the meeting he was going to attend later. He did not want to worry her. He was afraid that the meeting was a ruse by the oil company to get him out of his village so they could kill him. But then he told himself they could kill him any time they wished and nobody, but his own Mother would even know or care he was gone. He would go to the meeting with Ahmed and hear what this Westerner would say.

The meeting got underway with a mullah giving a rousing speech to the assembled young men about keeping themselves pure. They were to avoid allowing themselves to be corrupted by the agents of America the Great Satan. It was acceptable to take up paid employment with these oil companies but fraternizing with American or other western employees was forbidden for Yemeni men. The teacher acknowledged that they were young men and full of young men's desires, but these weaknesses were to be resisted. The teacher then instructed them to pray.

After a few minutes, the door to the small hall opened and a white man stepped through. This obviously was the western man Ahmed had told Ibrahim about. He walked to the front of the room and shook hands with the Mullah, exchanging murmured words with the fiery preacher. The teacher faced the group and introduced his guest, telling the gathered men that this Westerner was to be respected. He had travelled a long way to meet the men of Yemen.

The quietly spoken and well-dressed white man then turned to address the meeting. Through a translator, he introduced himself as Trevor Wilson. He explained that although he was white and spoke English, he was not a true westerner. He was from Zimbabwe, a nation he described as one that had been betrayed and oppressed by the Western world just as Yemen had been. He said that the Mullah had promised him all the men in the room were trustworthy. This was good news because he said he needed men he could trust.

He said he was in Yemen to recruit fighters to do a mission in a foreign land. Something to echo, to pay tribute to, the resounding success of the glorious September Eleven attacks. He needed strong men, resolute in the face of capture, unafraid of death. He claimed to have been advised that Yemen was the best place to find such men. The men he selected would be trained in the mission, and then they would be smuggled to the target nation.

On the special day, they would strike at the heart of the evil west. The objective was to inflict huge losses on their economy, damage their transport networks and maybe even collapse the government of the country they attacked. Trevor said he wanted nineteen men because he wanted to pay tribute to the nineteen holy martyrs that attacked America on the 11th of September 2001.

Trevor spent a few minutes in the hall, educating the gathered men about how America had invaded nations like Iraq and Afghanistan, using military strength to force regime change and to install the government they wanted. Then highly profitable contracts for rebuilding the nation's infrastructure were awarded to companies sympathetic to American interests. American oil firms, firmly embedded in the region since the very first days of oil exploration and extraction, were granted massive areas of oil fields containing proven reserves. As Trevor spoke, he noticed several men nodding their heads and shaking their clenched fists. These would be his recruits; they would be first to step forward when he asked for volunteers. Smiling to himself, he continued with the history lesson, stoking the fires of insurgency.

Years ago, the Saudi King had come in from the desert on the back of a camel, to agree to terms with Amoco executives who were looking to make commercial use of the ocean of oil, lying untapped under the sands of the Kingdom. The King, in those days, was said to be making purchases and paying his bills in coin from a metal box carried by his treasurer, who rode alongside the King on his own camel. The King was a simple tribal man living a simple life like most Arab people, but the Americans corrupted him in their evil ways. Down through the succeeding generations, The House of Saud and whichever American President was in the White House, had maintained this relationship. Muslim Arab royalty became more and more closely aligned with Christian Republican oil barons. Their common enemy was the atheist communists in Russia that had gotten above their station ever since they took the credit for defeating Hitler.

During the Gulf War, when the US congress refused to approve further funding for the Bush war machine, Bush called the Saudi King and suggested it would be in the Kings interest to make sure Iraq did not emerge from the war as any sort of viable nation. The King sent more millions of oil-soaked dollars just in time to keep the bullets, rockets and rations flowing from West to East. Saddam Hussein found himself in a hang man's noose. The Americans and their allies acquired new oil fields to work with, and the Saudis could finally relax about their crazy neighbor to the North.

Over the years, with the aim of making ever more profit from other nations' resources, America entered countries like Yemen. Using the pretext of invading the country to prevent terrorists using it as a base, the Americans destroyed whatever domestic industry was there. Then the invaders forced the Yemen government to seek aid from the world bank and similar institutions. The aid was given with terms and conditions attached and these were always weighted in favor of America and her friends. Once they had the country tied up in massive debt, they could then extract whatever natural resources were there to be taken, as payment on the loans. The whole campaign was conducted from boardrooms in offices on Wall Street, with not a single bullet being fired. The result of that activity was that an entire generation of Yemeni men were left jobless or employed in menial tasks with little prospect of advancement or of pay increases. The massive profits being extracted from the ground in the form of oil and gas were not being shared with the people of Yemen or with any of the other countries suffering similar exploitation of their own resources.

Trevor, having spent a few minutes riling up these already angry young men, now reaped the benefits of his rhetoric. He stood with hands outstretched and informed the room that he intended to make America pay for their behavior, both in Yemen and in his own homeland in Africa. Then he asked for nineteen men to stay behind after the meeting. Almost everyone at the meeting, over thirty Yemeni men, wanted to be among that chosen group, so practically every one of the young men volunteered.

Trevor made his nineteen selections, then took this group of men aside. The men that were not chosen were given a hundred dollars each for their time tonight and told that there would be other work for them in the future. He said this was only the beginning.

Trevor informed the chosen group of nineteen their families would each be paid $3,500 in compensation for the loss of each man's wages, as they would not be working in their usual jobs any longer. This large sum of money would be handed over on the day the group departed for the long, secret trip to the US. While the men were training and preparing for the mission, there would be a small weekly allowance paid to their families.

Training was to commence in the desert in two days. Of the nineteen selected men, Ibrahim Mahmoud was the second man chosen. Trevor liked him because he had shining eyes. He didn't ask questions or show any curiosity about the upcoming training. Trevor knew Ibrahim was a lonely young man, content simply to be chosen. He would feel special. He would be compliant and easy to manipulate if you told him he was part of a holy mission. If you had a few like that in a group, any of their fellows feeling a bit reluctant could be more easily persuaded by you pointing out that their friends were going along. Ibrahim's new friend Ahmed was the first man chosen. Ahmed had brought along a few others to the meeting, so they all stepped forward, too.

Just a few weeks later, with the nineteen picked men already immersed in firearms and combat training in a camp in the desert, the entire operation came to an abrupt halt.

Trevor had been trying to make arrangements with people traffickers in Yemen to secure covert passage for his large team of would-be jihadists on a freight ship. Trevor had the idea of smuggling them over land to India in trucks first, then getting them onto a ship there. Ships originating from India were less likely to be stopped and searched in US coastal waters than vessels showing Middle Eastern registration. Once they were in US coastal waters, the attackers would be lowered over the side in one of the ship's lifeboats and then wait offshore for darkness to fall. They could sneak ashore on an American beach or river estuary. It had all seemed so simple and straight forward when Trevor had imagined it.

Trevor found, to his dismay, that nobody would assist with this plan. All the usual contacts in the dark and dirty world of people trafficking deemed it far too risky, no matter how much money was offered. In this inter-connected world, it was common knowledge that to get caught whilst engaged with anything that smelt of terrorism against America would get you killed. There would be no trial, just execution. Most important, it would also mean severe retribution against the nation from which you came.

Dependent upon the seriousness of the crime the Americans caught you perpetrating, there might only be punishment in the form of short-term economic sanctions against your national government. But there had been more drastic examples recently of the US government investigating attacks against its interests. Having traced the source to a specific nation state, the US military was quietly tasked with revenge. A few drone-carried missiles fired at the largest power station in your homeland, added to a strongly worded letter of warning to your state department, usually proved a sufficient deterrent to similar behavior in the future. Even the hardest of criminals tried to avoid exposing themselves to that level of prosecution. Nobody enjoyed having their passport cancelled and their citizenship revoked by the country of their birth. There were easier ways to make a living. The word had been put around; Trevor Wilson was to be refused all assistance by anybody involved in people smuggling. Having to endure the weight of the US military pressing down on top of you was bad for business.

The US military was present on the sea, in the sky, and on the ground. They would not hesitate to stop, board, and search any vessel or vehicle anywhere they patrolled. The world's oceans were vast spaces, but that space shrunk considerably when you got close to the coastline United States, or if you approached their property. Their radar stations would pick you out from the ocean surface clutter. The radio queries would begin. If there was something even slightly off about you, your vessel, its passengers or its cargo, a US Navy Cutter would come out to take a closer look. They would invite themselves aboard your vessel, smiling politely and addressing everybody as `sir` or `madam`, while holding semi-automatic assault rifles, never removing their sunglasses and their heads constantly on a swivel trying to look at everything at once. They would ask for papers for crew members and papers for your cargo. If they were properly suspicious of you, they would do a headcount of your crew, compare it against the papers to make sure everybody was accounted for. As every smuggler and trafficker knew only too well, trying to explain the presence of nineteen undocumented Yemeni men to suspicious US Naval officers was the stuff of nightmares.

Three smugglers refused assistance to Trevor. The fourth one he approached, an old Somalian with more scars than skin, advised that it might be possible to bring them over in groups of three and four, disguised as crew on separate ships. But Trevor was unwilling to show any flexibility about the number in the group. It had to be nineteen because of the obvious symbolic connection to the 9/11 attackers. Anyway, he could not take the risk of having them pose as crew, as he knew these illiterate peasant boys would be picked out by the first security check they came upon. In any case, it would be impossible to get official passports or identity cards for most of the group, as not all of them were registered citizens of any nation. For Trevor Wilson, it meant his plan would fail at the first stage, as he couldn't see any way to get his nineteen men to America.

Trevor had planned to have the whole operation filmed, from its humble beginnings in the harsh desert of Yemen, through to glorious execution in the sky above New York. After a few days considering the problem, he decided he would not be stopped by his failure to smuggle his nineteen chosen attackers into America. Flipping the operation on its head, he decided if he was unable to bring his attackers to the US, he would go to America and source his attackers there instead. There was no shortage of disaffected young men in lots of communities across America.

That brought him to the next problem. The current training camp in the desert would have to be stopped. He called a meeting in the camp to break the bad news to the men. He told the nineteen men that, due to government interference, the operation had to be cancelled. He would contact them for an operation at some stage in the future, for now they were to return to their jobs and lives. They were to say nothing about where they had been. To soften the blow, he increased their pay by two thousand dollars. Trevor made some vague promises and left the camp with an armed escort immediately after the announcement, to avoid having to face the wrath of nineteen angry and motivated men. He had just denied them their one chance at doing something momentous in their uneventful lives. They would not be happy.

The training camp in the desert had been home to these men for three weeks. From there, they had expected to be departing for a glorious Jihad against the American pigs. It would now all be dismantled. It was getting cancelled by the very man who had filled their heads with tales of American imperialism and exploitation against the poor, uneducated folk of Yemen. These men had been angry already. That was true. They had known America was the main source of their discontent. But as angry as they had been while employed by the American oil companies, at least they still earned a wage. The wages were not very high, but it was enough to keep them and their families from starving. Having agreed to join Trevor's army, they had known there was a good chance they would not be returning alive.

Consequently, they left their jobs without giving notice. Their employers would already have replaced them with the next lot of desperate young men. Which left the nineteen rejected jihadists with no jobs and nowhere to go. The money that was promised to their families as compensation would still be paid and this would, of course, help. But it was little compensation without the honor that would have come from being part of the holy mission that had been planned by Trevor.

Five of the nineteen young men were deeply frustrated but had resigned themselves to forever being menial workers in low-paid jobs. This small group, which included Ibrahim Mahmoud, had families who were dependent on them to a much larger extent than the other men in the camp who were single with no dependents.

These five men decided to simply give up their chance for glory, instead accepting they were losers in life and always would be. As soon as possible, they would leave the encampment in the desert and return home. There, they would at least attempt to regain their old jobs, or they would seek similar employment elsewhere. The fourteen other men, however, bitterly disappointed at how their moment of glory had been snatched away, talked themselves into a righteous fury. They would not go quietly and meekly back to their impoverished existence. They decided to overpower Trevor's remaining security men, take the guns and other equipment, and then wait for Trevor to return to the camp. Trevor, before departing the camp, had promised to return with extra vehicles to get everyone across the desert and back to their villages. There was bad weather being forecast for the region later in the day, so Trevor said he would return in the afternoon of the next day, assuming the storm had cleared. The fourteen men would wait for Trevor and the convoy to arrive in the afternoon. Then they would attack and kill Trevor and his security guards.

On the day Trevor announced the cancellation of the mission in front of his nineteen would-be martyrs, reports had been received of a massive sandstorm coming in off the coast so all vehicular travel across the Plateau was restricted for that evening. The restriction was expected to be lifted early the next day. The five men that accepted their failure to be martyrs wished to leave peacefully and planned to do so under cover of the tail end of the storm. They were going to steal one of the spare pickup trucks. Trevor's men had parked vehicles in a shallow depression to the North of the camp for use in ferrying supplies, etc. The rugged vehicles lay covered in camouflage netting to prevent surveillance drones from spotting them from the air.

As there was almost no chance of anyone either leaving the camp or arriving at the camp during the sandstorm, the entire group tried to follow their normal routine, but with one group pointedly ignoring the other group. The five that would leave without a fight were being called cowards by their comrades. The fourteen that wished to put their newly learned fighting skills to good use by attacking the people who had been their teachers did not have the same family responsibilities as the other five men and so were more willing to die in a gunfight. It made for a tense, uncomfortable evening in the camp.

Unbeknownst to the nineteen men, or to the training officers left in the camp by Trevor, the whole base was being watched by men hiding close-by in the low hills to the West. Listening devices planted in every tent, in the toilets, and in the vehicles being used at the camp had been transmitting every word spoken in the camp since Trevor had briefed the men on their very first day there. Placed there by Trevor to keep himself informed of any issues, and as insurance if things went badly wrong in any way, it had proved to be the right move by him. From the moment Trevor had announced the abrupt ending of the mission, the armed men hidden in the hills had paid very close attention to the voices being unwittingly broadcast from the tents down below.

The hidden men heard the tone of the conversations changing from disappointment to anger to full-on rage. Most of the rage was directed at the organizers of the mission. Trevor's rhetoric had built the men up to the point of being ready and willing to die for that mission. Then the mission commanders had simply dropped the whole idea and left the emotionally charged men to find their own way back to their mundane lives. The listening men heard the voices through the small speakers as the men in the camp down below reached the fateful decision to murder those they felt had let them down.

The observers, sent by Trevor Wilson to listen and determine if the nineteen men intended to accept that their mission had failed, or if they were going to try to attack the people behind that aborted mission. If it proved to be the latter case, the watching men were to take decisive action. When they heard the boys speaking of overpowering their training officers, taking control of the weapons, and trying to kill Trevor when he returned to the camp, the men looked at one another and nodded. It was time for action. The small team of men lurking in the hills were not boy soldiers like the ones making their foolish plans in the tents below. These were battle hardened, mercenary killers. They would show no mercy, would not hesitate to shoot, and kill unarmed men in their beds. Not one of the nineteen men from Trevor's failed mission would leave this camp alive. The training officers, all local militia, would be shot along with their trainees. There could be no witnesses left to tell of the aborted mission. Trevor planned to leave Yemen without a backward glance.

Separate from the listening men, another man was also listening and observing, but he was not one of Trevor's hunters. He was hidden close to the listening men and had been secretly observing the team as they, in turn, spied on the training camp below. He had listened to their discussion of Trevor's instructions, and he knew that a decision had been made to execute the nineteen trainees.

This man had paid special attention to the movement of a particular young trainee in the camp earlier. He had watched and memorized the location of the tent into which this novice soldier had trudged to sleep earlier in the night. From studying the camp routine, the lone man knew that once the killers began their careful, silent descent to the camp, he would have a one-minute window of opportunity and it might be only as little as thirty seconds, to get down to the camp ahead of the armed men and to do what he intended. It was going to be close indeed, but this lone watching man intended to at least try. He figured the killers hiding and waiting in the hills above might not be too careful about counting dead bodies after they had fired a few hundred bullets through the thin canvas walls of the camp. They might not notice one victim had disappeared ahead of the gunfire. He hoped and prayed they would not search outside.

He intended to extract one man before the shooting started. If he could not get the lad out without waking the other sleeping men and causing a stampede out the exit doors, his nephew would die in the camp, just like all his comrades that would die there. Maamar could not allow his rescue attempt to put his own life or liberty at risk. He was important in a much greater cause than saving one pimple faced, foolish young man. But Maamar Hamidou wanted to be able to look his sister in the eye and tell her he had done his best to keep her only child alive. Maamar had not yet met his nephew in person, he was relying on long range reconnaissance photographs to guide him to the correct young lad. The pictures had been taken from the street outside the small house lived in by Emani and her son. Emani was embracing a young man of about her son's age when the picture was taken. Maamar just hoped the photographer had captured the correct subject with his camera. What a thing that would be if he succeeded in his rescue mission here tonight but brought out the wrong man!

Maamar prepared to make his move, aware that the men above his position would begin their attack in a few minutes. He had been watching them for hours and knew they were good at what they did. They were well hidden and kept very good discipline, but they weren't from this region and didn't know the environment like a local knew it. They smelt differently from the locals. Maamar had watched the goats grazing in the area and saw them avoid the hiding place of the men due to this unfamiliar scent. Goats act like they don't know or care about anything, but they're good watch dogs if you know how to read them. Maamar knew goats very well indeed.

Trevor Wilson paid the local warlords large sums of money to be allowed to run his operation in the area. Trevor expected complete discretion from the militia for the money they received. Nevertheless, Maamar had been informed by one well paid warlord that his nephew Ibrahim was one of the idiots chosen for Trevor's mission. It took a few days to determine the nature of the operation. But from questioning one of the local men, a training officer, to the nineteen novice soldiers, Maamar knew what Trevor Wilson was planning. Maamar told his own comrades that he intended to remove his nephew from the camp before the operation reached its conclusion.

Hearing that Trevor had failed to secure a smuggler to get his group to America came as no surprise to Maamar. His group had warned all people traffickers against accepting Trevor's money. Ibrahim wouldn't be going abroad to blow himself up in some foreigner's fantasy of being a terrorist. As relieved as he was, instinct told Maamar to start watching the secret training camp. Maamar discovered the foreign men hidden in deep cover above the training camp. He realized they had listening devices transmitting conversations from the camp to their position. And he knew then, just because Ibrahim wasn't getting shipped abroad to help carry out an attack, did not mean Ibrahim was going to be safe. In fact, Ibrahim's life had gotten shorter than ever. Unless Maamar was quick and brave.

Maamar got close to the tents in the camp earlier that evening and now knew what was being planned by a number of the nineteen men. Once he had that information, he then knew what the small team of men hidden in the uplands were planning. They were there to eliminate the witnesses to Trevor Wilson's failed plot. Trevor was probably going to try the same plan somewhere else and couldn't take the risk of these men in Yemen revealing this earlier attempt at an attack on America. The entire camp contingent would be shot to death, the bodies buried out in the sands. The camp could be left to decay on the ground, as it would not reveal the nature of the activity that it once contained. There were plenty of camps like this dotted around from the multiple military campaigns waged in these lands.

In his tent, Ibrahim Mahmoud sleepily opened one eye, and tried to look around the sleeping space. He was attempting to see, but he was in the darkest night he had ever experienced. Normally there would be some light from the moon, but tonight, the sandstorm had thrown a grey blanket across the sky.

Feeling sure that a noise, distinct from the sounds of the storm outside, had woken him, Ibrahim tried to sit up in the dark. Something like a hand was holding him in place. Panic threatened to take over as he struggled to move, and then he felt the heat from another person in proximity wafting across his face. A smell of goats and sweat filled his nostrils, and a voice whispered harshly in his ear, `grab the back of my belt and do not let go`. The hand holding him in place was lifted, and a gloved hand guided Ibrahim's hand to a rope-belt at the man's waist and he rose from his bed, holding tightly to the belt.

Ibrahim followed the mysterious stranger out through an opening that had been cut in the canvas rear wall of the tent. The leading man walked quickly up a shifting sand dune at the rear of the camp and continued out onto the sands of the open desert. Out here, the wind was gathering its strength and had begun to pick up fistfuls of coarse sand and fling it around. The stars above were barely visible through a veil of flying dust. Ibrahim kept his eyes and mouth shut and maintained his grip on the belt of the hunched over man in front of him. They were a few hundred yards away from the cluster of tents when Ibrahim thought he heard gunfire, carried faintly on the wind. With the fast pace being set by his rescuer, he couldn't risk looking back towards camp and probably wouldn't have been able to see anything, even if he had looked.

After what seemed like a couple of miles of wordlessly following, they finally came to a parked vehicle. When they were both strapped into their seats, the stranger started the engine, and the car was driven at high speed out into the dark desert, in the middle of what was now a proper sandstorm. After driving for nearly an hour, the vehicle skidded to a halt at a cluster of tents, smaller than the military ones they had left behind. How these tents were located by the driver was a mystery to Ibrahim. The driver told him to get out and to follow him once again. The stranger unzipped the front of one tent, gestured to Ibrahim to go inside the tightly roped dome. He then followed closely behind, forcing Ibrahim to scoot over to one side in the cramped space.

His rescuer sat down, rummaged in his layered clothing, removed a photograph from his inside pocket, and studied it for a moment by the shielded light of a torch. Finally, shining the light into Ibrahim's face, his grizzled saviour smiled and offered his hand for Ibrahim to shake. He introduced himself as uncle Maamar and Ibrahim finally realized who it was that had woken him and kidnapped him from the camp. And Ibrahim realized with a shudder what the gunfire behind them had meant. He had been pulled from his own deathbed by his mother's brother. He was alive, but his comrades were, without doubt, dead. And probably already buried by now.

Early the next morning, Ibrahim crawled from the tent to urinate out on the sand and discovered a large group of men sitting around the smoldering remains of a fire. They had been sheltering from the storm in the other tents when Ibrahim and his rescuer had arrived during the night. He was introduced to them as Maamar's nephew, and they were described as friends of his uncle. The men, grizzled and worn looking, looked at him for long moments, openly curious as to the nature of this gangly youth that Maamar had risked his life to rescue.

One of the men offered a battered cup of strong coffee to Ibrahim. The man said he hoped Ibrahim had slept ok in the tent and commented that it was better than being dead. In response to Ibrahim asking if he was correct in thinking his comrades were all murdered, the man confirmed his uncle had saved him from being shot to death along with his eighteen comrades in the desert camp. Maamar explained then that he could not rescue all the young men, as the people doing the killing would simply track down each man in their village and kill them there instead. They would also murder the men's families to silence them.

It was better if the eighteen men died in the desert and for the killers to assume they had gotten everyone. Now that the camp had been cleansed of potential witnesses, it was highly doubtful that the man calling himself Trevor Wilson would ever again show his face in Yemen. He would feel safe to go elsewhere and attempt to revive his failed terrorist plot. Maamar predicted they would be reading about it on the news websites one day soon. He was just happy his sister's boy was above the sand and breathing, instead of not breathing and buried beneath it. They all raised mugs of coffee in a toast to Emani's boy, and to the happy fact of him being not dead.

Hours later, having been driven across more miles of desert to the crossroads near his home, Ibrahim and uncle Maamar separated on the road. They would pretend to have just met on the road as both were travelling to Ibrahim's home. Now, sitting in the small room in the house shared by Ibrahim and his Mother Emani, Maamar admitted to them he had run away from prison in England a while ago. He said he hoped they would let him stay with them for a while, as he needed a place to sleep. He chatted away over sweet tea and home-made bread, telling them tales of his life in England.

Emani suspected her brother Maamar was talking a lot about his life in Britain, to avoid explaining how he had managed to arrive unannounced at her home with her son Ibrahim by his side. She suspected the two of them were sharing some secret. She felt sure they had been camped together during the night and had not only met that day, as Maamar insisted. They both smelt of the same fire when she embraced them, and when she washed their clothes later there were animal hairs stuck to the fibers that looked to be from the same goat. As a woman, she knew it wasn't her place to ask questions about what the men had been doing. Either they would tell her, or it was none of her business. She was simply glad to see her brother and very relieved and happy to have her son home from the work he had been doing up North. She assumed it was oil company work he had been engaged on, as he had been paid in US dollars. The money was most welcome and would be used to buy meat for a celebration dinner to welcome her brother to their home.

On their way into the village earlier, Maamar had warned Ibrahim to say nothing of the events out in the desert. To Emani, he simply said they had met on the road outside the village while Ibrahim was hanging out with some friends. Maamar had introduced himself and they had walked to the house together. Ibrahim had previously told his mother he would be working up North for a few weeks but that she would continue to receive his salary while he was away.

Much later, she found out how close she had come to losing her son forever. At the same time, she discovered that her own brother had been the one to rescue her boy. When she got this information, Maamar was no longer around, and she was far from home in drastically changed circumstances. Today, however, she simply thanked God every day for the close relationship that had somehow been forged between the two most important men in her life. Although she worried and wondered about the circumstances of their meeting on that first day, she knew better than to ask questions of the men.

After the evening meal, Maamar asked Ibrahim to join him outside the family home for a smoke, thus taking them out of the hearing of Emani. Having told Ibrahim some of his business earlier, Maamar explained in more detail that he was part of a group in Yemen. They carried out attacks all over the middle east on oil installations and on manufacturing facilities which were owned by western foreigners. They were trying to force these foreign-owned companies to leave Yemen by attacking their factories, refineries, and transport, thereby making it too expensive for them to carry on their business in the region.

Once the companies withdrew their operations, they left the actual buildings and hardware behind, as it was too expensive to transport abroad. Using politicians sympathetic to their cause, Maamar and his colleagues would persuade the Yemen government to take over the abandoned infrastructure and start processing the raw materials for export with the revenue being re-invested in the nation's well-being. It was happening in a small way in some areas of Yemen, but only very slowly. Too many government politicians were in the pay of the big business concerns and so, couldn't be seen to encourage the vandalism and outright attacks that were occurring.

Maamar's group were active in other parts of the middle east, and had sources of information everywhere. From the intelligence they had gathered so far, they were convinced the man calling himself Trevor Wilson, having recruited the nineteen Yemen men to be part of his terrorist spectacular in America, had not intended for any of them to survive the event. They were going to be a new type of suicide bomber, and their families would be left to face the consequences. If Wilsons plan had succeeded, the Americans would not have rested until the source of the attack had been traced. Once Yemen was identified it would simply be a matter of time until the villages and settlements from where the nineteen men had come would be pinpointed.

US air force drones or manned fighter planes would come in fast from the decks of a US carrier in the Gulf. Firing rockets and dropping bombs as they approached their targets. The result on the ground would be utter desolation and mass deaths. International condemnation would be loud and prolonged, but the American

President would happily ignore the protests. He would go on his twitter and boast about how his 'Air Force boys and girls had avenged America'.

Meanwhile, Trevor Wilson would be back in his life, free of blame. American oil companies would return to Yemen, offering exploitative contracts to repair and re-start the oil extraction and processing. Everything would go right back to the way it had been for years. The people of Yemen would again be excluded from the benefits of their own nation's natural resources.

These, then, were the reasons Maamars organization had blocked the attempts by Trevor to ship his nineteen recruits to America. The leaders of the loose coalition of militia and radical groups of which Maamar was a central figure, were influential in the entire region. They had spoken with the people smugglers and human traffickers and warned them not to cooperate with Trevor Wilson on any part of his plan. Maamars group certainly had no objection to Trevor Wilson or anybody else, killing Americans and destroying American property, but they would not allow an outsider to use Yemeni men as sacrificial goats, staked out on open ground, to be easily discovered by American investigators and quickly traced back to their Yemen homeland, where American vengeance would be swift and merciless.

Birmingham, England.
2019

It was this entire tale, from attending the meeting with Trevor Wilson to his uncle Maamar dragging him from the camp where he would be murdered, that Ibrahim left out while telling his story to the English cops and, by extension, to the American agents. He had meant to tell them all of it, but he still felt genuine embarrassment at the memory of needing to be rescued from the camp by his uncle. He didn't like thinking about it, so he certainly did not want to talk to the nice policemen about it. So, Ibrahim stuck to telling happy tales of his uncle and the bravery of the men in Yemen. When he eventually ran out of stories about Maamar's exploits, he then finally got around to telling them about his own adventure with Trevor Wilson in the desert. Of course, he made it all about how his brilliant, brave uncle had saved him from certain death.

YEMEN

2015.

Ibrahim, listening to Maamar explaining his involvement in the politics of Yemen, stared with awe at his clever uncle. These simple men, smelling of camels and goats, filthy with years of desert grime, were fighting a war against international companies, and even national governments, to try to regain some semblance of an economy for future Yemen generations. Ibrahim wanted to learn more and Maamar said he would be proud to teach his nephew. They would begin meeting with others who would help explain things to Ibrahim in better detail.

Maamar stayed with Ibrahim and Emani for almost a year after the incident in which he rescued Ibrahim from Trevor Wilson's killers. Ibrahim, now working in yet another shitty job in an oil company, but very happy to be alive, enjoyed spending his spare time with his uncle. The man had lived a real life and had many interesting stories to tell the impressionable Ibrahim. Maamar, perhaps seeing a young version of himself, saw a lost boy that needed a strong male presence in his life.

Maamar had only recently returned to Yemen after years abroad yet seemed to know everybody in the villages and settlements. Maamar explained to Ibrahim that he had grown up in this region, had gone to Europe and Britain to expand their network and to arrange new sources of funding for their war in Yemen. Part of his work had seen him getting involved with the radical group in England, sharing his skills with the devoted, but, inexperienced fighters. He had only intended to be in England for a year but had spent three years in prison after being caught with the bomb making materials. Now, having escaped from custody he was back in his beloved homeland. He was regularly going to meetings outside the village, where he and the other men discussed the state of their nation and tried to find solutions to their shared problems. Prompted by his sister, Maamar began to bring Ibrahim along to these meetings. They would travel by road to sit on cold, stony ground with men that lived in camps high in the mountains to the west of the country. There were old ruins up there that Maamar explained were the remains of old civilizations that had been destroyed in various wars and conflicts over the centuries.

Uncle Maamar was pleased that Ibrahim was accepted and welcomed in the gatherings. Ibrahim had some weapons and tactics training provided by Trevor's men in the desert camp and this helped him to bond with the mountain warriors. Before long, they had presented him with his own assault rifle, a battle-scarred Kalashnikov with ancient initials burned into its wooden stock. Maamar made it clear to Ibrahim that neither the weapon nor any of the conversation at the fireside in the hills were to be spoken of in the house while Emani was present. It was to remain between the men only. Ibrahim promised to keep it that way. Ibrahim kept that promise, but only until he got the opportunity to brag to English policemen.

It seemed to be the case that everyone around the camp had lost family members in various wars and battles against the Americans, Israelis, and Europeans. More still had been killed carrying out suicide bombings and gun attacks on targets in Israel, Saudi Arabia, and Iraq. Ibrahim's own father had deserted them when Ibrahim was still a child leaving Emani to raise the boy alone. Ibrahim now wished he had a father that had died in glorious battle so he could boast of him, in the same way the other young men did here. There was wistful talk among the men of attacking the Americans and the British in their separate areas of military operation in Iraq and Afghanistan. The men knew of militia groups that would welcome good fighting men from Yemen to bolster the insurgent forces in

Syria. The men that had been in combat in Syria, and survived, considered it a genuine badge of honor to have fought in that butcher's theatre.

From listening to the dramatic stories and from spending time with the families of men that had died in war, Ibrahim became convinced that joining an insurgency somewhere would bring new purpose to his empty life. He decided to focus all his energy on learning the fighting skills these men were willing to impart to him. He recalled his shame when he failed to join the regular army of Yemen, but he now felt that had been a blessing in disguise. For here, among these brave men, was an army that fought for the good of the people, not at the whim of some politician. Ibrahim felt sure that if he learned to be a good soldier, if he trained hard and constantly and fought well, he would make Uncle Maamar proud of him.

Ibrahim wanted to put the entire Trevor Wilson disaster out of his mind, and he just hoped Uncle Maamar would never again raise it in conversation. It was embarrassing to think of how close he had come to being killed in his bed like a helpless child. He would probably never see Trevor Wilson again, but if he ever came across him, he would gladly kill the white liar.

The day came when Maamar was preparing to leave the village for an important mission with his group of fighters. He took Ibrahim aside to explain things to him. He was going North to Saudi Arabia with six other men. They planned to attack an exclusive beach resort frequented by American and European embassy employees. They had information an American senator would be there, meeting with Saudi financiers. it was a rare opportunity to kill an American politician and Maamar and his men did not intend to let it pass.

Tensions between Yemen and Saudi Arabia were always running high. Relations were especially strained now due to the ongoing conflict between the two nations. The attack by Maamars group would be seen as the Yemeni response to news reports that America and the Saudi royal family had signed a new partnership agreement. The deal was a renewal of previous alliances between two of the biggest players in the middle east. Explicit in the deal that had been jointly announced by US and Saudi officials was that Russia was not being invited to join. It was the opinion of Maamar that if the Saudis chose to lay down with the American dogs, they should expect to pick up a few fleas. Maamar and his men were going to infect the Kingdom with a lot more than just a few fleas.

Previously boastful and cheerfully arrogant in telling tales of himself in battle, in stories of attacking the Western facilities, Ibrahim noticed Maamar now seemed somber, almost mournful. Placing a heavy hand on Ibrahim's shoulder, Maamar told the younger man that he did not have great hope of surviving this forthcoming attack. He had been hearing reports from other groups over the past few months about how Saudi Arabia had increased their surveillance and improved the security systems in their cities. Paranoid as they were, they were making more widespread use of informants to gather information on people from Yemen who might be in The Kingdom to do harm to businesspeople and foreign tourists. There were rumors of secret listening devices having been planted everywhere to gain advance warning of impending attacks.

In the hotels and resorts frequented by American and British businesspeople, Saudi security personnel were more thoroughly vetting people. They were quietly removing Yemeni people from their jobs without explanation or compensation. The Saudi government had recently announced a faith-based crack-down on homosexual, atheist and extremist behavior. This renewed religious fervor was used by the police to intrude into every aspect of people's lives. It meant increased scrutiny of anyone moving around the streets and roads of Saudi Arabia and made it far more difficult for people like Maamar to survey a potential target. Hence, the extra worry and anxiety on Maamar's part while talking to Ibrahim about the mission.

Maamar warned that if Ibrahim received a message that he, Maamar, had been killed or captured, Ibrahim was to use the written instructions and map that Maamar had given him. The instructions were that he was to take his mother and their belongings and head east, overland through Oman to India. He was then to rent rooms for the two of them and wait there for a month. Then, booking passage on a ship, they were to make their way to Britain. Maamar handed Ibrahim an envelope full of cash in various currencies. Also, in the envelope was the address of his council flat in Birmingham and two telephone numbers for his wife and his aunt in Birmingham. Those people would assist Emani and Ibrahim in finding their way around in their new homeland.

Ibrahim tried to argue that he could take care of his mother right here in Yemen. He did not want to leave his home for a foreign place. Maamar smiled gently at his nephew. 'The people that killed your eighteen comrades in the desert camp were contracted by Trevor Wilson to kill nineteen potential witnesses against Trevor and his failed plans, ' he said. 'I hoped they would not count the dead after they shot the camp to pieces, but I am hearing they took the time to lay out the corpses of your comrades and compared their faces to photographs. They know you were not among the dead. They have spent time sniffing around and following leads. They now know where to find you. They have been waiting for an opportunity to complete the job. They have not come for you so far because I and my men have been a constant presence around this village and near your workplace. They will attack without hesitation once they know we are not returning from the North`, he continued. 'There will be an observer with us in Saudi who will know if things have gone badly for us. He is not a fighting man. When he has confirmation of our capture or of our deaths, he will travel fast. He will come here to inform you and your mother and after here he will go to the homes of my comrades to give them the news. I have gathered this money and travel information to help you. Promise me you will use it if it becomes necessary`.

Ibrahim, close to tears, shook his uncle's hand and watched as the man walked out to the road to where a battered pickup truck waited with blue smoke trickling from its exhaust pipe. Maamar did not look back or wave to his nephew. Ibrahim simply stood there alone, looking after the truck until long after it had disappeared, from sight and from hearing. Emani had been trying to listen at the window and had heard some of the conversation. She now felt sure she had seen her brother for the last time as she watched from the window. After a while she went outside and, taking her son by the hand, she guided him into their home. By then, the smoke and the dust from the truck had long settled and there was no sign of it, or Maamar, remaining. Just over a week later, with a full Moon riding high in the night sky, Ibrahim shook his mother's shoulder to wake her. The messenger from the North had come bearing his grim news. The man had driven for almost seven hours to get to this tiny house in Yemen. He remained only long enough to impart his message, make use of the toilet and then he left. He had six more homes to call to, homes in which he would leave women and children crying in shocked grief, while the old men that remained, shook their heads in numb acceptance.

Before the Moon had fully risen on the night after, Ibrahim and his mother were well on their way out of Yemen and heading for a smuggler crossing that would bring them into Western Oman. Whatever scenery was there to be gazed upon and enjoyed along those roads went unseen by Ibrahim and Emani. Hidden in a secret compartment in the center of a sheep transport, they were unable to see anything outside. It was all they could do in the dusty, stinking truck to keep breathing and try not to sneeze while stopped at checkpoints.

They had offered to pay the truck driver for their passage, but he refused, telling them they would be insulting him if they persisted. He knew who they were and why they were leaving Yemen under cover of darkness. He offered his sympathy for their recent loss, and informed them with a quiet dignity that it would be an honor to assist in their escape. It seemed Maamar inspired loyalty and respect just as much after death as he had in life, even out here, hundreds of miles from his home.

Mother and son travelled as instructed by Maamar, Northeast across Oman. On the East coast, they would make a sea crossing to Karachi in Pakistan and from there, it would be a long road journey south to Mumbai in India. There, they were to meet a man, yet another link in Maamar's network. This man would arrange to get them both aboard a ship as fare paying passengers, while avoiding the need to show any documents of identification.

Ibrahim, before his uncle's departure, tried to argue with Maamar about their route. He said it would be more straightforward to have gone west from Yemen into Africa. But Maamar had explained that trying to cross that huge continent illegally would have been impossible. With the various famine, disease epidemics and humanitarian crisis in different African nations, the place was full of U.N and W.H.O. units, constantly on the lookout for villagers that might have crept past the disease containment checkpoints. The first patrol that stopped Ibrahim and his mother would demand their papers and that would be the end of their escape attempt. After being checked for any signs of infections such as Ebola, they would be deported back to their own country.

Maamar suspected that Trevor Wilson had government contacts and if Emani and Ibrahim were deported from an Africa nation back to Yemen, Trevor would be notified. He was undoubtedly still planning some sort of attack on a western target and would not want to leave any possible witness alive. Ibrahim was the sole survivor of Trevor's last attempt to raise an army, and Trevor would prefer to start any new operation with a clean slate.

Maamar continued his argument against trying to cross Africa by explaining if you managed to avoid all the official bureaucratic barriers, you also had to get past the warlords and their private armies that controlled each local region. Ibrahim was correct in saying it was longer and more time consuming going East from Yemen, but it should prove the safer route. And as Maamar pointed out, Ibrahim and Emani weren't really in a hurry, there was nothing waiting for them in Britain except the rest of their lives.

Almost two months after leaving their home in Yemen, Emani and Ibrahim arrived in the U.K. On the day they walked off the passenger ferry, in a slow-moving crowd of fellow passengers and stepped onto solid land, it was raining and cold.

After three years living in Britain, Ibrahim would often swear to his mother that the British weather had not improved even once.

Birmingham, present day.

Ibrahim finally stopped talking, took a long drink from his water bottle and glanced shyly across the table at the cops. The two English detectives were sitting open-mouthed and wide-eyed. This scruffy, simple-minded lad seemed completely unaware of just how crazy, dramatic and romantic the life he had been living back in Yemen really was. He possibly held the key to identifying the actual planner of the JFK airport attack. This Trevor Wilson fella had to be the brains behind the whole thing. The two detectives were both thinking the same thing, nineteen hi-jackers on 9/11, nineteen recruits in Yemen, and nineteen attackers in the most recent, but failed, attack on JFK airport. That was clearly the magic number, it was the ideological fingerprint of the mastermind from South Africa or Zimbabwe or wherever, it was smeared all over the thwarted attacks in JFK.

Nicholas King asked Ibrahim to excuse him and Mike for a moment. They would return soon. Out in the corridor, Nicholas was almost hopping around with excitement in front of his senior partner, Mike. The young detective ticked off the salient points on his fingers just to be sure that Mike got the significance of what they just heard in the interview room.

Out of the blue in Birmingham, this young man gets pissed off at police officers for the wrong reasons and finds himself arrested on assault charges.

He turns out to be the nephew of a rather big fish in the international radical cesspool. He admits to having been in training with members of one of the biggest known terror groups in the Middle East.

Then, to top all of that, he casually recounts the story of how he was invited to join and train for an attack, since aborted, on a significant target in the US.

Said attack being organized by a man who resolutely insisted upon there being nineteen attackers.

Supposedly because he wanted to pay tribute to Mohammed Atta and his little gang of helpers on 9/11 twenty years ago. Mike Farrell led Nicholas into a vacant office across the hall and, setting out sheets of paper on the desk, he plotted the timeline of Trevor Wilson and his terrorist plot as described by Ibrahim, and as known from the facts of the JFK attack.

Trevor Wilson's adventures in the Northern desert of Yemen appeared to have started out brightly enough. To the point of getting his nineteen martyrs into a training camp in the desert. His plans had then changed drastically, for some reason. They weren't sure what caused Trevor to pull the plug in Yemen, Ibrahim hadn't been too clear on the reasons. But they knew he'd been stopped in his tracks in Yemen four years ago.

Which gave Mister Wilson plenty of time to have made his way to America, to have come up with a new plan, to have recruited an entirely new class of nineteen idiots and to try to execute his new plan. Only to once again see it all come to a crashing halt right there in JFK, this time due to a nosy, quick-thinking Englishman and a Port Authority patrol officer, that acted first and asked questions later.

Mike and Nicholas returned to the room where Ibrahim was waiting. And from there, the US agents were contacted and had swiftly joined their British counterparts in Birmingham. And Ibrahim got to tell his story all over again, this time to a larger audience and in front of more cameras and recording devices. And to a more international audience this time.

Ibrahim, having been the center of attention, now found himself being led back down to the same cell they had stored him in overnight. The custody officer told him not to get upset. It was just a temporary stay while the bosses figured out what to do with him.

A young constable brought tea and toast along with an apology for there being no milk in the tea and nothing on the toast. He explained it was because nobody in the canteen was clear on whether Muslims were allowed milk and butter. Ibrahim, ravenously hungry at this point and caring nothing for religion or politics, ate and drank the lot exactly as it was. He had completely forgotten his earlier worry that police officers liked to spit on prisoners' food.

Upstairs in the office area of the police station, inside a soundproof briefing room, it sounded like the trading floor of the New York stock exchange. Two separate points were being noisily argued across the room. The American agents were attempting to claim sole custody of Ibrahim. They wanted to take him to the US for intensive debriefing. The British Home Office was adamant he was going nowhere until his nationality status had been established. If he was in the process of becoming a British citizen through an application for asylum or under his refugee status, then he would be under the protection of the UK government.

As it was currently fashionable to condemn torture and other forms of `enhanced interrogation`, the British Prime Minister would later attempt to get himself in a photo with the young immigrant so that he could proclaim his government to be a champion of immigrants' rights. An adviser from Ten Downing Street would quietly whisper that Ibrahim might yet prove to be a terrorist, and therefore it would be preferable if the PM did not go on the record or get photographed alongside the Yemeni man.

If he was in the UK illegally, he was technically still a citizen of Yemen, although there seemed to be some question as to whether he even had a passport from that nation. If he was illegally resident in the UK, and the US issued an international arrest warrant for him based upon charges of aiding and abetting a known terrorist, aka Uncle Maamar, then the American agents were welcome to take him. It would be done through the courts and the UK government could wash their hands of the whole thing while also claiming credit for catching and holding Ibrahim and extracting the information that led to the capture of the person behind the plot to blow up aircraft in JFK.

The British cops were in a position of strength in this debate. They had charged Ibrahim with the attempted assault of two of their police officers and he would have to face a British judge for that. As far as the British cops were concerned, that took precedence over anything else. It was now being used to protect Ibrahim from the American agents, who wanted to bundle him out the door immediately. The English weren't generally against Ibrahim being subjected to the Americans 'enhanced interrogation techniques'. But the Prime Minister had made it a plank of his election campaign recently that he would bring an end to any use of torture by British Armed Forces anywhere in the world. And he had said he would be against the use of torture by any other nation with which Britain had allied herself. Everyone took this to mean the US who were known to be using off-site security contractors to extract data from captured insurgents. The use of contractors was a legal move to remove any liability from agents and soldiers of the United States of America.

Detective Nicholas King was seated at the Police station briefing table among all the haggling but had not been invited to speak. Instead, he was quietly urging his senior officers to shout louder, to try harder to make themselves heard above the others. He did not want Ibrahim to be taken into the custody of the agents from the CIA. Ibrahim would not survive long if they took him as a suspect. Because they would be hostile toward him, Ibrahim would refuse to tell them anything further, which would make them more hostile. Nicholas, having spent time just talking with Ibrahim, before the madness had begun in the briefing room upstairs, felt sure he had a simple solution to all of it.

He believed Ibrahim was only too willing to continue to talk about anything and everything that had occurred in Yemen. Therefore, they did not have to drag him to one of their secret sites for ` real talk `, as he had overheard the American agents referring to it. They only had to offer him and his mother a trip to Disneyland or Universal Studios and he would willingly tell them his family's deepest, darkest secrets. Provided of course he had not already revealed everything worth hearing, he certainly did talk a lot.

There was also the urgent matter of identifying the man known now as Trevor Wilson. Nicholas was confident Ibrahim would be able to pick Wilson out of photographs if the American agents just gave him the time and space. And, if they weren't torturing and threatening him.

Two hours after the shouting between English and American cops had come to a halt in the police station, Detective Constable Nicholas King parked his private car in one of the designated parking places outside a rundown flats complex in Birmingham. His detective partner, Mike, had asked Nicholas if he could manage alone to carry out the task of escorting Ibrahim home. Mike said he had to go home to help his daughter deal with some sort of incident at one of her restaurants. She had been summoned to the closed venue by the security firm that patrolled the building. Her husband was away on a trip with some business clients, trying to secure some corporate entertainment contracts for their food service business.

Nicholas told Mike he would be fine alone. He laughingly said if he needed help at any stage, he could always call the CIA to come assist him. Mike asked him how come the yanks weren't going along to ensure their special guest didn't go missing. Nicholas replied that the American agents were leaving Ibrahim in the custody of the British cops as they had been warned of the legal jeopardy if Ibrahim got hurt or killed while in American custody. He was still on a charge by the British courts and was legally a British prisoner. More importantly, as it was accepted that Ibrahim genuinely wanted to go to America, he wasn't considered a flight risk. The CIA was happy to have Nicholas ferrying Ibrahim around town doing his errands. They would scoop him up just as soon as the English courts released him into their custody.

As a result, Nicholas was driving his own car and in the passenger seat was Ibrahim Mahmoud, formerly of Yemen, but for now, a British resident. He wanted to speak to his mother, to explain his absence overnight, and to explain why they both would now be going away yet again. Speaking to Ibrahim outside the flats complex, Nicholas repeated his earlier suggestion that the conversation between Ibrahim and his mother would be better accomplished without a police detective standing there. Ibrahim wholeheartedly agreed with that idea and headed for the stairs up to his fourth floor flat. As usual, the lifts were out of order and Nicholas smiled to himself as he watched Ibrahim appearing and disappearing above the brick parapet at each turn on the stairs, as he went trudging wearily up flight after flight of external steps. These were the same steps he had been carried down by police officers just over a day previously.

When Ibrahim finally reached the fourth-floor landing, he vanished from view and then, for just a moment, a bright light shone out onto the balcony. Nicholas, watching from below, guessed it was a relieved Emani opening the front door of the flat to welcome her son home. Most likely, the young man would face a dozen questions about his whereabouts for so long. What a story he had for his mother.

Nicholas sat back in his seat, rubbing his eyes to clear the grainy tiredness that had been irritating him for the past few hours. He was not yet accustomed to the long days that were expected of detectives. At this point, he just wanted to get home, shower, and fall into bed. While resting his eyes in the car, he smiled as he recalled his successful intervention amid the mad scenes in the briefing room earlier.

Having shouted at each other for quite a few minutes with both trying to persuade the other that their plan was the better one. The American agents and the British diplomats and cops finally settled back into their seats, having gotten exactly nowhere. Coffee, tea, and biscuits were brought in by Helen from the station cafeteria, and her timely interruption helped cool tempers even further.

Nicholas poked his sergeant, a bulky Jamaican by the name of Kennedy Brown, in the ribs, murmuring that this was an opportunity to get their point across. Brown put down his mug of tea, stood up and noisily clearing his throat, he addressed the room. He gave the credit for the idea to Detective Constable Nicholas King and his colleague, Mike Farrell, adding that he himself felt it was probably the best course of action. Nicholas had seen that the safest option for Ibrahim was if the Americans understood that Ibrahim was a prized asset and not a terrorist prisoner to be mistreated.

The idea put forward was that Ibrahim was to be moved to the US and put in the witness protection program with US federal marshals guarding him. The US agencies would then have access to him for continued questioning as needed. If they ever apprehended this South African or Zimbabwean organizer, Trevor Wilson or whatever his name was really, they would have their eyewitness in Ibrahim right there to do the identity line-up and pick out the most wanted man in the western world. In the meantime, Ibrahim could begin looking through police mugshots of criminals and terrorism suspects in the hope of picking out Trevor Wilson.

The senior people from the various offices and departments went into their usual huddle to discuss the suggestion and very quickly came out again to agree they could work with this arrangement.

At this point, two US state department officials were already in an office on the west side of the police building, with Ibrahim seated between them, examining book after book of photographs. The Americans had gotten an agreement to proceed with the photo examination while talks were ongoing upstairs. They were taking advantage of easy access to Ibrahim in case they lost the argument to take him into custody.

These photo albums contained numerous pictures of suspected terrorist figures, some of near studio quality but most of dubious origin. There were a lot of people in the photos that had their faces half turned away or else they were holding a mobile phone to their ear, thus obscuring the cameras' view. There were a few that kept their heads down and their eyes almost closed. A number of the pictures were of people now dead, and agents were interested to see if Ibrahim had been in contact with any of them before their deaths and, if so, in what circumstances had the meeting taken place.

Ibrahim would start at the top of a page, and with a slender finger to keep his place in the gallery, he worked his way down the page. If he saw a person that looked familiar, he removed that photo and placed it in a separate pile for closer examination and profiling later.

After three hours of this, Ibrahim had moved just five pictures to the suspect pile and two of these seemed to be of the same woman. Each time he saw a picture of interest, he leaned forward for a closer look and his two minders leaned forward with him, like puppets controlled by the same strings. At one point, two of the American agents that had earlier flown in from London had lost patience with the lack of progress. They felt if Ibrahim couldn't find Trevor Wilson, then he could at least help them with other suspects. They had gone into the room and shown Ibrahim a folder full of photos of those terror suspects that were priority targets, but he had shown no recognition of them.

Everyone involved was being forced to accept that the organizer of the JFK attack, which they believed was this Trevor Wilson, had not been photographed at any time, so his picture was not going to be in the system. Ibrahim had worked with police sketch artists and together they had gotten a drawing of a white man that might be from any one of twenty European nations, or from Russia, or could indeed be from South Africa or Zimbabwe. The face looked so ordinary; it was next to useless as a means of spotting Trevor Wilson on a street or in an airport. Ibrahim insisted it was very like the man that had recruited him and later ordered his murder in the Yemen desert.

One of the US agents spoke for everyone else when she stated, `we just have to hope that he gets picked up somewhere for something unrelated and we get a notification of it. I'm sure Ibrahim will be able to pick him out from a line-up then and once that happens, we can begin unravelling the scheming bastard's life`.

Due to Nicholas King having built a rapport with Ibrahim, and it was his plan they were following, it was agreed Nicholas was to drive Ibrahim to his Birmingham flat discreetly and quickly. Once there, Ibrahim was to collect clothes, shoes, and any identification he might possess. He was also to talk to his mother. Ibrahim would be allowed sleep in his own bed for the final time, and agents would collect him the following day. At this last part, Nicholas put his hand up to get the attention of the senior officers. There were a few chuckles from the US agents and some comments about school kids when they saw he had raised his hand, but it was effective in that it caught the eye of the most senior Embassy official, a pale and very thin woman of indeterminate age who might have been as young as forty or as old as sixty-five. She had the starved and tense look of a very heavy smoker. Her fingers were long and somehow spider-like in the way they were crawling around the tabletop, seemingly independent of the rest of her body.

She gestured at Nicholas with one creepy hand, while the fingers on her other hand opened and closed as if busy catching invisible prey. She spoke just four words in her raspy smoker's voice, but all other conversations died instantly upon hearing her, ` go-ahead young man.. `.

Nicholas acknowledged her with a half-bow and, turning to the rest of the table, told them the whole thing would go a lot smoother if they included Ibrahim's mother in the relocation to America. Nicholas said he would allow Ibrahim a few minutes in the flat to speak with his mother privately. Then Nicholas could enter the flat and join the conversation. He would explain to Emani that she was welcome to join her son in America, but if she declined, they would still be taking Ibrahim. She herself might be subject to deportation from Britain back to Yemen if she wasn't willing to accompany her son to America.

The career diplomats were nodding and agreeing to this proposal even while Detective Nicholas was still talking. They had been quietly impressed with this fresh-faced officer so far. He had managed to clear a way through what might have been a difficult diplomatic situation between American and British officials. Nicholas had kept his eye on the prize, which was getting Ibrahim to supply any other information he might be withholding, and to identify Trevor Wilson. Nicholas was determined to keep Ibrahim safe from injury and probable death at the hands of ruthless interrogators. Just so long as Ibrahim kept up his end of the deal by helping to capture Trevor Wilson.

Now seated outside the flats, Nicholas was watching the hands of his watch as they crawled up towards the hour mark. He had promised Ibrahim he would allow him one hour in the flat, an hour which comprised thirty minutes of speaking to his mother about America, and he was to spend the remaining thirty minutes gathering his personal stuff. Nicholas would honor his promise to the exact minute and would then head upstairs to explain the situation to Emani Mahmoud.

Nicholas had been taken aside by the Americans and reminded that he was not to make the mistake of thinking that Ibrahim or his mother were being invited to the US as guests. Ibrahim would be transported in the custody of armed agents just like any other prisoner. His mother was being allowed to accompany him and would be housed with her son in America, again in the custody of marshals in a guarded and secured witness house. They were to be granted the minimum of human decency while they got their possessions gathered in their flat.

Nicholas sat up straight in the driving seat of his VW Golf and did a swift mental checklist of things he might need when he went up to the flat to speak to mother and son. He had a canister of pepper spray and a loose bundle of plastic-cuffs in case things went badly upstairs. He smiled to himself at that thought, trying to imagine himself dragging a cuffed and struggling Ibrahim down eight flights of stairs, probably while the man's mother attacked and abused Nicholas at every step.

He checked his mobile phone and grimaced to note that as usual; it was down to just a few percent of battery. He never remembered to charge the thing at night like most people did. Conscious of this fault in his memory, he had gone out and bought a phone charger that worked in the car but of course he kept forgetting to plug the phone in while driving, which defeated the purpose of having a car charger.

He now plugged the phone into the socket on the console and the screen lit up. It displayed his favorite photo as the screen background. It was of himself at his graduation from college, holding the beribboned parchment up to his gowned chest and proudly flanked on either side by his parents. He opened the car door and lifted one foot out of the car. He reflected for just a moment on how much his career in the police had changed since graduation. He was at the center of an international case to catch one of the most dangerous people in the world. He was now on his way to go up to a flat where he would begin the process of removing two people from their everyday lives for them to be transferred to another country to assist in that case.

As his shoe crunched on the uneven, glass strewn tarmac on which he had parked the car, he glanced back at his phone screen, which was just now fading to dark, as sleep mode kicked in on the screen. The photo on his phone made him think of all the terrorist suspect photos the agents had been showing to Ibrahim in the police station earlier. Nicholas, now sitting half on the seat with one foot on the ground, and the other foot still inside the car, realized that there was another photo that he could show to Ibrahim. It had not been included in the mugshots earlier because this person was not a suspect in anything and therefore was not in the crook's gallery.

If Nicholas was asked his reason for doing what he was about to do, he would not have been able to explain. It was an idea, what they used to refer to as a "hunch" on the TV cop shows. He felt sure it would not amount to anything, but he also knew that he would not be able to forget it if he did not at least carry it to conclusion. Now that he had thought of it, he would not be able to un-think it. He would go to bed that night with that annoying sensation of having forgotten something. It would be like a fishhook lodged in his mind, pulling him in a direction he should have gone earlier. Far better to just get the bloody photo, show it to Ibrahim, watch him shake his head in negation, or shrug his bony shoulders to say he had never seen this person before, then Nicholas could put the whole thing out of his head.

Unfortunately, he was driving his personal car and had left his iPad on the desk he shared with Mike, which meant he did not have access to the police system as he would in an official vehicle. He would need to download the required photo from the internet. He could do that on his phone and show it to Ibrahim directly from the phone screen. It was yet another example of how much easier police work was in the modern world compared to previous generations of detectives. The process which Nicholas was about to initiate would take about five minutes from beginning to end, but in earlier times it would have taken a detective a large part of a day. In the days before the internet, he would have had to leave the flats complex, travel back to the station, arrange for the photo to be sourced, arrange for it to be printed, said print would be of bad quality. Then he would have to travel back to the flat to ask the witness if he recognized the person in the picture. Technology was indeed wonderful.

Nicholas had to disconnect the charger cable so he could sit up straight in the car seat. They never supplied long enough cables on personal devices for some reason, and he accessed the phone's internet browser. He navigated to a website of a national newspaper on the grounds that he knew they had an archive section for photos and news stories. This section had a search bar and Nicholas entered the name of the person whose photo he wanted. Once he had the required photo, he tried to save it to the phone's memory. Instead of being asked to which memory location he wanted to save the file, he got a warning banner across his screen informing him that the image he had downloaded was protected content. It was wholly owned by the newspaper website to which his browser had directed him. He could look at it as much as he liked, but if he wanted to save it for personal use, he would have to sign into his subscriber account. He did not have such an account and had no desire to have one. Deciding it would be fine if he just left the photo open on the screen, which removed the necessity of saving it to the phone memory, he completed his exit from the car. He locked the vehicle with the remote button, and headed for the stinking, graffiti covered stairs in full darkness. Whatever public lighting had once been installed in the flats complex was now vandalized and out of commission.

Nicholas noted the utter lack of movement in the stairwells or along any of the balconies as he climbed past each floor. He had patrolled this area and a dozen just like it in his uniform years. He and his patrol colleagues always said you could judge how good or bad an area was by taking note of any regular citizens moving around after dark. If old folk and couples were out walking dogs or exercising around dusk, the area was more than likely a decent, safe area. But it only took one unsavory incident to occur, and ordinary civilians would from then on stay home after dark. Sometimes it might only be verbal abuse of a woman or an old man, and that would be that. The entire area then became a dead zone, with people locking their reinforced doors and staying indoors once they got home after work. The instant that people in a housing estate or in a flats complex like this one got the idea that it was dangerous outside, the area never really recovered. It made the job of the police easier to a certain extent in that the patrols in areas such as this flats building knew that anybody moving around at night was more than likely up to some form of bad business.

On the fourth floor, as Nicholas reached the top of the stairs, he heard voices and laughter but could not determine from which direction on the landing the sounds were coming. He assumed somebody had their front door open while they said good night to a visitor.

Nicholas stopped at the door of the flat, which had once been occupied by a bona fide terrorist but was now being lived in by a young man who might hold the key to the capture of an even worse enemy of western civilization. He put his head up close to the door and listened for a moment. He could hear the murmur of conversation but could not be sure if it was the sound of a TV coming from one of the surrounding flats. The floors and walls were so thin and badly insulated you could sometimes hear conversations from the flat above and below as if they were in the next room in your own flat. Taking a deep breath, he rang the doorbell and stepped back a pace. His hand was on the pepper spray in his jacket pocket as he recalled moments like this from his days in uniform when they would be ordered to execute a search warrant or an arrest warrant on someone in a flat like the one he was outside right now. The most nerve-wracking part was the few seconds when the lead officer had rung the doorbell and everybody tensed up, waiting to see what sort of reception they would get.

He hoped this visit would be a peaceful one. He heard the door being unlatched, and then it swung open. Ibrahim was standing inside with a slight smile. Past his shoulder, Nicholas could see a woman he took to be Emani, standing in a doorway at the far end of the hallway. Ibrahim gestured for him to come in, offering black tea and enquiring ` if everything was all good in the police`. Nicholas stepped into the hall, pushing the door closed behind himself. Emani came forward to greet him, smiling and nodding as they shook hands. In passable English, she invited him to come through to the kitchen.

When all three of them were seated around the unsteady table in the corner of the small kitchen, Nicholas asked if they had talked about their situation. Ibrahim deferred to his mother here as Emani replied that they had discussed the idea of them being brought to America. `It's a good plan`, she said. ` I'm happy my son will have the chance to live in such a place`. And she herself would try to make a new home there. Maybe there would be other people from Yemen there for her to talk with and go to the market with. Nicholas reassured them both that there was quite a large Yemeni community in America. He was not entirely sure this was the case, but his words seemed to settle them both and helped make up their minds.

He asked Ibrahim if he would look at a photograph to see if he recognized the man pictured. Nicholas took out his phone and activated it to display the photo he had left on the screen. His phone was showing 2 percent battery, the number 2 was highlighted in red, and Nicholas knew from experience, this meant the device was on the verge of shutting down. He turned the phone to face Ibrahim. The young man glanced at the screen and then looked back at Nicholas. `There's nothing there, ` he said. Nicholas turned the phone back around to find the battery had died, likely helped on its way by him leaving the internet browser window open for all that time.

He cursed under his breath, but then realised he could return to his car, put the phone on charge, and leave it in the car. Then he could go up to the flat to help them finish packing. Once they were ready to settle down for the night, he would run back to his car, retrieve the phone, and could then show Ibrahim the photo and put his hunch out of his mind once and for all. Nicholas told the two of them to continue with their packing and preparing for their trip. He said he needed to return to his car to plug the phone into the charger, and that he would stay in the car for a while to give them time to finish saying their farewells to their home. The bulkier of their possessions would be collected by a van, and at that point, their flat would no longer be their home. They would be on their way to America, for better or for worse.

Stepping out into the hallway outside Ibrahim's flat, Nicholas stood for a few seconds to make sure he had done everything as scheduled. Ibrahim and his mother would get to travel to America, officially as prisoners. But Nicholas wondered if they might be eligible to collect at least part of the reward money on offer for information leading to the capture of whoever attacked JFK. He would ask one of the diplomats if he got the chance over the next few days.

He had been standing with the front door of the flat still open, and now he reached back into the hall, grabbed the doorhandle, and pulled the door closed. He looked around and realized the balcony area had been illuminated solely by the glow cast from their hall light. Now that he had closed their front door, the smelly concrete area was suddenly very dark. The public lights in their wire enclosures were all dead. In circumstances such as these, he would use the flashlight app on his phone, but of course the phone was not capable of providing light, as it had gone completely. Nicholas reached into his jacket and withdrew the phone, once again hoping to squeeze just a few seconds of life out of the dead battery to light his way across the landing to the stairs. No, the phone remained off, which meant he would have to try the stairs in the dark.

Using the distant glow of the city lights over the dark line of the balcony wall as a guide, he made his way towards the nearest stairwell, which was just discernible as a slightly darker rectangle in the almost total darkness of the corner. He slid his feet along the ground, feeling for the edge of the top step. The noise of the soles of his shoes crunching in the grit and dust on the hard surface sounded very loud in his ears.

Suddenly, he understood it wasn't only his own shoes making that scraping noise. There was somebody else sharing the dark with him. He started to turn in sudden fear, heart thumping up high in his throat, making it difficult to breathe. He'd forgotten the pepper spray. It remained unused, sitting uselessly in his pocket. Then, up close, shockingly warm on his neck, breath reeking of tobacco, and instantly, the bulk of another body on the opposite side of him, hands grabbing Nicholas's arm. Nicholas stumbled in the dark and, in moving forward slightly, the person on his right was dragged forward, cursing, but keeping his balance. They bracketed him, too close now for it to be an accidental coming together in the dark, and Nicholas opened his mouth to speak, to identify himself as a police officer but a voice rasped over his attempt to speak, blasting beer and cigarette fumes and bad breath into the side of his face, mumbling `fuckin Muslim cunt, gobacktoyourowncountry you pox, dirty bastards, here ye go, have some of this`.

The two figures, unseen, but moulded to him, one on each side, bent low together, two strong men that performed physical labor together and had developed routines for lifting, getting their arms around his knees and his thighs, with synchronized grunts, they hoisted him off his feet. Nicholas got a brief glimpse of his car parked down below as his head rose higher above the brick parapet that went around the balcony. In the distance, he saw three people walking past on the access road outside the car parking area. He had a split second to think, there are people out at night, it's not that bad here, then the men holding his legs tipped him bodily, over the parapet and down, cold air making his eyes water as he fell through the air, hot tears running in the cold, flowing upwards into his hair.

He hit the concrete, more than fifty feet below, headfirst, arms stupidly down by his sides, shocked out of providing protection to his head, and instead of the salt water of his tears flowing into his hair, now it was blood going in all directions. He lay there in confusion; all mental clarity having been left behind on the landing. The full understanding of what had happened to him was still happening to him, had not entered his awareness. Perhaps mercifully, it never would.

The part of his brain where police discipline was stored was screaming about a photo. What about the photo? The photo is important. His brain was telling him to call a police, phone his police, but he could no longer remember what a photo even was, never mind why one photo might be more important than another. He lay there, crying, but not knowing he was crying. His nose was mashed and broken, he was bleeding, and the blood from his nose merged with the blood from his broken head, and pooled beneath him on the dirty concrete. He lay there and lay there, and nobody came to help him. He was in the dark, both literally and in relation to his fading consciousness, just another shadow among many shadows.

For some time, nobody knew he was there.

After more time passed, he didn't know he was there.

After a couple of hours, photos, phones, and police no longer mattered. Not to Nicholas, anyway.

Nicholas had dropped his phone when the men grabbed him. In the darkness on the landing, after Nicholas was gone, a boy of fourteen, chased out of the family flat by his alcoholic father for being cheeky, was roaming along the landings. Hearing the sounds of a struggle, the boy stood still, listening in the dark, eyes nearly catlike in their night-seeing. He watched/heard two shadowy figures throwing somebody over the balcony. The victim's hair was silhouetted against those city lights, curls waving, visible in the wind and then gone. During the struggle, the men were calling their victim names, saying he was Muslim and a lot of drunken cursing. But the boy thought he had seen this curly-haired man come up the stairs earlier. The man had gone into a flat on this same fourth floor landing while it was still light outside. He was a white man and looked like police, or possibly an official visitor from social welfare. He had gone into the flat of the Arabs, had stayed a while, and when he had left the flat, he had come out to a landing that was by then, deep in darkness, because the sun went behind these buildings as it set, so this side was in shadow long before full dark fell. The curly haired man had been unlucky to be found in the dark by drunken racists, looking for a target for their hatred.

The instant the two attackers ran away, the boy picked up the dropped phone. While Nicholas lay dying on the ground below, the boy took the phone to a flat on the seventh floor of the building. There, he handed it to a fat man who smelt like cat's piss. The phone was dismantled into its component parts in a matter of minutes. The identifiable parts were dissolved in acid and the remaining material was added to a large carton of similar items. In the morning, it would be sold to a phone repair shop on the high street, with no questions asked. The teenager received ten pounds for his labor and spent it on takeaway curry and a bottle of cola. He went to the curry shop using the other stairs, well away from where the curly haired man had been thrown. And he didn't mention it to his mental case of an old man when he was allowed to return to the family flat later. It wouldn't do to set his father off in a temper tantrum again while he was still drunk. That shit only led to trouble for everybody. His dad hated Arabs and Muslims and did not appreciate being reminded that there were lots of them living around him.

Ibrahim and his mother sat with their cases and bags all packed and waited over an hour for Nicholas to return. They agreed with one another that it was strange that he had not come back to the flat. Maybe he would return in the morning. If he did not come back, they would be forced to call the station and ask for someone else to help them with their preparations for their move to America. Ibrahim took his mother's hand and told her how sorry he was for bringing all this disruption to their home. Emani touched his cheek affectionately, smiling at her son as she reassured him that it was not such a bad thing that had happened. They might find a good life in America; she had heard of such things happening for others. She did insist on a full explanation of who Trevor Wilson was, and how come her son seemed to be the only person that could find him.

She listened without reaction until her son told her how Uncle Maamar had rescued Ibrahim from certain death in the desert training camp. At this revelation, she sat in shock with tears in her eyes, and her face pale. She scolded her boy for being so reckless and for not telling her all this before now. And she wished her brother Maamar was here so that she could hug him and thank him for saving her son. But she was very much afraid Maamar had sacrificed himself for his cause. She still had no definite news of his death, but she presumed the worst had happened.

Ibrahim moved around the sparsely furnished rooms, turning out the lights and making sure anything electrical was unplugged. Neither him nor his mother remarked upon the flashing blue lights and activity outside their building. It was not unusual for this place to have police outside. They had left unpacked the essentials for their nighttime routines and for sleeping, so there was nothing left to do except go to bed. A couple of hours later, they were woken by police officers knocking on their front door. Officers wanted to ask about Police detective Nicholas King being murdered while outside their flats building. Police felt sure Nicholas had been in their building, had he made it to their flat? Ibrahim replied, "yes, but he left to charge his phone in his car. He was supposed to return to the flat but never came back."

With all the police activity outside, with the cops coming up and telling them that Nicholas was dead, added to their preparation for their new life in America, Ibrahim forgot all about the photo he had been asked to look at by Nicholas. There had been so much to do to prepare for their trip and his mother kept fussing about which clothes and possessions she would bring along. So much nagging, she made it hard to think. And now he was being told that his new friend Nicholas was dead! If asked how he could forget about the photo, he would have shrugged and said he thought that Nicholas was just tying up loose strings. Ibrahim had a lot of other things to worry about. Nobody could say what the photo was that Nicholas had asked Ibrahim to look at, because Nicholas had not had time to share his hunch with anyone. He had not told Ibrahim of whom the photo was that he needed Ibrahim to look at, so nobody knew to ask about a photo.

Down below in the car park, almost five hours had passed since Nicholas King had been thrown from the balcony above. Only minutes ago, the paramedics had skidded to a halt close to where he lay. They were frantic when they first arrived on the scene, but their movements had now slowed considerably. There was nothing to be gained by hurrying. The detective had been bleeding on the concrete for too long before a passerby discovered him. They took the time to get rid of the illegal drugs they were carrying, and finally, they phoned for an ambulance and the police. His injuries were such that he might not have survived even with prompt medical attention, but with the delay in getting to him, there was no chance for him.

The police investigators working under bright lights, bagged his wallet, keys and the loose cash from his pocket. They shook their heads when they pulled the pepper spray from his pocket, it remained unused. They noted the absence of a mobile phone on, or near the body. Officers had already been through his car and had not found one there, although there was a phone charger connected and ready on the console. They would have to call his phone service and get his phone records, plus any files he might have saved to the digital cloud. It might show something helpful, but they did not hold out much hope.

Detective Sergeant Kennedy Brown, having been up to the fourth floor to examine the landing from where it was believed Nicholas had been pushed or thrown, made the observation that with it being dark up there, the attackers probably hadn't known they were grabbing a policeman. He felt it might have been another totally random attack, there were more and more lately. Just some scumbags out causing trouble and looking for a foreigner to administer a kicking to. They saw a lone male heading across the landing and, on impulse, pushed, or threw him, over the parapet. They might not have been expecting such serious injuries to have resulted. Probably they were now hiding full of remorse and guilt. They might even hand themselves in at some point, at which point they'd plead guilty to manslaughter and get a nice easy sentence. And while they were doing that, Nicholas King would be going to his grave.

Six days after Nicholas King died and three days after his funeral, which the Mahmoud family had not attended, due to the fact they were now being held in secure custody by agents of the US government, a plain white van pulled up on the rubbish strewn tarmac strip outside the flats complex. A four-man team got out and checked the area around the steps. Seeing it was clear of any locals, one of the agents called to the other occupants of the vehicle to get out quickly. Emani and her son Ibrahim were surrounded by the four big agents, and the group marched up the stairs to the flat. Once inside, they began clearing it of the possessions and luggage, directed by the two residents. The senior man in the team carried the last bag out and ushered Ibrahim and Emani out on to the landing and pulled the door shut after them. They would probably never see this place again.

The agents would accompany Ibrahim and Emani on the delayed trip to the US. They were going to be flown out of RAF Lakenheath by US Air Force transport and taken directly, by car, to their new residence in America. There, they would be guarded by US marshals until such time as permanent arrangements might be made. If Ibrahim succeeded in identifying a suspect in the JFK attacks, he and his mother would probably be granted residency in the US. If Ibrahim failed to bag the mastermind, him and his mother would not be treated well at all.

Priority for the agents was to get them clear of this dismal flat complex, and back to the secure housing near the air force base, prior to flying them out of Britain forever. Two of the team came back up the stairs from the van, one taking a position half-way up while the other went all the way up to the fourth-floor landing. He took over escort duties from his commander to ensure safe movement for the guests. As they made their way down, a stone bounced off the wall just beside Emani, and a male voice shouted, `go back to your own country, dirty Muslim fucks!`. The agent that stood guard at the midway point, identified the location of the shouter, drew a pistol from his jacket and ran lightly up the stairs.

A minute or two went by in silence, then suddenly the head and shoulders of a man were seen being pushed out over the parapet, two floors above. His arms were extended over his head and his face was bleeding. A large hand was visible holding the front of the man's jacket and there was a gun being pushed into the man's throat. The man was screaming and begging for his life, shouting how sorry he was. He didn't mean it, it was just a joke. Some of his words were being shredded by the cold wind but enough could be heard and seen for the group halted on the stairs, to know the man was utterly terrified. A few seconds later, he disappeared as the arm dragged him back to safety and the screaming thankfully stopped. The grinning agent reappeared above them on the steps, and quickly rejoined Ibrahim and Emani on the stairs. They all resumed their descent to the car park. When they got to ground level Emani looked up at the American agent and thanked him for defending them from the abuse. The agent smiled and replied, ` it's no problem Ma'am, us dirty Muslims gotta stick together, that's all! `.

Two days later, the mother and son found themselves unpacking their meagre belongings in an anonymous, stale smelling house in America. There were now different agents guarding Ibrahim and Emani and these agents were not overly friendly toward the new arrivals. Emailed communications between the Secret Service and the marshals from this time showed a marked contrast in tone from the earlier messages between intelligence agency field offices in America and the agents that had guarded the two while they were still in Britain. In the earlier messages, Ibrahim and his mother were referred to as cooperative guests, working helpfully with the police and the Federal agencies to identify the man behind the JFK attacks and to help reduce terrorist activity in Yemen.

Now, with them in protective custody in America, the language in the inter-agency emails was markedly more hostile towards the Yemeni mother and son and spoke of possible future interrogation and coercion. At this point, most agents in the division had been in conversation with Ibrahim, either on the lengthy flight over, or during the hour-long drive to the safe house. They all had realized the same thing about the man, Ibrahim did not seem to care about anyone in the world, except his mother and himself.

To Ibrahim, there was himself and his mother, everyone else was secondary to that. If anyone in his orbit died or disappeared, Ibrahim tended to not even enquire about them after they were gone. It was like he had mental curtains that he could pull across the window of his memory and block out any grief, sense of loss or even simple human curiosity. The only time he mentioned Nicholas King was when he complained to agents that his own trip to America had been delayed because the detective had inconveniently died.

Agents made frequent mention during this period of their desire to shift Ibrahim on to s program of enhanced interrogation. Agents jokingly made reference to the rendition flights that had often been sensationalized in the western media as torture transports. These flights were being seen more and more as an attractive option for dealing with this fucking guy.

Certainly, intelligence officers involved in the question-and-answer sessions that took place in the safe house were of the opinion that Ibrahim should be pushed harder. He was looking at photos for a couple of hours each day in an attempt to pick out terror suspects. They also had him looking at maps to identify the locations up in the mountains of Yemen where he and his uncle had gone to meet extremist groups. They were now aware that Ibrahim, during his days in Britain, had knowingly withheld the very pertinent information that his uncle Maamar had very likely been killed in Saudi Arabia months before. Ibrahim had not revealed that fact because he was enjoying his place at the center of attention resulting from being the nephew of Maamar. They had begun to wonder what other little snippets he might have neglected to share with them. They were wondering what lies he might be telling. Or even what photos he had skipped past to protect people he cared about.

Life in America was about to get a lot less comfortable for Ibrahim. He would have to start earning his keep. Or they would take the information from him by much harsher methods. Through all these exchanges, the US agents still did not know about the photo Nicholas King was going to show to Ibrahim on the night Nicholas died. The photo that died when Nicholas phone went into a thiefs melting pot. The one photo that these clumsy Americans never thought to show to Ibrahim.

September 2021 Washington D.C.

Agent Harris Feldman of the US secret service had been on White House duty since the election of Edwin Stamp for the first term, had managed to survive in the post through those first four years and was still there now, well into the Presidents second term. Agent Feldman tried to be non-political in this job because you could never know for sure how an election would go. You could find yourself protecting a President that you did not vote for, or one you might not like on a personal level. It was better if you kept yourself neutral. Agent Feldman had in fact voted for Stamp, had attended Stamp rallies on his days off and broadly agreed with the policies that the President had enacted. On the other side of that coin was his distaste for some of the people that Stamp had in his inner circle. Falsely religious folk, sleazy lawyers and lying business failures, just seemed to gravitate to this President. Once they were in that inner circle, they stayed in until they said, or did something that annoyed or embarrassed Stamp in public. At which point, Stamp would turn on them like an attack dog. But while they were in his good books, God help anyone that spoke negatively about them where the President might overhear.

Agent Feldman, on walking patrol in the corridors of the White House just after three a.m., found himself summoned by someone on the two-way radio to a downstairs office in the East wing. When Feldman exited the elevator in the hallway downstairs, there was a White House staffer waiting in the doorway of an office. The guy was either highly stressed or very excited, as he waved frantically to attract the agent's attention. Feldman hoped it was the latter emotion, as that would mean good news, as opposed to some new scandal or PR disaster.

Feldman realized as he crossed the hallway, the office into which George was heading was the room in which the special assistance telephone was housed. George disappeared into the office and the agent followed, hesitating at the threshold, and taking a deep breath to steady himself. George, inside the office, which was so cramped it looked more like a closet, held the handset of a red telephone out to Feldman as he entered the space. The phone, being of an older vintage, was tethered by a cable to the desk. Agent Feldman raised his eyebrows at George in an attempt to get advance warning as to whom he was about to speak. George shook his head and, having managed to unload the responsibility, took a half-step backward til the backs of his knees touched the chair behind him, into which he slowly sank. Agent Feldman, meanwhile, was saying `Hello? ` while glaring at George for landing him with this. Then a voice came through the earpiece, speaking in a pronounced English accent, `Hallo, my name is Gerard Nolan, I was given this number by your President a while ago. He told me if I ever needed assistance I should call, and he would make sure I was helped. Can you be of assistance please? `.

Agent Feldman knew that name, as almost everyone in America did. He reassured the caller that he had reached the right number and that whatever assistance he required would be given. Was it an emergency? No, it was not, not really. It was something that could wait until morning. The caller had simply forgotten there was such a big difference in time between the two countries, he was happy to wait until daytime in America. The caller was told that the President would be given the details of the call first thing in the morning, over breakfast, yes. And the President would return the call at that time. The caller gave his own number, thanked the agent, and then hung up.

Agent Feldman put down the handset and sat staring at it for a moment. George the staffer was very excited now. He grinned happily at Feldman as he exclaimed, `that phone's never rung before, in my three years here, that's the first time, and it was Gerard Nolan. The most famous Englishman in America, not counting Ricky

Gervais and Piers Morgan. I cannot believe this; I can't wait to tell my mom`. George, in his extreme happiness, had stood up from his seat and was patting his pockets, like he had mislaid something. He was of course looking for his mobile phone, clearly having forgotten it was securely stored in a locker outside the staff kitchen. They were not supposed to have them in the House, unless necessary for their job.

Agent Feldman had remained hunched over the desk and was writing notes on a small notepad taken from inside his jacket. George tried to get past Feldman to get out through the office door, but Feldman turned and grabbed his arm to prevent him from leaving. Speaking slowly and enunciating clearly, he asked George if he hated his job and his freedom so much that he would be willing to get fired and probably imprisoned just so he could tell his mother about a celebrity phone call. George looked puzzled at first, then his face cleared when he realized what the secret service man was referring to. They all signed confidentiality and non-disclosure agreements with the lengthy contracts when they agreed to take the job. The White House staff, in particular, had to sign exhaustive agreements stating that they would never ask for autographs from the celebrity and political visitors that came through the house regularly. These agreements had been updated recently to include a prohibition forbidding the asking for selfie photographs with any of the famous faces.

The sitting President was the kind of guy that did not like to share his guests or toys with anybody. That included not allowing mere administration staff to waste the valuable time of guests of the President. God herself couldn't save you if you were found to have blabbed details of a special guest of the President to anybody outside the White House.

George the staffer was no fan of the President, but he liked working in the White House, and he needed the salary that came with the job. He returned to his seat with a sigh, knowing he would have to keep his mouth shut until he got home later. Then he could tell his mother all about the phone call. She was constantly nagging him to reveal White House gossip. So much so, he often made up slightly dramatic incidents just to have something to tell her. He never had the heart to tell her how boring and uneventful his job was. Well, he marveled to himself, at least tonight he would have a real story to share over dinner. He would tell his mother to keep it a secret, as nobody outside the White House was supposed to know about the special telephone call. A small voice of sanity in George's brain tried to warn him not to tell his mother anything, that she couldn't be trusted to keep it a secret, but he told the voice to be quiet. He loved his mother, and he just knew she wouldn't blab to any of her pals if he made it clear it was a secret.

Agent Feldman got down on to his knees, grunting and cursing the cracking sounds that came from his joints. He opened the two doors beneath the desk. He lifted out a small leather-bound book from the shelf, raised it above his head and placed it on the desk. Climbing back to his feet,he sat in the chair and pulled the book to him. The book contained the procedure to be followed in the unlikely event that a phone call was received on the special phone line. George was by now standing behind Feldman and trying to read the book over the agent's shoulder. Feldman firmly and deliberately closed the book and twisted in his seat to look up at George. `Oh, now you're interested, are you? after you landed me with the phone call, you want to get involved do you? `, he growled at the staffer. George grinned with embarrassment and apologized; `I wasn't sure how to handle the call earlier, I've never done it bbefore. I panicked. But I can help now if you want? `. Feldman shrugged and muttered, `now that you mention it, I've a small errand for you to run`.

Feldman turned back to the desk and, after reading and re-reading the instructions in the book, he accessed the on-screen menu on the phone. He keyed in some commands using the blunt end of a pen to press the miniscule plastic buttons on the front screen of the phone. He then told George to go down the corridor to the print room and retrieve the pages that should be on the printer tray.

When George returned a few minutes later, Feldman took the two pages from him, read what was on them, and then handed them back to the waiting George. `here you go, bring these to the President. He'll want to read them over breakfast. ` George recoiled from the paper being waved in his direction. He was not impressed with this task; he had never been inside the West wing and had no great ambition to change that situation. He had heard horror stories of people making mistakes while over there, and the President walking in right in the middle of some mess or other. George held a strong suspicion that he himself would be one of those unfortunate people. He had a feeling this President was the type that did not easily forgive errors nor forget the names of people that messed up in his White House.

Feldman laughed at the abrupt loss of color on George's face. He had seen this reaction many times before in these young staff members. They were all very eager to boast to friends and family that they worked in the White House. But they weren't as happy when it came to doing the work involved, such as bringing messages into the close personal orbit of the most powerful leader on Earth. He told George to relax, the President would not even be awake for a few more hours. Feldman pointed out it was not the job of secret service agents, or East wing clerical officers, to deliver important communications directly to the President. Feldman had voted for the President twice, but he had to agree with young George. Putting yourself in proximity to the big man was not conducive to long-term career advancement.

The printed transcript of the message from Gerard Nolan would be carried to the office of the White House chief of staff for summarization and then added to the president's breakfast briefing. The atmosphere in the oval office was toxic right now due to paranoia about whistle blowers and ongoing investigations into presidential abuses of power. Anyone going in there had better prepare themselves to be dragged into somebody else's argument. Or worse, you might find yourself later being questioned under oath by a Senate committee about a phone call or conversation you might have overheard while in the West Wing. Far better to stay away unless absolutely necessary. Feldman had personally brought a couple of printed communications through the hallways in the past just to save time, but it was not recommended activity for secret service agents, even ones with his length of service.

Feldman decided that today would be a good day to do things strictly according to White House protocol. He called for an in-house messenger and handed the responsibility off to the skinny intern that came down in the elevator. The lad arrived pushing an empty mail cart that looked like overkill when Feldman handed over the single envelope for delivery. The cart was prescribed in health and safety manuals to avoid the possibility of injury due to lifting parcels and packages. Any time a parcel or package was being moved between offices in the house, an intern would be called into action. The interns never knew how much or how little they would be collecting from various desks and offices around the White House until they got to the desk of the sender, so they were warned to always bring a cart, every time they were summoned to collect any mail.

Agent Feldman, postal chore done, and with less than an hour remaining of his shift, told George to have a good night and headed for the elevator. While he waited for the elevator to come down, he glanced back at the door of the office he had just left. George was standing there looking after him and Feldman turned to face the younger man, "hey Georgie, " he called softly, "any more calls come in on that phone, why don't you go ahead and pass them to some other asshole eh? ". Laughing quietly as he saw the red color that suddenly flared in George's cheeks, Feldman turned away and entered the lift car. He would do a final walking patrol of the corridors, hallways, and kitchens before checking in with his shift supervisor, Sergeant Jim Kennelly to see if the man needed a lift. Jim was currently without a car of his own due to it developing engine trouble two days before and would be glad to see Feldman finishing up his shift at that time. Jim would be able to grab a lift out to the bus station with Feldman. Kennelly only had to await the arrival of the Sergeant currently assigned to day shift cover. This agent, Nicola Ortega happily made a habit not only of being on time but of arriving early and ready to begin work fifteen minutes ahead of shift start. Kennelly could save himself twenty dollars on taxi fare if the day shift Sergeant kept to that habit this morning, as this would allow Jim to catch that lift in Feldman's car.

When Feldman got back to the security room to turn in his radio and equipment, he told his supervisor about the call he had been involved with earlier. With other agents in the room listening to Feldman's report, everybody had the same question: What the hell did Gerard Nolan want from the US President? Nolan had become very wealthy as a reward for helping to stop the JFK attack, so why he was calling the special assistance line at three A.M. was an interesting mystery. Ortega, the day shift supervisor, had arrived at this point, and put an end to the speculation by saying that they would all find out in due course. The President would receive the transcript of the phone call and would decide on a course of action. Until then, all it did was make for interesting conversation that provided a welcome distraction in an otherwise boring job.

Two agents from the day shift, having just arrived in the control room, waited until supervisor Ortega had left the room, then suggested the agents open a betting pool on the reason for Gerard

Nolan making contact. They asked for suggestions from those present as to why a British citizen was making contact through this channel, probably without the knowledge of his own Government. There were suggestions and theories thrown around the room by various agents, the main one being that Gerard Nolan had decided to escape the English weather and move to Beverly Hills with his bulging bank account, and wanted the President to grant him US residency. There was a suggestion that Nolan had gotten fed up with being hounded by British charities looking for big donations and wanted the privacy of a gated community in a New York suburb.

Amidst all of this and un-noticed by the laughing agents, Special Agent Ortega had re-entered the room and had been listening to the conversation. She weighed in with her own suggestion that maybe Gerard Nolan was being hunted by the people behind the blocked attack at JFK airport. They had finally tracked him down after all this time and were now coming after him for revenge. Nolan was reaching out to the US President for rescue and protection.

The agents lapsed into a thoughtful silence when she finished speaking. As he got up to go home, Harris Feldman growled, `I bet a hundred dollars I get tagged to fly to England and hold his goddam hand on the return flight back`. Feldman and Sergeant Kennelly left the office on a wave of laughter and shouts of `bring us back some Limey whiskey and, `send us a postcard`.

Agent Feldman was in the middle of a switch over from night shift to dayshift and was scheduled to have the following day and night off. He was then to report for day duty on the second day. The morning after the night of the phone call from Gerard Nolan, he ate a light breakfast, showered, and went to bed, earplugs in place and heavy curtains tightly closed to keep out the sunlight. He awoke late that afternoon, in his usual state of disorientation, while making the transition from nightshift to dayshift. He went through to the kitchen to make coffee, reminding himself not to burn the toast.

As he passed the console table in the corner of the sitting room, he noticed the message light was flashing on his answering machine. Probably a white house staffer calling to confirm some details of the phone call from Nolan. Which reminded him to check if there were any work-related messages on his cell phone. Sometimes, they asked for off-duty agents to come in as emergency cover if there was any sort of situation, or if an agent fell ill. The tiny mobile phone was not to be seen on any of the surfaces as he moved across the room. While waiting for the coffee to be ready, he returned to the sitting room, went to the infrequently used answering machine and pressed Play. There was a voicemail from White House chief of staff Dwayne Fort.

Fort was a man previously well known for having a sense of humor regarding his own job and politics in general and could always be relied upon to supply a joke about past Presidents. However, just lately Dwayne Fort had become a very different person. He was very serious, particularly in any conversation that contained any combination of the words President, investigation, or impeachment. Which happened to be just about every conversation these days. Feldman replayed the message twice more and took a moment to consider what it meant. The mere fact the Chief of Staff had made this call personally was a big red flag. The content of his voice message set off even more alarm bells.

On the voicemail, Fort greeted agent Feldman by his first name, and requested that Feldman attend for duty twenty-four hours earlier than scheduled. Feldman was not to go to the usual briefing room upon arrival in the White House. Instead, he should go directly to the office of the Chief of Staff in the executive suite. Fort signed off by advising that it would be preferable if Agent Feldman kept quiet to colleagues about why he was entering the White House on his day off.

Agent Feldman ate his toast and drank his coffee while compiling a mental list of clothes, equipment, and documents he would need for a trip to the UK. He hadn't been told this was the

reason for the early summons to Pennsylvania Avenue, but he was pretty sure he had it right. It would be just like the White House to want the same agent that had answered the phone call

from Gerard Nolan to be part of the team that got sent overseas to collect the man. They just loved circularity. When he finished eating breakfast, Feldman went out to his car and found his missing cell phone. It was still on the console and connected to the car charger, where he had placed it on the journey home from work. When he powered on the phone, it showed four missed calls from two different numbers, both with Washington, DC prefixes. Those would be the Chief of Staff in the White House trying to make contact while Feldman slept through the day, which explained why the man left a voicemail on Feldman's landline machine.

He went back inside and dumped the nearly full pot of coffee down the kitchen sink. He would have to at least attempt to sleep tonight so he could be up and about during the next day like a regular person. The day was going to be planning meetings more than actual activity, and he did not want to fall asleep in front of the senior people that would be present. Especially if one of those was POTUS himself.

Feldman had been married for a few years when much younger. Divorced now, for more time than the marriage had lasted, he still kept in touch with his ex-wife Linda. Neither of them had remarried for the same reason their marriage had ended. They were in careers that required long hours and being on call at weekends and during holidays. Linda had progressed from being a general doctor to a surgical discipline. She was in constant demand in three separate clinics and hospitals. Feldman sent Linda a brief text message. The message said he hoped her day was going well, and she was doing ok. He mentioned he might go on a work-related trip, he couldn't say more. He signed off with his usual five kisses and then got ready for bed. He awoke in darkness, needing the toilet. The illuminated face of the clock on the bedroom dresser showed 3:09, and he had to think for a moment to make sense of the numbers. Was it pm or am? The small window in the bathroom was a dark square on the tiled wall, which told him it was nighttime. He had fallen asleep and remained unconscious for five hours. He would not sleep again this night, so he went back into the bedroom, got dressed in a clean suit and prepared for what he was sure would be an eventful day. He opened his phone and saw a reply from Linda to his text message. She used only a few words, as was her habit. `So, they are finally letting you out in public, are they? Be careful out there`. The last part was an in-joke between them from the early days when he was a trainee agent and she worried about him on the job. The quote was the warning given to patrol cops by the sergeant on Hill Street Blues, an old cop series on TV when Harris and Linda were much younger. She had made it her mantra when he progressed to being on close protection duty with POTUS after he admitted he would be required to take a bullet for the main man if there was an assassination attempt.

Feldman had been around the Obama White House but had never been out on the car cavalcade and crowd walks Obama liked to do. Harris had come up for selection to run alongside newly elected President Stamp's car, and became a regular in the tight group of agents that went everywhere with President Stamp. Linda had never been a Stamp fan, even in his TV hosting days. She could not understand how America had voted to put him into its highest office. However, she respected her husband for his dedication to the job of protecting the nation's leader. Linda said she had never feared for Obama out in public. He hadn't raised the political temperature high enough to bring out the proper crazies.

Edwin Stamp quickly annoyed just about every section of American society and seemed more likely to be the target of an assassin. Feldman often commented that he wished he had the brains to be a doctor like Linda, so he could help and protect lots of people the way she did. But all he had was his body to throw in the path of would-be assassins. It had not proved necessary yet, but as some wit pointed out, that was only because all the gun-toting crazy people were stamp voters and supporters. They wouldn't kill one of their own.

Agent Feldman drove in from Fairfax and around to his exit for the White House. It was a commute of just over half an hour and allowed him to live in a nice place well away from the insular madness of those areas inside the Beltway. One had to adopt the hipster cool lifestyle to live among the real insiders of Washington, DC. Harris Feldman refused to buy into that shit. Approaching the entrance to the White House grounds, he went through the myriad of checks and questions, with security getting progressively tighter as he neared the big house.

He parked his car and hurried through the lower levels of the house. Once inside the west wing, he made his way to the office to meet Dwayne Fort. Entering the designated office, he found three agents from the same shift Feldman had just completed. Feldman had dressed in the same style as his colleagues, an observation that brought a resigned grin to all four agents' faces. They were incapable of dressing casually in a situation if it contained even the slightest chance of being in the same room as POTUS or any senior government officials.

The three agents had sat on one side of the table, so Feldman moved around to that side. It left the table looking lopsided with one side empty, but they were aware from previous experience of how that would change if the President sat on the other side of the table. The man wasn't just big-bodied, he also had an immense presence and a loud voice, and seemed to fill far more than just the chair he sat upon.

The four agents had multiple years' experience, so there was zero chatter among them as to the purpose of their being called to this meeting. A senior person would tell them everything they needed to know in due course. That person would tell the essentials and nothing more. After a few minutes of expectant silence, the door at the opposite end of the room opened and Chief of Staff Dwayne Fort stepped through. He smiled tightly at the four carefully blank faces that turned toward him. `Good morning gentlemen, let's get this show on the road. Please follow me through to the other room. We have a meeting to attend. `

To the surprise of the agents, the President of the United States of America had sat down and was waiting in the office. President Stamp was sitting halfway down on the left side instead of at the head of the table. His position meant the agents moved together down the other side of the oval table so that POTUS could speak to them as a group and avoid shifting his focus back and forth.

As usual, there were no greetings or introductions. The President began speaking even before the agents sat down. He stated that Gerard Nolan requested entry to the United States to prepare for his becoming an American citizen. Nolan had offered to fly to America by private chartered jet, if that would help expedite the process. However, the President had told him that by a lucky coincidence, the G8 summit would take place in Paris in just ten days' time. The American President would attend the summit and would arrange for Air Force One to make a stop off in London on their return journey. They would collect Mr. and Mrs. Nolan and fly them to America in presidential style. Gerard Nolan had regretfully informed the President that he would travel alone as his wife had remained in the UK for the immediate future.

The President informed the four secret service agents across the table from him he wanted them to be his advance party. They were to travel to England, meet with Gerard Nolan and make sure he felt safe, loved, and cherished as a hero and as a future American citizen. They would stay with him at his home. They were to be ready to escort him and his belongings to London Heathrow Airport a few days after from where Air Force One would collect them after the G8 conference. Prior to take-off, there would be a brief ceremony in the British Airways VIP lounge in which President Stamp, alongside the British Prime Minister, would make the public announcement of Gerard Nolan's move across the Atlantic.

The president asked if there were questions on the mission and there was just one from Harris Feldman. `Mr. President, do we know why Mr. Nolan is getting out of the UK? `. The President, automatically assuming there would be no questions from mere federal agents, had risen from his seat on his way to depart the room. He stood to his full height, frowned across at Feldman, then growled, `Gerard Nolan is not getting out of the UK. He is coming to America! He's not running away, he's running toward! `. With that, the President swept from the conference room, gesturing sharply at his chief of staff to follow him out.

The agents remained there after the door swung closed behind the chief of staff. They had been called in between shifts. Federal agency bosses gave no instruction about when they were to travel to the UK. Agent Kenneally suggested the White House travel office might be the best place to make enquiries, so they agreed to head there in a group. The travel office was one of only a couple among federal agencies that still made travel arrangements on behalf of federal employees going abroad on official business. Most other federal agencies used commercial travel agencies, which operated by agreement with the federal government. The White House operated like a small city in most respects, and this was one more example of its individuality. The four agents walked up to the waiting area of the travel office where there were a couple of other federal employees sitting around, also waiting.

Assuming they should take a number and wait to be called, three of them took seats while Feldman went up to the front and pulled four numbered tickets from the dispenser on the wall. However, he had only just gotten himself seated alongside his colleagues when the woman behind screen beckoned them forward. She told them she was waiting for them and she handed out four folders, each with an agent's name on the outside. This was their tickets, gun permits, and letters of introduction to security agencies in the UK. They were to travel the very next day.

The four agents headed for the exit doors, and once outside the White House, they went directly to the surface car park to retrieve their vehicles. Before they went their separate ways, Harris Feldman called them close together and reminded them they weren't to speak to anyone about the details of their mission. He suggested they travel to Washington airport together the next day to catch their flight to London and the other three agents readily agreed. Feldman would drive his personal vehicle and collect each agent from their homes. The President wanted their presence in England to be kept low key until he himself could make the public announcement. They would fly on a commercial airline to the UK. They were travelling as Federal agents and would have their guns on the plane as carry-on luggage, but they were to be as discreet as possible. Later, of course, they would come home to the US by rather grander means on Air Force One. Of the four agents, Feldman and Jones had flown on the Presidential jet before. They promised the other two it was an experience to savor.

They would have a few days in London to relax and play board games with Gerard Nolan before gathering him and his baggage and shipping out to Heathrow. Agent Kenneally reminded Feldman of his prediction from the other day about getting tagged to fly to England to hold Gerard Nolan's hand on the return flight. It had proved accurate. Feldman smiled at that and said he should have tried to get people to take his $100 bet. He would have made a bit of spending money. They parted, laughing about Feldman's prophecy, with each agent promising to be on time the next day.

The following day, the four Secret Service agents boarded the plane for their flight to London. Casually dressed in shirts and jeans, they were recognizable to any American passengers as federal agents. Most people assumed they were those sky marshals. These passengers dismissed the quartet from their minds, while also feeling safer that the burly agents were on the plane. The agents stowed their bags, removed their jackets, and fell into their seats with identical groans of relief. The very instant the drinks trolley came down the aisle, they each ordered two doubles with ice, raised a glass to one another, and drank it down in one long swallow. They sipped the second drink and conversation naturally turned to the man they were flying toward.

Gerard Nolan was almost as much of an unknown quantity now as he had been when he and his meek and silent wife had intervened to prevent what might have been one of the most devastating terrorist attacks in history. The people had feted Gerard Nolan as a hero, not only in the US but worldwide, because of the international mix of passengers that would have died on the planes and, on the ground, if the attacks had proceeded as planned. The airlines had avoided incalculable financial losses. Because of his revered status, there had been just the lightest examination of his personal history. A few papers and magazines had done background pieces on the Nolans, but they usually did these in that fluffy way of treating high level celebrities. They had written articles as part of bigger pieces about the attack on JFK airport and did not delve too deeply into Nolan's life. But what they knew was that before the events in New

York, Nolan had been married to his first wife until her death several years ago. There had been no children from that marriage.

He had taken early retirement from his accountant job, cashed in his pension and collected a large payout from a life insurance policy. He sold his home and began travelling the world on what appeared to be endless holiday cruises. He met the woman who would become his second wife on one such cruise. There followed a brief engagement and a wedding in Tenerife with a secular celebrant and two hotel guests as witnesses for the happy couple. The FBI had that much in their files and not much else. After the wedding, a long honeymoon comprising more trips ensued. Gerard Nolan had caught the travel bug and was just as happy to have his new wife along. The couple were passing through JFK airport on one of those trips when Gerard was looking in the right direction to notice a surreptitious exchange between two men. The rest, as they say, was history.

Now, according to the President, Gerard Nolan and his second wife Alice were no longer married. Reportedly, she had gone her own way with Gerard's blessing and a sizeable chunk of the airline's reward money to ease her way in life. The phone call from Gerard Nolan using the special White House line had come out of the blue, with people having mostly forgotten Gerard Nolan existed. President Stamp had suggested to the agents at their pre-trip briefing that he suspected boredom had persuaded Gerard Nolan to change his situation. He had used the special phone number because it amused him to activate such a service instead of simply applying for a travel visa, booking a flight, and moving to America. He could have sent a message to the President at the White House once he was in a residence in America. Stamp suspected Nolan had gotten a taste of being famous in the weeks following the JFK drama and was now missing the attention. His move to America would re-ignite media interest in him.

Agent Peter Kenneally, emboldened by a couple of drinks, remarked on the strangeness of how quickly Gerard Nolan had slipped into obscurity. Following the JFK attack, it seemed as if the Nolans were the most watched guests on just about every television show in the world and were hardly out of the newspapers and magazines. They were both modest people who never claimed to be experts on terrorism or politics. It didn't stop the chat show hosts and the journalists from constantly seeking their opinion on news reports involving hijackings and suicide bombings. At one point, Time magazine named them on a One hundred most influential people list. That article followed on from Gerard Nolan, being named Citizen of the Year in the same publication. But the fanfare fizzled out, and the couple swiftly faded from the headlines, and from the showbiz news. Harris Feldman joined in on Kenneally's train of thought. `Nolan was probably the most famous person on the planet at one stage. All those Instagram and Facebook loonies go to crazy lengths to get their own fifteen minutes of fame. Yet Gerard Nolan seemed pretty eager to take himself off center stage as soon as possible. A cynical person might think he had something to hide`. Agent Chris Jones leaned forward so that he was included in the discussion and asked quietly, 'do you think he had something to do with his first wife dying? It sure made his financial situation better, and when they asked him about it on that show, he didn't want to get into it. Feldman and Kenneally glanced at each other and nodded. Kenneally seemed to answer for both when he said, ` yeah, there's definitely a skeleton in the guy's closet. After months of privacy and quiet seclusion, he upends his life in England for a move to the US. It's gonna put him right back in the tabloid's crosshairs. I wonder if Nolan got a warning. There's finally somebody rooting around in his past looking for dirt. Our President is gonna fly Air Force One, plus all of us, into a media shit storm to go collect his new best pal. Stamp will parade Nolan and his UK passport in front of the cameras as an example of why Stamps America is the greatest nation on Earth. Having Gerard Nolan in our country is gonna make the country an even better place to live in, at least that's how President Stamp will tell it. I'm not sure if Nolan has some shit in his back story, but I sure as hell hope none of it backfires on our President. Because we will be the ones that get it in the neck from the President. He will blame us for bringing Nolan over! `

Feldman raised a hand to the steward with the drinks trolley and as she approached their seats, he smiled and looked at all three agents; `Anyone feel like getting drunk with me? we might as well enjoy our trip. We won't get too many opportunities like this. ` When they all had fresh drinks in hand, Feldman raised his glass, `here's to Gerard Nolan wanting to make a fresh start in the land of hope and glory, may he find happiness away from the tabloids and from suspicious, cynical fucks like us. `

Present day.

Virginia, U.S.A.

In a farmhouse, a mile from any neighbor, and roughly halfway between Langley, Virginia and Washington DC, a group of six men had quietly taken up residence. The house had been on the sale market for almost two years following the death of the elderly owner, John Madison. The locals were aware the house was for sale but hadn't heard it had found a buyer. They had seen lights on at the house and the realtor was in town a lot more just recently, so they assumed she had gotten a private offer from a purchaser and was in to complete documents etc. Old John Madison had been born there. His father had lived and farmed the land before him, and John had taken over the farm when his father died over fifty years ago. John's two sons had never been the farming type and had moved away as soon as they were old enough. They would not refuse their share of the money if somebody bought the house and land, but they had done nothing to add value to their inheritance. They would come to town to sign the property transfer documents. They might buy the few surviving old timers a beer or two, shake a few hands. They would then depart to whatever city life they had were living.

The locals, some of whom had been letting their own livestock graze in old John's pasture fields, spent a few minutes speculating on the new owners. There were differing opinions and predictions made about them, but the old guys sitting around the bar all agreed on one thing: whoever had bought the place most likely would not be a farmer. It might be a writer looking for a getaway or a congressional representative looking for a weekend drinking den where they could entertain financial donors. They would be the type of person who bought property in a rural place like this but would not spend any time mingling with the locals. Nor would they spend much money in the local stores or bars. It was the way things were these days. Farming was still vital, but nobody wanted to work in farming. It might mean one of the local farming families would get to buy some of the land on John's farm at a knockdown price. Other than that, very little would change. Conversation moved on to more pertinent subjects, football and politics being the two topics that everyone could agree to disagree on.

The team of six men had arrived separately to the farm property in a fleet of unmarked vans and cars and unloaded the vehicles from the dusty yard directly into the house. They brought with them bags of groceries from the big Walmart twelve miles down the road. They carried rolled up sleeping bags and bottled water. The second day saw a truck marked with the logo of a well-known DIY warehouse and this time the delivery was of lengths of timber, paint, and various tools and equipment. Another van arrived soon after and five men in worn overalls got out, stretched in the sun warmed yard, and, following the path taken by the warehouse delivery crew, went inside. For the next couple of days, locals could hear the sounds of construction. When the sun rose on the fifth day, all was quiet in the yard and on the road that went by the property. In the house, the men had cleaned all the signs of construction up, and the working people had all departed. Throughout the house, the smell of fresh paint, cut timber and newly plastered walls was clear.

One week after arriving, the original team of six men were sitting around the farmhouse table eating breakfast washed down with strong coffee. The work had gone faster than expected, but it meant they now had to wait longer than scheduled before the next phase of the operation would begin. They would bring their guest from another house in less than twenty-four hours, but the men were impatient to get started. However, the US Marshalls worked to their own schedule and had their own rules. The marshals were under strict instructions that no civilian contractors were to set eyes on this prisoner.

As soon as they received word that Ibrahim Mahmoud was coming, the six men would change from the easy-going guys they appeared to be now into hard faced and ruthless interrogators. The US government, or the part of it that operated beneath the surface of legal and human rights, had finally lost patience with Ibrahim and his attitude of ' I really want to help but I don't know what you want to know'.

Most of the agents handling the daily sessions with Ibrahim felt sure the skinny fucker knew exactly what they wanted to hear, but they suspected he was stringing them along to keep his American vacation going for as long as possible. The more cynical agents suspected Ibrahim had already seen their most wanted man, Trevor Wilson, in the photographs they had shown him and had skipped it deliberately.

Ibrahim wasn't sure what would happen to him if he identified the Zimbabwean. He only knew that they hadn't shown him a photograph that had the scheming bastard in it. He also knew the Americans didn't believe him when he said he wanted to help, but couldn't. His mother, Emani, was now living with a distant relative in an apartment, in Ohio of all places. Her freedom was part of the allowances and freedoms they had given Ibrahim to keep him talking. The cozy chats in the UK with the English cops had gone well. They had heard local gossip from both Ibrahim and his mother. The naïve pair kept talking to the local officers about their home, and how hard their lives were in Yemen. They spoke of the various men that stayed as guests in the small village. Ibrahim had picked out two men from the photo files as men that were allied with Maamar. He confirmed they had been in the mountain camps at least twice.

With a bit of prompting from the cops, Ibrahim began speaking about his uncle Maamars' activities there. By asking certain questions, agents could cross-reference Ibrahim's answers with other information they already had, which then allowed them to confirm the identity of men that might have worked with Maamar on attacks. Ibrahim spoke of how long it took to drive a vehicle from his own village to the camp where Maamar held meetings with other fighters. Using satellite imagery and GPS mapping, the agents could make rough estimates of where Maamar and Ibrahim had gone. Ibrahim and Emani did not realize the chat sessions were being recorded for later study by the Americans.

This was the sort of seemingly aimless chatter that gives US defense contractors enough background so that they can locate a village or camp where a suspect might join his family for a brief holiday while he is resting between terrorist attacks on American interests in Yemen and elsewhere. Ibrahim's stories of camping trips with Maamar had led the contractors to uncharted valleys in desolate mountain regions where groups of men met with other groups of men, in areas too remote for the US and Saudi drones to catch on camera. Several raids had already taken place using the locations gleaned from Ibrahim's musings to his handlers.

But there was more to be gotten, and the only way to extract the really serious information was to remove Ibrahim from the comfort and safety of the UK. The Brits were friends of America, but they had this strange hang-up with legal action and human rights. Ibrahim was not cooperating to the full extent of his knowledge; he was holding back the big prize. The American agents were after this organizer Trevor Wilson, as they assumed him to be behind the JFK attack. They knew Ibrahim had personal knowledge of the Zimbabwean, but he had failed to pick the man out of the photo files. They also wanted to break up uncle Maamars' group in order to halt the attacks on US interests in Yemen and Saudi Arabia. Ibrahim would have to give these group members up, one way or another.

The agents intended to show Ibrahim how good life could be for him and his mother in the west if he cooperated fully. Once they both became accustomed to that comfortable existence, the agents would snatch it all away. That way, Ibrahim would finally understand that betraying uncle Maamars comrades, who were thousands of miles away in Yemen, was much better than allowing his dear mommy to be thrown in a filthy prison just a couple of miles away, right here in the United States of America. Ibrahim did not have to worry about the men in Yemen ever catching him and taking revenge for his betrayal. They would all be dead soon. Ibrahim and his mother would meet the same fate just as soon as Ibrahim helped to catch Trevor Wilson. Loose ends and all that.

Borehamwood, England..
Present day.

Meanwhile, in a large country house near London, England, four Secret Service agents were slowly getting used to the sad fact that the next seven days of their lives would probably be the most boring time they had ever endured. They were now ensconced in the huge empty house owned and lived in by Gerard Nolan. He had paid off and let go the few domestic staff at the house to prepare for his move across the ocean. He opened the door himself when the agents rang the bell. Gerard welcomed them in and apologized for not having staff to assist in their arrival. They had a room each but had to dress the beds themselves using bedding taken from the enormous closet on the second-floor landing. Gerard Nolan had not expected to have guests before he departed for America. So the agents would have to make their own beds and prepare their own food for the few days they were there. The Secret Service men were well used to looking after themselves.

The realization that boredom would be their constant companion came as they reached the end of their first day in Gerard Nolan's house. They had cooked dinner, all four agents sharing various tasks in the spacious, well-equipped kitchen. They had joined Gerard at the long dining table in a room that looked far too large for a man and his wife to have dined in and must have been positively daunting to the husband after his wife had left.

After they had eaten and cleaned away the dishes and saucepans, Gerard Nolan invited the four agents to join him for a drink in the smaller sitting room. Upon entering the room, each of them walked past a large oak table which was situated along one wall. On the table was a game of monopoly, set up and ready to play although there was a layer of dust on the board. There were boxes of jigsaws and more board games in a tidy pile on the table, all with dust on their lids. Gerard Nolan obviously lacked willing playmates. Harris Feldman made the mental connection between Gerard Nolan, having been an accountant before the JFK events, the monopoly game probably appealed to his money managing nature.

Feldman remembered the President had warned the agents they would in effect be ambassadors for America, and he had told them to entertain Nolan and to keep him happy. In accordance with those orders, Feldman pasted a smile on his face, accepted a glass of wine from Gerard Nolan and said in a booming, cheery voice, ` anyone for a game of monopoly? `. The smile that lit up Nolan's face told Feldman he had said exactly the right thing. Feldman felt he should receive the congressional medal of honor for this sacrifice in the face of extreme boredom, and if he didn't get one, there would be hell to pay. His fellow agents were looking at Feldman in disgust from behind Gerard Nolan's back. They knew they were going to be stuck here for a week and their visit had gotten off to a poor start. Flying all the way to England to play board games and act like housemates with this rich idiot had sounded like the duty that agents would kill to be added to. But it was already shit.

It occurred to the agents that a week was not necessarily only seven days long, it could seem to be a much longer period. They had been playing monopoly for just a few minutes when Gerard Nolan began telling endless, pointless anecdotes from his days in the drab world of accountancy. The four agents, screaming inside, but outwardly nodding and smiling, saw the forthcoming few days, much as how a newly sentenced prisoner sees the next five years stretching in front of him. Playing monopoly might yet prove to be the high-point of their week.

It would be of some consolation to his Federal agents in England to know that in Paris, France, the G8 summit was just as boring for President Stamp. He could barely contain his impatience at how slowly the talks and meetings were moving. He was looking forward to the un-scheduled press conference he was going to hold before they flew out of Paris. He would announce that Air Force One would make a stop in London where they would pick up a passenger and then going on to Andrews Ai r Force base in the US. He could hear himself addressing the gathered media;

`No, sorry, I cannot tell you the passenger's identity. I will reveal all in London at a press briefing there. You will just have to wait until then. `

Before that glorious moment though, he had to endure these foreign fools going on and on about a lot of unimportant stuff. Why he had to attend these things in person, he could not understand. He had staff that should sit here listening to these speeches and lectures. He took out his phone and sent a text message to Agent Feldman in England to ask how it was going with Gerard Nolan. Minutes later Feldman texted back that things were ok. They were keeping Nolan entertained. He seemed happy to have the agents as guests in his home. He was looking forward to his new start in America. President Stamp replied with smiley face and thumbs up emojis. Agent Feldman had to smile at certain surreal aspects of his job while this man was President. Text message emojis and presidential Twitter announcements were the norm now.

Stamp allowed his attention to wander again as the foreign accented voice at the podium droned on and on. Stamp had heard a rumor that Justin Bieber might consider applying for US citizenship. It might be worthwhile having someone reach out to see if the rumor held any truth. He wanted the world to see how the greatest people wanted to be part of Stamps America. Justin Bieber wasn't to Stamps musical taste, but the guy sure was popular with a certain age group, a group that would be old enough to be voting soon.

Stamp thought it would be funny if he could send Vice-President Lance Worth to have the exploratory meeting with Biebers people.

Worth was so uptight; you could almost hear his butthole clenching when he was forced to spend time with distasteful people. Stamp had a quiet laugh to himself as he remembered the time he had ordered VP Worth to play host to the Irish Prime minister, an openly homosexual man. What a laugh that had been, Stamp genuinely thought Worth would explode from the indignation. There was a rumor afterward, Worth had his home fumigated following the visit, which certainly seemed like something Lance Worth would do. Certainly, his wife had bought whole new sets of sheets and pillows in the days after that state visit. The used bedding probably went into an incinerator.

Back to the Bieber situation, though, on second thoughts, the weird little guy would try to bring that goddam pet monkey with him. The FDA and the animal rights people would have a shit fit at that idea. Stamp was in enough hot water with Federal agencies as things stood. He didn't need to invite further hassle. Bieber would remain Canadian, regardless of Canada's desire to be rid of him. Gerard Nolan would serve as notice to the world that America was open for business, that she welcomed people that wanted to come and live there. Worthy people only obviously, not those huddled masses the liberals tried to welcome. Stamp wanted only the brightest and best in his America.

Edwin Stamp automatically presumed people would judge him and his family to be right there among the best and the brightest if it ever came to a test.

Virginia, U.S.A.
Present day.

In the farmhouse in Virginia, among the rolling acres of grassland, Ibrahim Mahmoud's mood had gone from being content to terrified. His mother had written to say she was doing ok and Ibrahim had convinced himself he could endlessly drag his heels in the questioning sessions. But the day before, things had utterly changed. The marshals that were his keepers since they had transferred him from England to America had been gone when he awoke at six am. In their place was a group of hard-faced men without uniforms or any official insignia. They were clearly military, but that could mean a lot of different things these days. Ibrahim had seen the private security firms that operated on the edge of legality to protect the oil companies and other American interests in Yemen. They were mainly former US military, big, tough men with specialist training in nasty disciplines.

His captors were like that and they scared the shit out of Ibrahim. They told Ibrahim that the deal he made to keep his mother and himself safely in the US was now void. He had not kept up his end of that deal. They would move Ibrahim to a new location shortly. They told him he would find his situation much less comfortable.

True to their word, they marched him through the house and out to the carport. There, a van awaited him. In the rear cargo compartment was a single seat, bolted to the floor and looking like the electric chair Ibrahim had seen in a movie he had watched with the marshals when he first came to the US. A massive, hard faced guard pushed Ibrahim into the chair and pulled a chain out from under the seat. They looped the chain around Ibrahim's legs and wrists and the guard took a pair of steel handcuffs from his pocket, shaking the cuffs in Ibrahim's face while grinning at him. The cuffs were used to secure the ends of the chain to a steel ring on the van's floor.

Ibrahim knew his situation had deteriorated to its lowest point. He had to give up everything he knew about the insurgent group's leaders in Yemen. There would be punishment, even torture and pain, if he did not answer their questions. But worse than that, they would bring his mother back from Ohio and hurt her, too. These men, so like the US and Saudi contractors he had hated and feared in Yemen, would not balk at hurting a woman. They were outside the law, and now they had him. He himself was beyond the protection of the law. He had withheld important information, mainly the details of Maamar's operations. He eked it out to the questioners, a piece at a time, so he and his mother could enjoy the luxury of a few peaceful months. He could measure his remaining life only by how long it took for him to tell his last few secrets. He would attempt to get a deal for his mother from these new jailers, but they had already convinced him it was no use. The men were in no mood for deals. They would drain him of information and they would kill him. His corpse would go into an unmarked grave or an incinerator. His mother's dead body would be right there with his. Nobody would ever question their disappearances; they were non-citizens from a region of Yemen that had thousands of similar people inside its borders. The world would not remark on their deaths, their killers would go unpunished.

Ibrahim began begging and pleading with his captors at every opportunity. He wished he had put names to more of the faces they had shown him in the photographs. He would identify anyone they wanted him to identify now. He would no longer hold any information back; he would try to prove his worth and he would pray they would spare him and his mother. He hoped and prayed there were still some questions they needed him to answer. He wanted only to show how cooperative he could be.

They took him to this freshly painted house, and the questioning continued. Soon, they would bring in a specialist. A man they hoped would unlock Ibrahim's memory and give them access to his memory. To the secrets he was carrying. This man would fly from a place close to Ibrahim's homeland, and he would persuade Ibrahim to betray everyone he knew back home. This man would be the last chance for Ibrahim to save himself and his mother. Neither Ibrahim nor his American captors knew there was a photograph that, if shown to Ibrahim, would hand them the man that attempted to bomb all those planes in JFK. That secret had died with detective Nicholas King.

Borehamwood, England.
Present day.

Although the Secret Service agents staying in Gerard Nolan's house felt like the time was endless, time passed. The agents conversed Gerard Nolan for hours, and decided he was as boring as he seemed on the surface. They had gotten over their suspicion that he might have killed his first wife and covered it up. Gerard explained she had been sick for a short time with a nasty type of cancer and had died in hospital, in the company of her husband and her family members. Gerard Nolan was a genuinely normal guy who had gone flaky after losing his wife. The agents realized he wasn't a scheming murderer so they got bored with him again.

Chris Jones was cheeky enough to ask Gerard about his marriage to Alice and why they split up. Gerard had little to say on that subject, any more than he had said about his first wife passing away. He merely stated that Alice was badly affected by all the fame and intrusion into their private lives following Gerard's intervention at JFK. She had wished several times that it hadn't happened and that they had simply remained a married couple living their lives. He had made an agreement with her to turn down any more media appearances and to refuse any further magazine interviews. They deliberately worked to let the story die and to allow their lives to settle back into anonymity. That helped the marriage to survive for a few more months, but it seemed the damage was done, and they agreed to go their separate ways. The Federal agents were mostly relieved to hear the man explain the whole thing in such normal terms, there was no big conspiracy of lies going on. Just a couple of people finding themselves at different points in their lives and having no idea how to meet in the middle. Consequently, each went their own way with no hard feelings.

Gerard had a couple of barely interesting stories about being on the television chat shows during his period of worldwide fame after the attack on JFK airport, but they were mostly the same story, repeated over and over again but with different chat show hosts. It was clear to the agents sitting with him that he missed being in the TV studios and sitting in front of journalists. His enthusiasm as he recalled the weeks he had enjoyed as a celebrity had not waned very much, and if Alice was indeed fed up with all of it, there was no surprise they had clashed so badly.

Finally, thankfully, the last day of their stay in England arrived, and the federal agents helped Gerard move his luggage and possessions from the house to the mover's van waiting in the long driveway. There was a professional moving firm standing around in the garden, but the Secret Service men were restless and needed to be up and moving, and so they volunteered to carry out the lighter items. The moving crew carried the bulkier boxes and chests. One crate, tightly strapped to keep it securely fastened, made it necessary for all four of the young men to gather around and perform a countdown before attempting to raise it. Grasping a grab handle each, they grunted in unison when they lifted the box off the ground. One man was heard to fart loudly from the strain, causing the agents to burst out laughing. Harris Feldman was still grinning as he turned to Gerard Nolan and asked, ` what the hell is in that box, gold bullion? `. Gerard Nolan returned Feldman's smile and said, `no, nothing like that, just some statues and rare books that I collected on my travels, very heavy obviously`.

They got the van loaded and then they accompanied Gerard Nolan around his empty home to ensure he had missed nothing. Gerard had reserved a limousine to take them to the airport and when the mover's truck had cleared the driveway, the long black Mercedes drove in and turned to face back out to the road. The driver got out and opened the doors and then returned to the driver's side door to await their entry into the luxury vehicle. The four agents had kept possession of their personal overnight bags and gun cases, and they carried them with them when they got into the limo. The driver closed the doors, folded himself into the driver's seat, and the big car moved away. Feldman noted that Gerard Nolan did not turn to look at his home one final time before they turned the corner, after which the house could no longer be seen. Feldman thought it was another sign of just how wealthy Nolan was that he could leave such an expensive house behind without so much as a rearward glance. Either that, or it showed how determined he was to leave his life in England behind and look forward instead, to a new life in America.

They would be on the road for almost two hours before reaching London city where Nolan had some meetings with his bank and his legal representatives. He asked the Federal agents if they would go have some lunch somewhere so that he could conclude his business without having to explain the presence of four big American gentlemen by his side.

For their part, the Americans were only too happy to leave Nolan's presence for a while. They would find a restaurant to park themselves in for a couple of hours. If Mr. Nolan would be so good as to phone one of them when he was ready to depart, they would join him, and all could return to the limousine together. From there, they would make their way to the Heathrow airport complex.

President Stamp planned to hold a press briefing at Heathrow in which he would announce Gerard Nolan's decision to emigrate to the US. The President seemed to be treating it as something like a soccer team poaching the star player from their main rivals. Harris Feldman wasn't convinced the US were getting such a good deal out of the exchange. In the few days they spent in his home, it had become clear to the federal agents that Gerard Nolan was making the move to America, in the hope of reigniting the flames of his fame, to get the magazines writing about him and the talk shows discussing him again. He probably expected to have the lifestyle shows all over him once he bought a new home in America. President Stamp was only too happy to accommodate the Englishman in his transition to US citizenship. This was exactly the kind of occurrence that Stamp bragged about in his rambling monologues. His America was the best country, it was the place to which all the best people desired to emigrate.

Upon landing in the UK a week ago, before they went to Gerard Nolan's house, the four US agents had paid a courtesy visit to their counterparts in the UK security service MI6. The Federal agents wanted to talk off the record with the Brits if there was any sort of threat against Gerard Nolan which might have forced him to request the move to the US. It was information that they would like to have so they could mount some covert protective surveillance of the man once he was in the US. The feds wanted to be aware if their guest was likely to get shot a week after landing in America. President Stamp would not find that funny at all.

The British agents had been brutally honest about Gerard Nolan and his not-so-secret decision to move to America. They would be glad to see him leave their jurisdiction as they had been expecting some sort of attack on him and his wife ever since they returned to Britain from the US. Following the Nolan's intervention in the planned terror attacks in New York, the British cops had assumed there would be a very annoyed terrorist chief somewhere who would eventually come gunning for Gerard Nolan to exact revenge for the Englishman's thwarting of the attack.

In fact, when Agent Feldman of the Secret Service had called ahead to set up this meeting, and had mentioned Gerard Nolan's name, the Brits had thought Feldman himself was coming with a report of an impending threat to the former accountant. They had been ready to dispatch their armed response units to Nolan's country home. It was a relief to the UK intelligence agents that Nolan was leaving for another country. Gerard Nolan had done nothing to assist the security services in protecting him. He refused to install or allow them to install shielded windows and doors on his home. He never varied his route while driving,. He allowed reporters and well-wishers onto his property any time they approached. It was almost as if Nolan didn't care if he got attacked. The legal shit show, and public relations disaster that would result from his being killed or even injured on British soil seemed entirely lost on him. He did not care that people's jobs might be under threat due to Nolan's lack of safety awareness. So, it was now a case of let America take him, the Brits were fed up with him being their responsibility.

Agent Feldman had a suspicion about just why Gerard Nolan did not worry about his personal safety, but he said nothing to the British agents. The two groups of agents wished each other the best and said goodbye. The US agents had spent the week in Gerard Nolan's house and Nolan never once mentioned having any discussions with the security services in the UK regarding his personal safety. Feldman tried during the week to open a conversation about the people that had planned and failed to attack JFK airport, but Gerard Nolan showed very little curiosity as to who they might be. He certainly didn't seem worried they might come after him for thwarting their plans.

During their lunch in the afternoon while they waited for Nolan, Feldman caught Jim Needham glancing at him once or twice as if he wanted to say something, but the other man stayed silent. This was really the first time the four US agents had been together without Gerard Nolan present, so Feldman felt like they might talk about any worries or concerns any of them might have. Feldman thought Jim Needham might talk about their meeting with the British agents a week previously and about the fact that Nolan had refused protection. Needham had been slightly cool toward Gerard Nolan during the days they had stayed in the man's home, but he had never said anything to the other agents as to whether or not he had a reason for disliking the Englishman. Feldman thought maybe there was some jealousy there over the large sum of money Gerard Nolan had been rewarded with by the airlines. Did Needham feel like Gerard Nolan didn't appreciate his good fortune, that he should do more with his money than simply using it to live the good life?

The other agents in their team, Peter Kenneally and Chris Jones, seemed to just go along to get along, probably a sensible approach to life in a federal agency. Beyond their idle gossip on the flight over to the UK, they did not have any questions as to why Nolan was leaving his own country to live in America. It was simply the action of someone with plenty of money, someone that did not need to worry about working for a living. Feldman tried to convince himself he was over thinking the whole thing. And he was reading too much into Jim Needham's sidelong glances in his direction. If the man had something to say, he would say it.

G8 summit Paris, France
Present day.

In Paris, President Stamp had been counting the hours through each monotonous speech, lecture and talk during the mind-numbing days of the summit. It had finally finished the evening before, and he had gone straight to bed in the hotel suite, leaving strict instructions he was not to be disturbed. Waking early as was his habit, he finished eating breakfast and sat back with a satisfied smile. He could finally leave this dusty, boring place and fly home. And on the way, they would stop off to collect Gerard Nolan in London. Nolan was the bright spot in this trip. The man was a genuine hero and he wanted to come and live in Stamp's America. It was proof that the country was in a good way under his stewardship, and it would be a fine rebuttal to throw in the faces of the Democrats when they claimed he was ruining the country.

There were days when Edwin Stamp wondered if he really needed to be doing this job at his age, but the call from Gerard Nolan had reinvigorated his drive and enthusiasm. It was confirmation that America still had the old magic. That strong force of attraction that had brought the worlds brightest and best from every country on Earth. Stamp's election slogan of Bringing the Great Back had been ridiculed by his opponents, but it was a simple fact now that he had done exactly that. They would all have to acknowledge his vision and brilliance. Stamp was that oppressed, loser kid in school who dreams of being a successful adult so he can go to school reunions and rub the bullies' noses in his wealth and success. The world would recognize him as a great American President now. He had won a second term in the White House, and it was proving to be even better than his first term. That he had broken and bent practically every rule, protocol, and law in his stampeding run through global politics went completely over his head. It was both the curse and blessing of Edwin Stamp that he utterly failed to understand just why people disliked him. He would never improve as a person because he believed he was already the best person in the room, in every room. In classic denial mode, it was the world that was wrong, not him. And he intimidated everyone around him to such an extent, they would never tell him how to correct his faults. The few that did venture an opposing opinion got divorced or fired, depending on their status or relationship to Stamp. All he had around him now were people that echoed his opinions, said yes to his outlandish ideas, and never criticized him in any way. Stamp kept his high opinion of himself, and his staff kept their high paying jobs inside his inner circle.

American area of operations.
Afghanistan.
2011.

Danny Curran had joined the US Marine corps a few weeks after he turned eighteen. He had been in his first gunfight four months after his nineteenth birthday in which he killed two enemy combatants and in the same engagement, pulled two squad mates from the wreckage of their armored truck after they hit an insurgent booby trap on the road back to base. The CIA recruiters observed him from a distance for a few days following the enemy engagement. Clearly, he did not show an adverse reaction to the incident. He was observed on the base and in the field doing patrols and reconnaissance on insurgent strongholds. The recruiters were particularly interested in his temperament, in how he behaved around other soldiers and around the local people. He was observed chatting to the local faith leaders and sharing candy among hordes of local children. In all his interactions with the various people in his sector, he was polite and respectful and seemed to have a good accord with the locals. He spoke their language and knew their customs. He did not treat them like uneducated peasants, he enquired about the wellbeing of their children and their elderly relatives. He asked their opinions on how the weather would be over the next days, he asked about their crops and animals. He respected their faith and never referred to any local as haji as so many soldiers did.

Under Danny's niceness, though, was a hard streak that was never too far from the surface. There was an incident one day where Danny and his unit were on the street in their patrol area and four men walked into the village square right in front of the Marines.

Three of the man were openly carrying assault rifles and Danny was first to respond to this clear threat. He shouldered his own rifle and spoke loudly in the Pashto language, "to the armed men, put down your weapons, you are in danger of being shot." He repeated the command once more to no verbal response from the men. It became clear that the men were preparing to engage the Marines in combat. Danny fired one round into the shoulder of the oldest looking man in the small group on the assumption that in this society, the older men were usually in charge of younger males. The man was spun around from the impact of the bullet, dropping his own gun, and falling into the dust of the street. Danny's squad, having spread out across the space when Danny first spoke to the locals, were now in prime shooting positions to kill all three of the men that remained on their feet. The man Danny had shot rolled onto his back and spoke to his comrades telling them not to surrender to the American dogs. The man made a move for his fallen weapon and Danny shot him again, this time in the head. At this, the other three men threw down their rifles and stepped back with hands by their sides. Marines took them into custody and called up a transport to remove the body of the man Danny had killed.

Back at base, a translator questioned the three men and discovered they were simple farmers from one of the valleys to the West. They reported that the Taliban had come to their village three weeks previously, gave them weapons, and told them they were now fighting in the war to liberate Afghanistan from the pirates of Europe and America. The men were warned not to try to return to their farms or their families would be killed. The older man that had led them into a face-off with a full squad of US Marines was their Taliban captor. He had forced them to travel to this far-flung part of the country to where there were heavy concentrations of Alliance forces. The man Danny killed was on a list held by the non-uniformed operatives that worked out of the same base as

Danny. These operatives flew in and out of the base on Blackhawk helicopters. One of Danny's officers told him they were CIA black-ops contractors. The Taliban put out large cash rewards for any Afghani that could capture alive one of these non-uniformed killers. If the Taliban got their hands on an American operative, they would make a video of the captive. On the video, they would tell the world how America used mercenaries to kill Afghan people, in direct violation of the Geneva Convention. Then, they would execute the American. Also, in direct violation of the Geneva Convention.

Danny found himself in the shadow of two large, bearded men while filling his dinner tray in the cafeteria. They invited him to join them at their table in the corner of the spacious restaurant. Danny followed his hosts across the room and saw his squad mate, Pete, staring at him with raised eyebrows. Pete looked concerned at the company Danny was keeping. Danny shrugged his shoulders to reassure Pete that all was ok and looked ahead to the table they were walking towards. Already seated there were two more scruffy looking guys. They all seemed to share a certain look, an aura of having seen and done things that regular soldiers would never experience. US Marine corps officers seemed to tolerate these men on the base as a necessary evil in today's military conflicts. But mostly the officers acted as if the operatives were not even there. They respected each other's work, and both disciplines cooperated to achieve mission objectives.

The men shuffled their chairs around so there was room for Danny at the table. When he sat down, the big man with the bushy red beard and unruly ginger hair offered his hand across the table, telling Danny, 'good work out there earlier. Your kill was a nasty bit of Taliban for sure. He's off the list now, thanks to you and your squad. Those three farmers will go home to their families tomorrow`.

`I'm Rusty. These monkeys around the table are Jim, George and Stanley. We've heard some good things about you, Danny. There are senior people that really like how you carry yourself, how you do your work. Interested in a career change at all? `

Over Rusty's broad shoulder, Danny could see Pete still staring over, clearly trying to figure out what the meeting in the corner was all about. Danny turned his chair slightly to one side so that he could no longer see Pete trying to catch his eye. Danny turned to Rusty, grinned and said, `a career change would be nice. What exactly did you have in mind? `Rusty grinned back and told Danny to stay safe until his tour ended, somebody would make contact back at home.

As he found out later, recruiters had picked Danny out as the type of soldier they liked in their agency. Danny completed his first tour in Afghanistan and went home to Boston on leave. He attended a lecture by a professor of military history from Harvard. Afterwards, in the lobby of the theatre, a grey-haired man approached Danny. The guy dressed like Danny's mental image of how a college professor would look. He even had the elbow patches on his well-worn jacket. He exuded a powerful aroma of pipe tobacco as he moved. Danny wondered if he had an old dog that lay under his desk in his office. There were coarse white hairs on the man's clothes that looked like Jack Russell's hair.

This man introduced himself as being from the government. He gave his name as Alan Thewson and told Danny he wanted to talk about Danny's career as an analyst in the CIA. Danny took a step back and replied that he had never worked for the CIA, he was just a Marine. Alan smiled and said, `I was referring to your future career in the CIA, the one you can develop today if it's something you would like to do. `Alan offered to buy Danny coffee at the café across from the theatre. Danny realized the man was continuing the courtship begun by Rusty and his team at Delaram Marine Corps Base, Afghanistan. He accepted the offer of coffee, and the two men moved to the warm dining room.

Over coffee and delicious pastries, Alan Thewson told him they saw special talent in him, and they wanted to know if Danny wanted to continue firing rifle rounds at other humans. Or, he could make a real difference to the American war effort. Danny Curran began his career as a senior analyst at the CIA that very day. He quickly understood there would not be much on the analyst side of his position. They were merely putting that title on his ID badge and his tax return.

They put him into an intensive training regime. Specialist training officers shoved into his brain languages, chemistry, psychology, weapons training, and a myriad of other skills. He didn't know what he was being trained for, but he felt sure he wouldn't be out in the dust riding around in a troop carrier or driving an armored Humvee again. His days of carrying a rifle seemed to be over. The weapons he would use would be less obvious, but probably far more deadly.

He learned how to inflict pain and cause suffering while hardly touching his opponent. They showed him how to bring a man to the edge of madness and to hold him there until the man emptied himself of his secrets. They were making Danny into a specialist interrogator, a breaker of resistant minds, and the chief confessor to tortured souls. He would prove to be a very effective questioner of the most fanatical insurgents that were captured in Afghanistan and Iraq.

Danny got sent into a room with a man born to hate all white westerners, to despise the very existence of America and Israel, a man that was completely willing to die before answering even the simplest questions put to him by infidel interrogators. And within a couple of days, Danny was in the man's mind, digging deftly, and with infinite skill, at the secret knowledge held there. It was not magic, but one could forgive an observer for believing in sorcery when witnessing the transformation taking place during questioning by Danny Curran. Danny understood just how lonely these men were, how suspicious they were, not only of their sworn and hated enemies but also of the Imams that sent them into battle, while the supposedly dedicated clerics stayed safely in their homes, having promised eternal reward for victory against the infidels.

Danny used that distrust to create paranoia in the men he questioned. He persuaded the man that their own leaders had betrayed them, suggesting their leaders received a financial reward from the American agents working in the area.

There were different approaches for different men, but with most of these fighters not being well educated, it was mostly a matter of planting doubts in their minds about the actual situation they were fighting in. Once Danny convinced the man that everybody else was getting rich while the ordinary fighter was simply being used, he could then begin using those doubts to convince the men they were being badly used by people in the al qaeda or ISIS leadership.

Occasionally, Danny placed himself in a group cell with a dozen captured insurgents. He would pose as a Westerner that had converted to Islam, had been caught while fighting for ISIS, and now faced interrogation, torture, and execution just like everyone else in the cage. It allowed him to build a small rapport with some of the stronger willed men that might not be easily susceptible to the verbal persuasion techniques Danny used on others.

Later, these men would share a double cell with the white westerner, and Danny would continue the work of breaking them open. There was never any fear of these prisoners speaking to each other and revealing Danny's methods to each other. For most of the men that were questioned by Danny Curran, the next, and usually final, stop after the interrogation centers, was somewhere like Guantanamo Bay in Cuba.

Once there, it did not matter who the men spoke to.

Danny's skill in languages, dialects and customs, were why they sent him to various far-flung bases and centers around the world any time they had detainees requiring special handling. Those skills were why his commanders put him on a select unit searching for Trevor Wilson and whoever else had been behind the attempted hijack of nineteen planes in JFK.

Baghdad, Iraq.
Two days ago.

Danny was in a bar in the green zone in Baghdad, having a couple of beers and playing cards with two Saudi agents. They were waiting for a phone call with the order that would send the three of them to Jeddah in Saudi Arabia. There had been a gun and grenade attack by insurgents at a resort hotel complex in which they had wounded several European energy company executives. Security guards at the hotel had returned fire when the attackers came through the gates, and they had killed three of the five gunmen. Civilian casualties were lower than usual, but even better was that the remaining two attackers were in custody.

The Saudis had already found evidence that the gunmen had travelled to Saudi Arabia from Yemen. They were possibly from the same groups responsible for many similar attacks on Gulf resorts. US intelligence agents hoped to get solid information on the active groups from the interrogation sessions.

Danny Curran had been told to be ready to fly to Jeddah as soon as the Saudi authorities called. He would be there to assist the Saudis in extracting the maximum amount of information from the two survivors. Left to their own devices, the Saudis would physically ruin the men while clumsily attempting to extract information, then they would publicly execute them, losing any information forever.

Information gathered by such brutal methods as those employed by some of the Saudi interrogators would be mostly useless. There were some good people working for the Kingdom's rulers and they got excellent results. Experts like the people that had been Danny's instructors had taught them well. However, good questioners were often outranked by over-zealous types. These showed nothing but brutality towards anyone caught attacking the Kingdom.

Instead of the expected summons from the Saudi authorities, Danny received a call from a CIA supervisor that he remembered from his training days. Pamela Byrne was one of his instructors and had impressed Danny with her ability. She was an officer who refused to fall into the trap of trying to be tougher than the surrounding officers. Instead, she simply did the job in an efficient, clear minded and precise manner at her own pace. She was a highly skilled judo fighter, too. Students often thought they could have fun on the combat mats, at the expense of this five-foot one-inch instructor. They regretted their confidence when she put an arm-lock on them, approximately thirty seconds after the bout began.

Pamela told Danny she was currently overseeing an interrogation at a location in Virginia, and she was requesting Danny's help. Her guest was the nephew of Maamar Hamidou. She got to the point, `are you available to come to the US to put this guy through the mill. We'd like to find out for sure if there's anything more to learn from him. My guys here in the house are of the opinion that Ibrahim already saw this Trevor Wilson guy in the mugshots but skipped over him. Maybe you can ask him nicely if this is true. He and his mother are due to be shipped somewhere less nice than Virginia, most likely Guantanamo Bay. Command believes it's too risky to simply ship the pair back to the UK or to Yemen. So, that will be the last we'll see of them. `Danny, aware of the past link between Ibrahim and Trevor Wilson, knew the interrogation in Virginia could be vital in the search for the attackers at JFK so he would go to Virginia. He made his excuses to the Saudi agents, apologizing for abandoning the card game and for leaving them on short notice.

He had an overnight bag and passport in his quarters in readiness for what was now a cancelled trip to the Saudi Kingdom, but he only had Saudi currency in his wallet. He had a gun in a shoulder holster and a knife clipped to his belt. He would need English pounds for the stopover and then US dollars for the last stop on his trip. He would have to leave the gun and knife behind in his room here. British Airways did not take kindly to passengers trying to board their planes while armed to the teeth. The special friendship between the US and the UK only covered so much. He knew he wouldn't need to be armed while on the ground in the US as an agency car would collect him from the airport upon landing. Passing through the UK without a gun, though, that was a frightening prospect.

Virginia, U.S.A.
Present day.

Twenty-nine hours later and thousands of miles from the hot, sandy place in which he had first learned and later perfected the dark arts of interrogation; a very different Danny Curran walked into a newly painted room in a farmhouse in Virginia. Danny was now wearing an odd ensemble of layered jackets and vests, which appeared to be made from animal furs and hides. His flared trousers were of a bright red material, bloused out over broken leather boots. By coincidence, he had not shaved for three days before getting the call to come to the US, and he had a heavy shadow of beard on his cheeks. Other personnel had earlier been told to leave the room so Danny could work. Danny strode in, greeting Ibrahim Mahmoud by his first name in a traditional Yemeni greeting. He gave a firm hug and double cheek kisses to the amazed young man.

Ibrahim, overwhelmed by this affectionate treatment, promptly burst into tears.

Until that moment, Ibrahim had not realized how depressed he had become lately, mainly because of the uncertainty about his future and that of his mother. The hostile treatment by the men in the house. Danny suggested he knew how Ibrahim felt, how he knew it was difficult to be away from your homeland and living among foreigners. He spoke Ibrahim's language, and he sounded like he had just come down from the mountains of Yemen. He smelled like goats and smoky campfires, and his entire appearance invoked fond memories of nights spent in the cold mountain camps with Uncle Maamar. Ibrahim instantly felt better about life in America.

When preparing to interrogate a prisoner, Danny aimed foremost to become the man's best friend. It was only later, if they failed to cooperate, that he would change and become their enemy.

For Ibrahim's part, he was relieved and happy to have this new man Daniel in the house and in his life. It was just like it had been in England with the English police officer Nicholas. The American agents had been getting rough with him recently, but Ibrahim assumed they must have realized their error. They had obviously remembered how valuable Ibrahim was to their search for this Trevor Wilson and the other terrorists. Now things could return to the way they had been. His new friend Danny would make sure of that. Danny respected Ibrahim and valued his contribution, that was evident in the way he spoke and related to Ibrahim. The man had even brought a paper wrapped packet of Bint al Sahn, Yemen honey cake. It was an unexpected taste of home, and Ibrahim wished he could share it with his mother.

Ibrahim slept properly that night for the first time in weeks. He might not have slept so soundly if he had known how badly his situation had deteriorated. His new pal Danny would chip away at him tomorrow and that process would eventually leave a man like Ibrahim without belief in anything real, unsure anymore of what was true. He would edge very close to being suicidal. He would soon reveal everything he knew about life in Yemen with his Uncle Maamar. He would tell his deepest secrets. He would tell the secrets of everybody he had ever spoken to. Danny would hollow him out and leave him empty.

They would then discard Ibrahim like yesterday's newspaper, read completely, and no longer capable of imparting any new information.

Paris, France.

Present day.

President Edwin Stamp loved to fly on Air Force One. In his life as a private citizen, before being elected President, Stamp had owned his own private jet, which he secretly nicknamed Stamp Force One. But he had to admit, Air Force One was the real deal. The plane assigned to POTUS was levels above anything used by himself, or by most wealthy people. There were two planes with that designation, both with all the bells and whistles and carrying the instantly recognizable Eagle emblem of the United States alongside the US Presidential seal. Edwin always felt at home once he sat in the lounge on the spacious jet. He objected to a proposal to build a brand-new presidential plane because of the cost involved. He felt they should just keep repairing and servicing the existing craft. But the upgrade would happen soon, whether he agreed or not. These current aircraft had been well used by previous Presidents and were now old and getting older.

Having finally escaped from the stodgy fools at the G8 summit, President Stamp was now walking out across the tarmac in the French airport. He casually saluted the US Marine guard at the bottom of the stairs and gripping the handrail, slid his hand along the rail as he climbed, panting, to the high landing. It was yet another tradition he had needed to learn upon taking over the Presidency. That the President should pause there on the landing, turn to the people waiting below in the airport, and wave goodbye. He did so now and then ducked his head through the doorway and entered the aircraft interior.

Air Force One.
Present day.

There was the usual receiving line of air crew and stewards. They either saluted or curtsied to him, all smiling and full of cheerful courtesy. He wondered if any of them had voted for him a couple of years ago and then quickly decided he did not care. They were crew and staff of the presidential plane, and he would have the benefit of their services for two more years. After that, he would have had his two terms in office and that would be the end of it.

He would never have to worry about campaigning for election again. He had money in the bank and his businesses had all gotten a boost from being associated with the Stamp name. He might write a book when he left the White House, as some modern Presidents had done. He often fantasized about writing a nasty memoir detailing how much he truly despised the people that protocol had forced him to be nice to, while President. Other world leaders would get the worst of it. Some of them were real assholes. It didn't occur to him that the people he might target had the same fantasy regarding him and his behavior. Diplomacy hid a lot of unpalatable opinions of our fellow humans.

Stamp shook himself out of his toxic reverie and sat up straight. His wife, the First Lady, was usually there to prompt him not to slump, but of course, she was back home in the White House hosting some charity event. He glanced up as other people came down the wide aisle and began joining him in the lounge and in the comfortable chairs there.

US Vice President Lance Worth was in Mexico holding meetings with the Mexican government about a possible relaxing of US entry requirements for migrating Mexican citizens. Worth had volunteered to go, but they both knew there had never really been a choice. It had to be the VP that went. Stamp was not capable of going to Mexico without causing a diplomatic storm because of his well-aired views on illegal immigrants. He never failed to mention the infamous border wall he kept threatening to build, to keep Mexicans and other nationalities out. Lance Worth spoke Spanish and would smooth any ruffled Mexican feathers on behalf of his boss. The other side of the coin was VP Lance Worth couldn't do the trip to Europe as Stamp couldn't trust the fanatic to keep his Christian fundamentalism to himself. Letting Worth loose in Liberal Europe would cause a storm of negative publicity among the left of center European media. Worth wouldn't be able to resist telling them God doesn't love gays.

Members of Stamps' government cabinet and their advisers came on board now, most of them laughing and joking with the aircrew. There had been a lot of wine at the farewell reception given by the French in their horrible airport building. Stamp never drank alcohol, and he wasn't happy that some of his administrations, more senior people, were well on their way to being inebriated. The French hosts had insisted on refilling glasses every time the person took a sip, and some of his people had emptied a couple of bottles during the hours they had spent with their French counterparts. Stamp felt some anxiety because of this flight being of a short duration. There wouldn't be time to sober anyone up before they had to face the British government representatives and the media. They were going to be stopping in London before making the much longer trip home to America. The drunken fools could sleep it off over the Atlantic before arriving back at Andrews air force base. But the London stop over might be a problem for some of them.

The President looked around at the glassy eyes and flushed faces of US government figures, some of them falling into chairs, sprawling across couches, and slumping over in their seats and he wondered if maybe he should cancel the press briefing in London.

It might be better if he simply sent somebody anonymous to grab Gerard Nolan and his Secret Service babysitters. A quick dash to the plane and got them all back into the air as quickly as possible to avoid any possible embarrassing scenes on British soil.

Stamp wasn't so egotistical that he didn't appreciate the value of a no-show over a shit-show. Those British tabloid newspapers would slaughter him if there were any drunken incidents at Heathrow airport involving Americans.

Stamp beckoned his favorite presidential aide over to the adjacent seat. The aide was a young lady called Hazel Burns, and she came from Arlington, Texas. She had started as a young White House intern in Stamps' first administration. Hazel had graduated college in the final year of Stamps' first term and had applied to join his staff the very instant he won re-election. She proved to be utterly incapable of panic or indecision in the most trying circumstances and was better than any computer at handling the hundred details of the President's schedule. Even the White House Chief of Staff, Wayne Fort, left a lot of the daily scheduling details in her hands. Stamp relied upon her so much, he had already invited her to come with him into his business when he completed his term as President. She had consumed nothing stronger than coffee at the reception earlier and was stone cold sober, bright eyed and awaiting instructions from the boss.

The President quietly asked her to go around the various cabinet members on board, have a quick chat and try to find out just how intoxicated they all were. Stamp told her she had less than an hour to get the information. After an hour, they would be on approach to London, and he would order anyone slurring their words or unsteady on their feet to remain on board until the landing party returned. Hazel moved quietly among the seated officials, murmuring questions to each passenger.

The President watched and listened to each brief interaction with interest to see if any of his staff would voice an objection to being questioned on his or her level of drunkenness by a mere presidential aide. No one did but whether this was because of Hazel's interpersonal skills or because they knew the President had sent her. Still, she completed the survey with no fuss and returned to Stamps' side with a satisfied smile on her face.

`Mr. President, some of them smell strongly of wine and look flushed in the face, but they are mostly ok. The Agriculture secretary might need help on the aircraft steps. Are we all disembarking in London? Maybe some strong coffee and some breath mints would be in order before then`. President Stamp smiled across at her and asked, `what do you think? Are we all sober enough to get through a press briefing and swiftly depart along with one of the most famous men on Earth? ` Or will one of our colleagues embarrass us in front of our British pals by tumbling down the aircraft steps? `.

Hazel kept her face carefully neutral, but secretly she thought it would not be the possible drunkenness of the passengers on board that might embarrass America. It was the one completely sober man among their group that would do that, Stamp himself. The man would never understand just how cringe-worthy he was in public. She valued her current job and saw a career in political life as a natural choice for her, but she was determined never to work so closely with anyone like this President again. She would try to attach herself to the staff of an ambitious female Senator as soon as Stamps presidency ended. Hazel looked forward to that, it couldn't come soon enough. She had gained valuable experience working within the highest office in the nation, but she would be more than happy to step down a few levels for her next job.

Holding on to her smile, Hazel reassured the President he had nothing to worry about. The stopover in London would go just as he wished, and they would be safely airborne, en route to America in no time at all. With their V.I.P. guest on board.

England.
2019.

`May I say it's been an honor and a pleasure to have had you and Mrs. Nolan as customers at our branch these past few years and we are heartily sorry to see you going away? The staff have all signed a farewell card just to say good luck in your new life wherever you may settle. We wish you both all the best`. They had given the bank manager just a couple of days' notice that Gerard Nolan and his wife were leaving Britain. They were closing their account at the branch office in which they had banked for the past few years. The loss of business from such wealthy people would have been far more damaging to the bank if the Nolan's had kept all the reward money there. But they had lodged the vast bulk of their new wealth in a London investment firm where it was managed by specialists. The Nolan's had left only their savings, an amount that had been boosted by Gerard Nolan's lodging of the proceeds of the insurance on his first wife, at the bank branch which was nearest to their home. That money had only been lodged a few years ago but had been steadily withdrawn as Gerard Nolan paid for his worldwide travels in the years between his first wife dying and his meeting with Alice, who became his second wife. It was a quite substantial sum of money, but nobody would lose their jobs at the bank as a result of this particular account getting closed.

The branch was in one of those areas where a large number of near retirement age couples lived, the sort of people that collected insurance policies and still trusted banks to care for their money. So, there were many accounts just like the Nolan's and they wouldn't be the first people to take their money abroad to begin a new life in warmer climes.

Gerard Nolan, arriving alone at the appointment in the bank, had provided all the documentation required to close the account. He had withdrawn the savings as a bank draft that he could lodge to a bank anywhere in the world. Alice Nolan had pre-signed the documents, and their solicitor had duly witnessed all signatures. Gerard explained Alice was already abroad and that he himself was finishing up their business in the UK before flying overseas himself. Gerard spoke as if he was joining his wife abroad. In the chat over coffee in the manager's office, not once did the bank manager realize that Gerard Nolan and his wife had not been in the same room together for several months. Gerard Nolan did not lie to the bank manager; it was just that he left some things unsaid which allowed the banker to draw his own conclusions, and those conclusions were incorrect.

Alice Nolan was now living a new life under her maiden name and, while she held no hard feelings toward her former husband, she would be totally ok if they never crossed paths again. He enjoyed being the center of media attention while she preferred to live quietly and in private. They had been married; they were not married anymore. She had accrued wealth from the marriage and would enjoy spending the money. She did not feel her former husband even cared about the money he had received as a reward for stopping the terrorist attack. Instead, it seemed he took an almost grim satisfaction from being on speaking terms with Presidents and Prime Ministers. And from being invited on to talk shows. It was the almost constant talk show appearances that had killed any joy she might have felt at their sudden fame. All that false niceness and insincerity had driven her crazy, but Gerard seemed to thrive on it. He was welcome to it all now. She was very glad to be away from that circus.

Gerard came out of the bank, turned left, and entered through the front door of a charity group that helped women and children escape domestic abuse. Gerard had done his research on this group, and they were as genuine as it was possible to be nowadays. The charity owned a large tract of land twenty miles from the town center upon which they had built several comfortable chalet style lodgings at well-spaced intervals across the property. These were emergency housing units for women and their children that had fled from abusive husbands and partners. It allowed the women to gather their belongings and to regain their sanity until they could return to work and get their children registered to a school.

There was a high fence topped with razor wire surrounding this land. The farmers that worked the land adjoining this property on three sides supportive of the work by the charity group and all three farmers showed they were willing to point a shotgun at, or set their dogs on, men that might come to the property in search of their former partners. The founders of the charity had approached the farmers years before. They asked if the farmer would be willing to sell a piece of land for use by the clients of the charity. No money changed hands as the three farmers signed over a few acres into the foundation. They chose the three plots of land in such a way that the entire donation formed one area. The farmers simply re-drew the borders of their farms and continued farming.

In the sparsely furnished office that was the main street location of the charity, Gerard went directly to the receptionist, who was behind a screen like that which protected bank cashiers and asked to see the manager. His business would take just a few seconds, but he did not have an appointment. The receptionist picked up her phone and whispered into it. There was clearly a security protocol in place here, probably triggered by a code word or phrase used by the receptionist. The manager came out of an office at the rear and she nodded to the receptionist. When she faced Gerard Nolan, a large security officer stood slightly in front of her. The charity had been the subject of visits by irate ex-husbands and violent boyfriends before. The management had learned the lessons from those encounters.

Gerard knew to keep his hands out in the open and he made sure to inform the smartly dressed lady that he was going to reach into his inside pocket and remove an item. The guard's left hand rested on the handle of some sort of baton clipped to his belt and his right hand was holding an object which Gerard assumed to be pepper spray. The guard's eyes never left Gerard Nolan's face during the conversation with the office manager. He clearly expected something other than a paper document to be in Gerard's hand when it withdrew from the jacket. Gerard handed over the cash bond and told the manager he had chosen her charity because he himself had grown up in a home with an abusive father. He asked her to make good use of the money and to keep up the great work. He turned and walked out and was gone before she recognized him. After the door swung shut and locked behind the man, she looked at the gilt-edged paper in her hand. It was in the amount of three hundred thousand pounds, and she suddenly felt the need to sit down.

An hour later, she had calmed down and informed her board of management of their sudden good fortune. Then she retraced the same route Gerard Nolan had taken before her. She lodged the donated bond into the account maintained by the charity at the very bank from where Gerard Nolan had withdrawn the money earlier that same day. The cashier at the bank, Bernadette, had been the same person that issued the cash bond to Gerard Nolan and recognized the document. In telling her friend Una about the donation that night, Bernadette remarked that it was the sort of behavior one heard about from somebody that was terminally ill and about to die and was divesting themselves of their worldly goods. Una snorted in derision and said it's more like the behavior of somebody with more bleedin' money than sense. If it was really Gerard bloody Nolan, he had dozens of millions more pounds to keep him in the style he was accustomed to. He probably found the money in his spare jacket and didn't know what else to do with it.

Virginia, U.S.A.
Present day.

A CIA instructor, when asked why he thought Danny Curran was such an effective interrogator, jokingly replied that it was because of his surname. To uneducated farmers and fighters, his surname sounded like Quran. Confused, in pain and scared half to death, they thought they were speaking of their holy book. To which they found it impossible to lie or refuse to speak truth.

Danny was effective because he waited until other interrogators had wasted their time hurting and abusing a prisoner. He waited until there was blood and tears and sweat and piss. He waited through all the denials and the beatings and the screaming. He waited until finally, inevitably; the prisoner began praying. Danny heard the prayer for the dead recited in the sobbing voices of the broken, and he knew the prisoner had given up. The man would not respond to more assaults or mental torture, for he had already begun withdrawing from this life. He was preparing himself for the next life. They would remove the original interrogator from the room and Danny would enter. Seating himself next to the beaten prisoner, Danny would join in the praying. He prayed and sang and whispered with the men. Gradually, Danny would persuade the prisoner that, in fact, it was not time to die. He brought men back from death's door. Many of them ended up wishing he had not.

He would talk to the prisoner, and he would find out from where the man came. He would find out about their family and their friends. Slowly, over time, bringing food and water and clean clothes for washing, he would find out about the men still free in the desert and in the valleys and in the hills, men the prisoner knew that had gone to the North with guns and grenades hidden in their camping gear. He asked about any foreign men that had come through their local region or that might have stayed in the area recently. And slowly, Danny built up a picture of the local area in which the prisoners lived. The tacticians in the operations department could then plan observation posts and run camera drone flyovers to take advantage of Danny's information. In most cases, drones attacked insurgent camps without any human troops having to set foot on the ground.

Danny spoke in a quiet murmur in perfect Pashto, to which he had added a slightly regional pronunciation to suggest he had a mountain upbringing. He spoke Farsi and other languages perfectly well, and these languages were used in other places. Somehow, Danny always managed to sound like he had grown up in a small rural area of the country from which whatever natives he was dealing with came. It was a trick he had learned from previous generation politicians in America who, when addressing the public in person at town halls and church meetings, sometimes spoke with an exaggerated hillbilly drawl to appear like simple folk, and therefore sound more trustworthy to people who were themselves, pretty simple. He learned their language, their jokes, their customs, and it seemed like he learned how to read their minds.

Virginia, U.S.A.
Present day.

By the time Danny met Ibrahim Mahmoud, the Yemeni man had already become withdrawn and distrustful of Americans. Danny spoke to him in Arabic, greeted him in a traditional Yemeni way, and by vague suggestion and no clear answers to Ibrahim's questions, made Ibrahim think that Danny was there to help Ibrahim leave the farmhouse in Virginia and move to new lodgings to begin a new life.

There would be no new life for Ibrahim. There would be new lodgings, though nothing like Ibrahim imagined. He was fast approaching his sell by date and his American hosts had already made preliminary moves to have Ibrahim moved to a detention site where he would probably live for the rest of his life. They could not return him to Yemen because they had shown him exactly who and what they were most interested in. He knew about Danny and other agency people, and he knew they had drones or aircraft with cameras because they had shown him photos taken from above camps, villages, and towns.

He could sell the information to the wealthiest warlord in Yemen. Immediately, the militia groups would change their travel routes and meeting places. The insurgents were well aware of the threat from drone strikes but it wouldn't be advisable to allow them to know just how accurate those drones really were, and Ibrahim could tell them exactly that. That would make it more difficult for the US and her allies to spy on or to attack the insurgents from the sky. It might mean more troops having to be sent into trouble spots, which would result in more casualties on both sides of any conflict.

Danny, having been in close quarters at the farmhouse with Ibrahim for four days, was fed-up talking to the man. He decided they should have a day off from all the questioning and the viewing of photographs of terrorism suspects. He informed a delighted Ibrahim they would go to a bowling alley, and they might also watch a movie at the cinema. Ibrahim went to get dressed for the trip and Danny then went to wait in the sitting room where the tv was located. While Danny was waiting for Ibrahim to rejoin him, he idly flicked through television channels.

Ibrahim came into the room, flanked by his two escorts. The burly agents always stayed close while Ibrahim was moving around in the house. Security guards could relax during those times Ibrahim was in the photo viewing room, as there was no chance of Ibrahim escaping. Danny changed channels to Sky world news where there was a developing story being broadcast. US President Edwin Stamp had made a stop-over in London while returning from the G8 summit in France. The information ticker at the bottom of the tv screen said President Stamp had called a press conference in Heathrow airport. The President announced the immediate move to the US of British citizen, Gerard Nolan. Mr. Nolan's picture from previous news footage was shown with a brief paragraph about the attack on JFK airport to remind viewers why Nolan was special enough to warrant a trip on Air Force One.

Heathrow airport, London.
Present day.

The news program was broadcasting from Heathrow Airport in London. The night sky was visible through the large windows of the airport lounge, airport floodlights casting a bright glow into the sky on the outer edge of the picture on screen. The camera zoomed in on the group of people standing at a temporary-looking podium, the obligatory small forest of microphones bearing various media network logos in front of them. The imposing figure of President Stamp loomed over a much shorter man standing beside him, Stamp's overly long arm clasped firmly around his guest's shoulder.

In the flashing of cameras and the glare of the tv lights, Gerard Nolan looked unwell, his eyes sunken in dark pools of shadow, and he was repeatedly licking lips that appeared to be chapped and dry. A reporter asked a question about why Nolan was leaving his homeland and moving to America. They also wanted to know how it felt to be getting the VIP treatment from the President of America.

President Stamp stepped up closer to the microphones and smilingly announced that Gerard Nolan was a genuine all-American hero that had simply been born in the wrong country. He was now correcting that mistake by moving to the US. And he was being flown home in proper style aboard Air Force One to start his new life among his fellow American patriots. They well knew the smug grin on President Stamps face, but it was still annoying despite its familiarity.

In the tv room in the farmhouse, Ibrahim stepped from between his two escorts and walked closer to the tv screen. Ibrahim spoke English at a conversational level, but he still could not read a lot of words written in the English language. He hadn't really been following the news text as it scrolled across the bottom of the screen.

The agents on either side of him had stopped to watch the news report, so Ibrahim had to stop with them. Ibrahim was impatient to get out for their trip to town but was looking at the screen along with everyone else. The news channel showed Gerard Nolan's face in close-up. Ibrahim got agitated and began jabbering in Arabic. Danny heard the Arabic words. His brain translated the words, but Danny couldn't make sense of the words.

He went over to Ibrahim and gently turned him so he could look at his face while he talked. The Yemeni man was crying, but it seemed from his words that the tears were of happiness. `They caught the terrorist, Trevor Wilson; how did they catch him? Did I help with this? Was it my help that helped to catch him? Am I good guy now?
`

Danny, confused by the excited chatter from Ibrahim and the questions from the two other agents in the room, had to shout at Ibrahim to get him to explain who or what he was talking about. Ibrahim jabbed a finger at the television screen. `him, him, it's Trevor Wilson, the man that got my friends and comrades to be killed in the beds. How they catch him? Was he doing more attacks? Did I help catch him? Did I help with this? `.

Danny, looking over Ibrahim's shoulder at his fellow agents, said, `Gerard Nolan is Trevor Wilson. And he's about to board Air Force One with the President of America and half of our government. We have to call them, stop them getting on the plane`.

The other agents were staring at the tv screen, identical shocked looks on their faces. One man turned to face Danny Curran, and he almost choked on the words trying to say them aloud, `you're wrong Danny, he isn't about to board that plane, the timestamp on the screen says that news is over an hour old already, they are already on board and most likely in the air as we speak`.

Danny pulled his phone from his pocket and ran for the front garden, where he knew he would find the strongest phone signal, punching numbers into the keypad as he ran, already praying and hoping for a miracle.

. Heathrow airport, London
Earlier, same day.

Agent Harris Feldman, if asked, would describe himself as a rational man. He valued hard work, adherence to correct procedures and good, old-fashioned police investigation when it came to catching criminals and preventing crime. He had full confidence in the factual science of DNA and fingerprints and forensic evidence. He did not believe in hunches or bad vibes or any of that hippy shit that police detectives seemed to use to solve crimes on television or in movies.

But, on the day he and his Secret Service colleagues escorted Gerard Nolan to Heathrow to meet President Stamp in preparation for flying to the US, Feldman was unable to shake the distinct feeling of having forgotten something important. It was that feeling you get when you have been extremely busy in work, and you are now at home resting. In the back of your mind, almost too far away to see clearly, there is a tiny fellow jumping up and down, waving his arms and shouting to get your attention. He is saying you didn't do everything on the list of tasks, you didn't complete the checklist, you didn't turn off all the switches. Feldman patted himself down for the fifth time since they had driven out of London City. He rummaged in his bag, in his pockets and in his gun case and still couldn't see what he had missed.

Agent Chris Jones leaned forward in his seat and asked Feldman what was wrong. `Have you lost something? cos you look like you have ants in your pants`, Jones said with a grin. Peter Kenneally agreed, saying he had noticed Feldman rooting in pockets etc. Feldman shook his head and reassured them both that he was fine, he had thought he had mislaid his passport but had found it nestled down the side of his bag. Jones nodded and went back to staring out of the car window, but Kenneally gave Feldman a lingering look that told Feldman he hadn't entirely convinced the other man all was ok. Feldman's anxiety seemed to be becoming contagious.

Upon arrival at the commercial warehouse complex on the runway side of Heathrow airport, the Secret Service agents checked in with Airport police, showing their service credentials and confirming the reason for their presence in the airport. The furniture removals company truck had gotten there ahead of them and had been held in a waiting area by airport cops. The limo driver was instructed to drive at fifteen miles per hour directly behind the Police escort vehicle and the truck was to follow the limo. They would move to their next destination which was the loading bay from where the furniture and belongings of Gerard Nolan would be transferred to the special cargo pallets prior to loading onto Air Force One.

At the loading area, there were four other secret service agents that were part of the massive advance party that always travelled ahead of the POTUS entourage. The two groups of agents greeted each other, Feldman and his colleagues grinning a bit sheepishly due to the easy mission they had enjoyed at Gerard Nolan's house. The other agents ribbed them for a minute or two, but all eight men very quickly settled into the task of assisting in the unloading of the furniture truck. Gerard Nolan remained in the limo guarded by the airport cops, drinking coffee, and browsing news articles on his phone. They would bring him through the secure warehouse complex to meet up with the President once the pallets were in place and ready to be loaded. Agents would stay with the load until airport staff lifted the pallets into the Presidents aircraft and the planes doors were fully secured. The secure chain of possession from furniture truck to aircraft would be kept intact.

The airport management sent three airport employees to help. They were told to have a smoke break somewhere else for a while. The Secret Service agents had security clearance to enable them to access everything going on board the President's plane and they never allowed civilians to enter that process until it came time to forklift the load on board. The loading process was proceeding smoothly until they came to the strapped and secured heavy crate. The one Nolan said was full of statues and books. Feldman recalled his feeling earlier that he had forgotten something.

He instructed the other agents they were to open and thoroughly examine the contents of this crate because he wasn't happy not knowing what it contained. He thought, `here and now, this is what's been bugging me all day`.

He had a niggling feeling something just wasn't right about the crate. The four advance group agents didn't argue, and one of them went to the furniture truck to get a crowbar. Before the agent could get to work on opening the crate, Jim Needham protested loudly at Feldman's suggestion. He was almost shouting in his eagerness to put the point across that they had just spent a week enduring the most boring man on Earth, laughing at his dirty jokes, and nodding interestedly at his endless anecdotes about accountancy and business. They had done all of that because their President had ordered them to keep Nolan happy. But now, just as the mission was ending, they were finally about to be rid of the man. Feldman wanted to open the guy's private stuff almost right in front of him and to rummage through it. Nolan would be unhappy, he would not understand they were doing their jobs, he would likely complain to the President. The President would be unhappy. He would want to know why Nolan was not being entertained and kept happy by the Secret Service agents ordered by the President to do just that.

Why would Feldman do that to his fellow agents? He would ruin any chance they might have of being selected for future trips like this trip. And for what? A feeling, a fucking hunch, he forgot something. Needham said he didn't give a shit if Nolan was smuggling rhino horns and elephant dicks in the crate. Needham just wanted to get home with no trouble. Jim Needham grinned and commented, ` Old Feldman probably left a door unlocked back at home. That's why he thinks he forgot something. `

Needham, speaking as if he had settled the argument, shouted, ` guys, it's all good here. Let's just get the pallets loaded and get Nolan to the meeting point before POTUS comes looking for his new best friend. `

Harris Feldman, hesitating, almost said more, but shut his mouth abruptly when he saw Jim Needham's face. The thunderous expression on the younger agent's face was enough to make Feldman understand he might get punched in the mouth if he persisted in trying to get the crate searched. Fuck it, he had a bad feeling, with no evidence for it. Life was too short to be fighting with people about a rich man's shitty art treasures. Feldman twirled his finger in the air and shouted, ` let's get it done! `

Feldman knew Jim Needham mostly by reputation. He had heard the stories about him being on disciplinary leave twice for losing his temper at other agents that had fucked up on the job in ways that made Needham look bad by association. Secret Service bosses had treated Jim Needham leniently out of compassion because he suffered a personal loss. He was a newly qualified agent in his early twenties, and he lost his brother in a terrorist bombing of a hotel in Kuwait City. His brother had just married and the happy couple were enjoying a honeymoon. Frank Needham was on leave from his Marine Corps unit. They had just returned to their room on the ninth floor when the entire front section of their hotel had come crashing to the street.

The devastation was because of a huge bomb in a delivery truck parked almost directly under the honeymooning couple's room. Investigation revealed the group behind the attack was avenging an American drone strike. The drone had blown up the desert home of a Yemeni tribal leader responsible for terror attacks. Jim Needham took a career break for a few months to help his elderly parents in Arkansas deal with their bereavement. He returned to work and immediately got into a fistfight with a senior colleague. Suspension followed and after he returned from that, he seemed to have calmed considerably. But he was involved in a heated verbal row with a supervisor a few weeks later and received a week's suspension for threats he made towards the senior agent.

The agent reported that during the argument, Needham had yelled that he held the US President responsible for the deaths of his brother and his brother's new bride. The President had ordered the drone strikes while issuing no advance security alerts to service personnel in the region. Needham's brother Frank might still be alive if they had made him aware that American troops would be under threat. Secret Service directors arranged for Jim Needham to meet the President. President wanted to explain his reasons for his not warning American personnel about the drone mission in Yemen.

US agents knew Saudi police officers had access to the alert system used to warn American military people of increased threat levels. Some of these Saudis had allied themselves to insurgent groups that operated against Americans. To send out a general warning was to give corrupt Saudi officers notice of an impending operation by US operatives. To maintain operational security, they sounded no alerts.

At the meeting with the President, Needham acknowledged he was wrong to blame anyone for his brother's death. He apologized to the President and to his own commanding officers for his previous behavior. After six months back on duty, he transferred to the presidential security detail. The President was asked how he felt about the transfer request, and he approved it. Needham had been on the team for two years and had not been in more trouble.

It was seen by Secret service supervising agents as another example of the extraordinary gift for persuasion that Edwin Stamp possessed. He seemed able to make widely different people feel like they could trust him and follow him anywhere. He certainly seemed to have rescued Jim Needham's career in the service. The young agent had settled down nicely.

Heathrow airport.
Freight handling area.

Now, on a windswept runway in a secure area of Heathrow Airport, Jim Needham seemed determined to complete their babysitting mission, join their Commander-in-Chief on the presidential plane and get back to normal life in the US. He saw Feldman's gesture and heard his shout to the other agents to get the work done. He nodded his approval at Feldman's positive action and apparent change of mind about the crate. Maybe that old guy wasn't such an asshole after all.

They rolled the final pallet up the loading ramp and secured it on the rack in the cavernous belly of Air Force One. The secret service agents prepared to escort Gerard Nolan through the passageways for President Stamps' press conference.

The air crew were at their stations and preparing the massive jet for departure. They were mostly relaxed as they had performed all the required checks only a few hours ago prior to departing Paris. They had green lights across their boards, and the crew expected a nice, easy flight across the dark Atlantic Ocean to North America. They were all looking forward to some well-earned down time and trips home to visit family.

There was a running joke between the different air crews that operated Air Force One when POTUS was aboard. President Stamp had a habit of asking a different variation of the same question each time he boarded, 'how's she looking today ladies and gentlemen? '. And the Captain would come out with some technical jargon bullshit that meant absolutely nothing in reality. Each time they did it, Stamp would nod wisely and agree that they should definitely get the experts to check it back in the US. He sure hoped it wasn't serious.

With all the pre-flight checks completed once again, the crew drank tea and ate light snacks while playing solitaire or chess on their iPads and phones. The stewards took the opportunity to do one last sweep through the President's lounge to ensure everything was perfectly tidy. They deployed air freshener spray to clear the lingering smell of exhaled wine fumes from the guests that had flown from Paris. This stop-over would be a short one and then homeward bound.

HEATHROW AIRPORT
PRESS CONFERENCE

Inside the airport buildings in a roped-off area of the British Airways VIP lounge, the assembled representatives of the various media outlets were shuffling in their seats and fidgeting with cameras and recorders. Finally, the British foreign secretary came from the rear office area and stepped to the podium. She tapped the microphone and without preamble announced, 'ladies and gentlemen, The President of the United States of America, Mr. Edwin Stamp. '

The office door opened again, and the very recognizable figure of Edwin Stamp lumbered into the brightly lit room. Flanking him were two Secret Service agents of a similar height and build as the President. They positioned themselves to block potential lines of fire from outside the glassed-in lounge. The corridors, hallways, and external areas of the airport itself were being patrolled and controlled by British security service officers, but close protection for POTUS was by his own Secret Service.

Reporters pushed cameras and voice recorders further forward, and everybody sat up a little straighter in their seats when Stamp cleared his throat and greeted the room. President Stamp seldom used a teleprompter and veterans of his press briefings knew to expect a certain amount of waffling and verbal wandering, but tonight was even worse than usual.

He began by complaining about the G8 summit in Paris, from which he had just escaped. He claimed the speeches were boring and the whole thing was a waste of his valuable time. He then extolled the virtues and values of his America. He bragged about how great things had become under his management; no previous American

President had improved things as he had done. He claimed there was a list of non-American celebrities waiting to come live in the greatest nation on Earth. A reporter cheekily asked for the names of these celebrities, Stamp named three film stars and a writer. Journalists noted three already lived in the US and the fourth was an Englishman. He had lived most of his life in America but had died two years previously. There were some groans, laughter, and a noticeable rolling of eyes in the room.

President Stamp took a breath, looked out at the assembled members of the press with a smile on his face. 'There is a very famous, the most famous... great man, the greatest in fact. A big friend of ours, we really like this guy, he did a good job for us in New York, at the airport. He called me up, you know, he called and said, hey, Mr. President, come get me, I'm ready. Ladies and gentlemen, America's great hero, Mr. Gerry Nolan.

President Stamp had clearly been expecting a huge response to his announcement, and he made no secret of his disappointment at the distinct lack of reaction from most of those present. Tipped off by their usual sources in the security services, some journalists were not surprised by the name of the celebrity. Others were not interested enough to show much emotion. Most of them were simply there on the orders of their editors, as they had nothing better to cover that evening. Stamp kept his smile, but it was looking strained now. Gerard Nolan came through the door and made a slight gesture like a wave with his hand towards the journalists to acknowledge their having shown up. He looked embarrassed at the fuss and became even more so when President Stamp gathered him into the most awkward hug ever witnessed by anyone there. Stamp lifted Nolan's hand aloft and jerked it up and down twice like a boxing referee pronouncing the winner of a boxing fight. A fight which nobody cared who won or lost. When the cringe-worthy display finally ended, President Stamp asked if there were questions.

One journalist wanted to know why Gerard Nolan had gone down the route of calling the President personally to arrange his move to the US. Why not simply apply for a visa, and then move to America like anyone else? Before Gerard Nolan could form a reply, Stamp stepped to the microphone and growled, 'he called me because I gave him my card and told him to call me if he ever needed anything, it's what we do for our very best, the finest people that are our special friends. American heroes don't queue with everybody else in an Embassy somewhere to get a form stamped ' There were a couple of other questions directed at Gerard Nolan and again, President Stamp took it upon himself to answer. The President then turned his back on the press corps, but the reporters heard him asking Gerard Nolan if he was ready to get out of this place. When Gerard nodded, Stamp took him by the elbow and steered him off the stage, away from the bright lights and out through the door at the rear. Secret Service agents in front opened the door and more agents closed the door behind them. The doors were closed just in time to block out the sound of journalists laughing and groaning at how embarrassing the evening show had been. They began gathering their equipment and preparing to leave.

Sadly, for the journalists, none of them was still at the airport when the genuine news story developed just a short time later. As they departed the airport complex, not one of them had any clue they would all be racing back to Heathrow that night, to cover a real news story.

Virginia, U.S.A.
Present day.

In rural Virginia, they put a frantic Danny Curran on hold for the second time, as his call got bounced from one government office to another. The call was finally caught by a Secret Service agent who had been part of the President's travelling party. Unfortunately, as he was not on the team on Air Force One, he was on the ground in London and just as helpless as Danny himself.

At this point, over eighty minutes had passed since the press conference had concluded in London. Danny was praying aloud in three different languages to the gods of all faiths that the President's would suffer catastrophic engine failure on the runway and could not take-off. He wished severe diarrhea on the pilot and on the co-pilot and on anyone else aboard qualified to fly that plane, such that they would be unable to fly for a further twenty-four hours. Danny was cursing and swearing, hoping, and praying until finally an irritated American voice broke into his mutterings to inform him that `he was too goddam late, the bird had flown. Now quit that foreign jabbering and explain to me in English what the fuck is the problem with the plane? `.

AIR FORCE ONE
LATER.

The President's aircraft had been sitting, ready to go, since President Stamp had departed from it to collect Gerard Nolan and to do his smug bragging to the media horde in Heathrow. Its loving crew had held it at partial readiness for ninety minutes. It was then moved up to take-off readiness within a couple of minutes of the pilot being informed that the President had left the VIP lounge and was now making his way back to the plane. The captain throttled the massive jet up to engines-hot and brakes-free just three minutes after President Stamp, his new friend, plus the entourage settled in their plush seats with seat belts fastened. There was no delay once the massive plane moved away from its stand, as they gave it A1 priority taxi privileges at most airports in the world. Its call sign showing on the ATC radar was the reminder to the tower to clear a path through their airspace regardless of how busy they might be with other flights. Nobody wanted the responsibility of having this aircraft on their concrete, and everyone breathed a sigh of relief as soon as the American eagle and flag emblem had disappeared over the nearest horizon into someone else's area of responsibility.

On board, with the plane having climbed steeply into the London sky and began levelling out, Stamp unbuttoned his jacket, pulled his red tie down from his throat and slumped back in the chair with a grunt and some deep sighs. Gerard Nolan, sitting opposite, watched the President unwinding and settling himself and smiled at the difference in the demeanor of this powerful man while in private compared to his public persona. All around them, the staff were bustling up and down with drinks and snacks for the senior government people and their corporate guests. A couple of seats held snoring old men and over these, the stewards gently placed a blanket. The steward would check back regularly to ensure the sleeping figures did not suddenly awaken to find themselves unattended. Gerard Nolan raised a hand to a passing steward and requested a small gin and tonic. The steward hesitated before leaving the plush lounge area, trying to catch the eye of the President. When President Stamp finally looked up at the young man, Stamp raised a questioning eyebrow but said nothing, forcing the nervous steward to address him. `Mr. President, can I get you a drink Sir? `. The President frowned as if thinking about what drink he would most prefer, but then the frown changed to a smirk and he just said, `No, nothing for me`.

To the watching Gerard Nolan, it was an example of what he had heard was a nasty, regularly shown side of Stamp's personality. He liked to be the center of attention and always wanted to feel that others waited for him to be served first. Gerard Nolan's wife Alice, before they separated, told Gerard she had been told by a British diplomat that President Stamp had stood up from his seat at a state dinner, intercepted a plate being brought to the Queen and taken it for himself. His excuse was that his blood sugar was low, and he needed the nourishment quickly. Then he joked he could be sure they hadn't spat on as it was for the beautiful Queen. He clearly was not confident of the same deferential treatment toward food destined to be on his own plate. He smirked during the incident. The Queen kept her face expressionless and waited patiently for a new plate to be brought to her. The rumor afterwards was that staff had indeed messed with the food destined for Stamp, but because of the switch around, had to dump the plate and prepare a new one for Her Majesty.

The steward on Air Force One returned quickly with the drink as ordered and Gerard deliberately did not toast Stamp when he took the first sip. The President appeared not to notice any change in the atmosphere between himself and his VIP guest as he asked,

`So, Gerry, have you decided where you want to live in the United States of America? You have the fantastic thing of being able to settle anywhere. It's great for you. I don't have that. I've gotta stay in Washington, or when I'm back in my companies, doing business you know, being just a regular guy, I need New York at my front door. But you, you can go North or South or West. It's great, really good that you can do that. Such a great, really wonderful country, the best place really`.

Gerard Nolan had continued sipping at his drink, still saying nothing while President Stamp rambled on about the great country to which Gerard was coming to live. The plane had by now fully levelled off. People moved around the polished conference table and in the various booths around the spacious interior of the plane. The social activity had increased to the level of any business convention that Gerard had attended over the years. There was a constant murmur of conversation and even the occasional loud burst of laughter. It was all so normal, just like any long-haul flight might be if passengers had smoothed take-off nerves with alcoholic drinks. Gerard Nolan excused himself and stood to visit the bathroom a few feet away from their seating area.

President Stamp signaled to a steward hovering nearby and made eating motions to ask if dinner was ready. The steward nodded to acknowledge the question and hurried away to find an answer.

Gerard Nolan returned from the bathroom a few minutes later to see President Stamp slumped in his seat with his double chin resting almost on his chest. Nolan was still standing when Secret Service agent Jim Needham put his head around the partition wall and asked if everything was ok. The query seemed to be directed at Gerard Nolan rather than at the President. Stamp had not reacted as if he had even heard the agent speak. Gerard Nolan replied, `Yes, all good here, thank you. ` Agent Needham nodded and withdrew to his own seat. President Stamp had not moved or lifted his head from his semi-slumped position during the verbal exchange between Nolan and agent Needham, but then abruptly dragged himself to an upright position. Looking at Nolan from half-closed eyes, Stamp mumbled, ` You don't like me much, do you? You pretend to, but I know you don't, not really. You want to come to America, and you've used me to make it happen. Did you do it so it'll get headlines in the papers? You could have gone through the channels like any rich man. We would have let you in, no problem. So, tell me, what's the idea? You're using me? For what? `.

Gerard Nolan smiled and nodded. `You're right, I don't like you. You're an obnoxious prick and you treat people like dirt. I've heard rumors and stories about you and your inappropriate behavior, and I assumed it was exaggerated shit being spread by your enemies, but I've seen you in person and it's all true. And it's just another thing on a list of reasons we chose you. I wanted it to be the Prime minister of my homeland, the UK, but he persuaded me it should be you`. Stamp demanded to know what the hell Nolan was talking about, who was this `we` he referred to and who persuaded him to choose Stamp over the UK leader? Chose him for what?

Gerard Nolan stood and walked over to the partition wall, leaned around the side of it and called softly, `Jim, you're needed here. Can you join us, please? `. Secret Service agent Jim Needham walked into the close confines of the Presidential lounge and looked down in contempt at his boss, the President. For Edwin Stamp, suddenly the space was too small. He wanted to stand up and run away but felt himself weighed down in his chair. He felt the heaviness of a pending announcement, just like he had felt when they had announced his unexpected election triumph six years ago. But he felt sure this time it was not good news he was about to hear. Not good for him, anyway.

Jim Needham had his hand inside his suit jacket and the reason became clear when Agent Harris Feldman came around the corner of the same partition from where Jim had come. Feldman took a moment to look around at the tableau before him and drawled, 'well now, what do we have here? '. Needham withdrew his hand and in it was now a short-barreled revolver, gleaming blue steel under the ceiling lights. He turned it slightly, so its lethal aim was now in the space between Stamp's slumped, seated figure and Feldman's tightly coiled, standing position.

Gerard Nolan stepped to one side, well clear of Needham's gun, and smiled down at President Edwin Stamp. 'The attack on your JFK airport was a decoy, a big red flag for your federal bulls to charge at. While all along, the real danger was standing off to one side waiting to step into the spotlight, to be cheered as a hero and to be welcomed into your great country as your new best pal. From the very beginning, we have predicted your actions and behavior, like we were reading an open book, and now here we are. You've followed a script you didn't know was written', Gerard said.

Gerard Nolan continued speaking, 'I assume you are familiar with the story of the Trojan Horse? A big wooden horse sent to the besieged city of Troy, posed as a peace offering, but actually full of attackers. The impenetrable city opened its gates to take in their gift horse, and they opened the doors to their own destruction. You, Mr. President, have opened the gates to the same thing. I am both the Trojan horse and the attackers hidden inside, in this story. You've invited me on board your highly protected aircraft, inside your defenses, beyond the ring of steel that normally surrounds the President of America. '

'The nineteen 'attackers' at JFK were each carrying a device, an electronic trigger for a bomb on the plane that each person had a ticket for. There were nineteen people with triggers, and agents quickly recognized that number as representative of the nineteen attackers that carried out the 9/11 attacks. But everybody seems to have forgotten about Osama Bin Laden. Accused and assumed to be the man behind those attacks. So, that makes twenty people, not nineteen`.

At this point in his tale, Nolan removed an object from his pocket and showed it to President Stamp, who, having slumped again, had to drag himself into an upright posture. Harris Feldman leaned in to see it. Feldman noted that Agent Needham showed no interest in the object. Clearly, he knew what Nolan was showing. The President looked puzzled and asked, ` that's one of those trigger gizmos from JFK. How did you get it? Did the FBI give it to you? `. Nolan smiled and shook his head. `it's not actually from the JFK incident, although it does the same thing. This is from the same batch as the other ones. They were all produced in a small electronics factory in Poland on my instructions. There were nineteen at JFK, this is number twenty. This is my personal trigger device. I am the twentieth attacker, ` Gerard said.

Gerard Nolan was lecturing now, his voice rising as he spoke. Members of the crew of the aircraft, assuming it was a political argument, stayed as far up the plane as they could. The other agents from the team that had spent the week in Nolan's house, Peter Kenneally and Chris Jones, had heard his words and come around the partition. They were standing alongside Harris Feldman so that all three and the President were now under the gun held by Jim Needham.

Nolan continued, `The nineteen people hired to be the attackers at JFK were unknowing, fake tributes to the nineteen 9/11 martyrs. So that being the case, I am a tribute to Osama Bin Laden. I consider him the twentieth martyr of 9/11. Your hunters took so long to catch and kill him, people forgot what America accused him of doing. Your government accused him but never tried him in court. You simply declared his guilt. Your soldiers executed him without trial, just like they have done so many other people that have crossed swords with American interests around the globe. A pattern of illegal

behavior by American agents that has become so commonplace in
the world it barely gets mentioned on the news.

I've watched news coverage of American agents as they carried
out murders of foreign and domestic so-called terrorists. ` I've seen
the reports of military coups in Central American nations in which
the elected leaders get killed and America instals a new leader,
backed by American guns. I've listened while you and the people
that surround you have lowered the level of political discussion in
America and in the world to one of childish name calling and jeering.
You insult journalists and accuse them of publishing lies. You lie
and cheat and blame other people for your failings. The world is
becoming more nasty and stupid by the day with people like you
in charge. All of it used to bother me a bit, but like most people, I
let it go over my head. It wasn't something that really affected me.
I had my wife and my career, and we were happily married. Then
my wife got killed and everything changed for me. I finally saw how
bad things had gotten, how corrupt everything was now. I saw world
leaders deliberately caused much of it. You and the leaders of Britain,
and others in Europe and abroad. You're all complicit `

` We have some time remaining, so I'll tell you where I've come
from to get here, to this point in life. My wife and I went to live
in Zimbabwe when we got married twenty years ago, because my
wife was from there and she wanted to be near her parents. I agreed
to move abroad as I knew I could practice my profession anywhere
in the English-speaking world and I will do whatever I could to
make my new wife happy. Around this time, Zimbabwean President
Mugabe started his land grabbing and re-allocation of farms, taking
the land out of white ownership and placing it into black ownership,
my wife's family were naturally very concerned as they owned a few
hundred acres of very good agricultural land in the South. Their fear
became reality a few months later when men in masks and armed
with guns entered the family property.

I had recently set up my new financial consultancy, and I was trying to establish myself in business, with my work being mostly in South Africa. I had gotten a large contract with a firm there and I had been away in Johannesburg for months doing audits for that firm's separate divisions. I was so involved with getting my new business off the ground, I barely heard the news of land grabbing and the rumors of persecution of white people in my wife's homeland. My wife would travel down each month from her parent's place in Beitbridge in Zimbabwe and we would spend quality time together in the small apartment I rented in Jo`Burg. She selflessly tried not to tell me anything about the worsening situation in Zimbabwe so as not to worry me while I worked to build my new company, to make a success of the new business. Nobody knew just how bad things would get in Zimbabwe.. `

My wife had returned home from visiting me, and she was at home with her parents when a group of men in paramilitary uniforms arrived at the family farm. These men told my wife and her parents to gather their personal possessions and leave. The land was being returned to black Zimbabwean ownership by order of the President of Zimbabwe. Growing a few crops did not entitle whites to the land as they were interlopers, invaders. They had stolen any land that they owned, and so they were to be treated as thieves.

I heard the details later from a South African man named Henry. Henry had been installing new shelves in the cellar of my father-in-law's home when the men came and Henry heard everything that happened that day. Henry worked for my wife's parents on their farm and when he realized what was happening upstairs, he stayed quiet and just hoped the men wouldn't come downstairs to where he was hiding. Henry assumed the men would deliver their threat along with a warning, and they would then leave. They would return later to take over the property once the white folk had left. Henry said it seemed from the conversation between the men that my father-in-law had tried to grab a gun from the kitchen closet to protect his farm and they shot him to death right there. The men obviously decided they couldn't leave witnesses, so they also killed my wife and her mother. They burned the farmhouse to the ground and Henry almost burned to death in the cellar. The men fled from the scene soon after starting the fire, and Henry could escape through a storm door from the cellar to the rear of the property. He got to a neighbor's farm to raise the alarm. The Zimbabwean police summoned me to identify the bullet riddled corpses of my wife and her parents. The pathologist took the time to tell me that my wife had been about eight weeks pregnant at the time of her death`.

Gerard Nolan was telling his terrible story to a shocked audience in the small seating area and Chris Jones saw a chance to overpower Jim Needham. He lunged across the space and grabbed the gun, pushing it down to the floor as he crashed into Needham's big frame. The two of them went down in a tangle, grunting and growling like dogs. In the middle of this, it became apparent that Jim Needham was laughing loudly. The wrestling ceased as Chris stopped attempting to get the gun. Getting to his feet, Chris asked, `what's with the laughing, are you crazy? Jim replied, ` it's just funny, you`re trying to grab an unloaded weapon, to take control of an airplane that's already fucked! ` Harris Feldman heard what Needham said and replied, `you don't need bullets to control us because the planes got a bomb aboard, is that what you`re saying? `

Needham grinned and said, `let the man tell his story, eh? He's been waiting a long time`.

Gerard Nolan, deep in his memories, barely reacted to the scuffle that had broken out in front of his seat, as he simply continued talking, `I was grief-stricken, in shock. I shut down the office in South Africa and walked away from my fledgling business. An insurance policy on my wife paid out a large sum, and I took the money and left Africa behind. I went travelling, aimlessly booking trips just to keep myself occupied, not caring where I went or who I saw.

In my grief, I blamed President Mugabe for the deaths. It was his policy that brought armed men onto the property and resulted in my wife being murdered. But on my travels, I did a lot of reading, mainly history books and political stuff. I wanted to fill my head with facts and dates to stop myself from thinking about all I had lost. And I discovered Robert Mugabe couldn't have done any of it if he didn't have the support of Western nations. On my travels, I read an account of a missile strike fired from Israeli war planes in a Palestinian village a few years ago. The villagers found the remains of the missile that had killed their neighbors and stamped in bold lettering on the side of the missile were the words, Made in the United States of America. The Palestinians already hated Israel for attacking their village, but now, they understood that the greater evil was American companies shipping advanced weaponry to Israel with the full support of the White House. Support from the West gave Israel an unfair advantage in the Middle East. And from my reading, it seemed to me to be the same situation all around the world. Dictator regimes curried favor with the most powerful nations and received financial and military support. The dictators were not the problem. The rich nations that sponsored those regimes were the real threat.

Britain and America were the two countries that had the most influence on Zimbabwe over the past decades. The World Bank funded Mugabe for years with American money behind a lot of that backing. And it was American direct aid that allowed Mugabe to arm his thugs and to think he could get away with the things that he did. Then Mugabe stopped playing the game the way the West wanted him to play. America pulled the plug on all of it and imposed sanctions, supposedly to punish Mugabe and his cronies.

The sanctions did nothing but starve poor Zimbabweans and cause a crazy rise in crime.

You people seem to pull strings in every trouble spot and disaster region on the planet. Even in places where you claim to be against the regime in charge, you are pumping money into the country as part of counter-insurgency programs and other ridiculous covert operations. And you, Edwin Stamp, as President of America, have refused to learn, or you could not learn, any lessons from the failures of your predecessors. You have continued to meddle and mess in other nations' affairs, trying to mold the world in the image of America the great. Somebody has to say that's it, enough is enough. I'm saying it and Jim here is saying it. We are sending a message and you are going to be the page we write it on. ' Nolan sat back for a moment, deep in thought. Then, taking a sip from his glass, he continued talking.

'On a cruise ship on one of my trips, I met Jim Needham, a federal agent on compassionate leave from his job in the US because of family bereavement. We realized after a conversation over drinks we had the loss of family in common with one another. He had lost his brother, and his sister-in-law and I had lost my wife and unborn child. After more drinks, we understood we both were suffering from a deeper type of sadness.

We were both sick and tired of how humanity had sunk to such low depths in recent years. There seemed to be very little to cheer about anywhere. The TV news was full of doom and gloom and newspapers seemed to only appeal to the mob mentality in people. Stirring up hatred of immigrants and people in poverty and feeding a constant diet of spite, corruption and greed seemed to be their chief occupation.

I turned the conversation toward Jim's job in law enforcement and I asked him about all the horrible things he had probably seen while investigating crime in America. I spoke to him about various methods of murder and suicide. I deliberately let slip that I had thought about ending my own life, and I felt I might do it very soon. Jim empathized with my feelings and then shocked me when he asked, `why waste a good suicide though? `

He planned to say something about his brother's death. He wanted to do something that would affect the US President. To make him pay for the neglect that had gotten Jim's brother and wife killed. Jim had devised a crazy plan that sounded like the plot for a Jason Bourne movie, and he suggested I could play a part. I laughed at that at first, but then realized he was at least partly serious. After more drinks and a lot more talk, I postponed any further thoughts of suicide, just long enough to have a proper, sober conversation with Agent Jim. `

`Jim Needham had reason enough to detest you, his nation's President, after his brother's needless death and he had a vague notion of finding some way to discredit you as President. He began watching you and listening to your speeches and briefings, hoping to catch you in a serious lie or maybe even in criminality. He compiled a comprehensive dossier of your lies, but then again, so did a lot of left-wing media outlets. All of them trying to knock you down a few points. You lied and lied, and your supporters refused to acknowledge any of it. Towards the end of your first term as President, Jim became convinced instead that you were just a couple of bad decisions away from starting an all-out nuclear war with a foreign power, so he was most relieved when you completed that Presidential term without serious incident. In common with most of the world, he assumed you would lose the election and that would remove the threat you posed to world peace.

But to the surprise of everybody and the utter dismay of many people, you somehow won the vote. You began your second term in a triumphant and even more unstable frame of mind, so I really needed little persuading when Jim showed me his crazy, brilliant plan.

`My role was that I was to become a South African radical named Trevor Wilson. I could speak in that accent rather well after living in South Africa and Zimbabwe with my wife and her family years before. After the attack we staged in JFK, oh my, how we laughed at the news reports of the search for this terrorist mastermind that nobody knew anything about. And all the while, Gerard Nolan, the mild-mannered English tourist, was being feted on American TV shows as an all-American hero. The plan Jim and I agreed upon was that I was to travel to Yemen to recruit nineteen ignorant peasant boys, get them all riled up about America being the evil empire and then, using people smugglers, get them all to America where they would blow up nineteen passenger planes in the sky above New York. The original plot didn't work out as planned because of my failure to get anyone to agree to provide transport from Yemen to the US.

I probably should have been more flexible on the whole nineteen-Jihadists-all-at- once, decision but I needed to frame the thing as the work of a fanatic, intent on paying tribute to the September eleven martyrs. But, you have to admit Jim's back-up plan was even more brilliant.

Jim got the idea partly from training scenarios he worked on with the Secret Service. The plot he devised wasn't specifically in the training, he simply took some parts of other plans and made a whole new plan. Funny how your worst-case scenario in the training never involved a Secret Service agent being the instigator of the attack. Jim himself had become the absolute worst-case scenario, and you idiots were paying his salary and welcoming him into the White House on a daily basis!

`I deserve an award for my acting, Mister President, pretending to be your best pal while attending all those bloody lunches and award ceremonies at the White House, when what I really wanted to do was stab you with my dinner knife. The gifts you gave us were lovely and the reward money from the airlines was an unexpected bonus. Alice will certainly enjoy spending her share of it. She was so understanding when I told her I wanted a divorce. Undoubtedly the millions of pounds in her bank account helped take away the slight sting of rejection. She doesn't seem to have suspected I had only married her to be a respectable married couple travelling the world in early retirement.

I hope there won't be any legal moves to deprive her or Officer John Corcoran of the money. They certainly both earned it, and neither of them ever suspected they were part of a set-up. Poor Officer Corcoran was so panic-stricken at first when I approached him at JFK, I thought he would totally freeze up in that airport lounge. I had to tell him what to do next, otherwise we would have been standing in JFK even now! ` But once I got him primed, he followed police protocols to the letter, exactly as we had expected.

Chinese neighbors. `

Using Jim's inside knowledge, we knew most of the systems and protocols that are rigidly adhered to by law enforcement departments. We were able to plan our moves in advance using Jim's knowledge of what the response would be from police and federal agents to each incident. And of course, we had the actual handbook for Secret Service responses to threats against the President. The federal government is so smugly complacent in the faith it holds in the recruitment and vetting procedure used to select federal agents that there is little consideration given to attacks by corrupt agents from inside the establishment. Jim Needham told me this fact early in our friendship and I did not fully believe him. It's true though. The CIA seems to be the only agency that routinely distrusts its own operatives and they've had occasion to feel that way. They've been breached in the past. I imagine there'll be new recruitment procedures and training scenarios devised after our little adventure, eh? `.

Nolan addressed Harris Feldman next. `Agent Feldman, you were of course correct in wanting to open and search that heavy crate in my luggage. Unfortunately for all of you, you just weren't forceful enough to override Jim when he argued in favor of leaving the crate unopened. The crate holds a ninety-kilogram stack of powerful industrial explosive compound. It requires an electrical current to detonate, and that explains the other reason the crate is so heavy. There are two car batteries wired together in the crate and they will provide ample power. And that, gentlemen, is all she wrote. America has been carrying out regime changes all around the world in dictatorships and in nations unfriendly to American interests. It's now time for regime change in the greatest democracy on Earth. We think Vice-President Lance Worth could be an improvement on what's gone before, but he surely won't be any worse. And there's always the hope of a new direction for American foreign policy once the elections take place in two years. Maybe a young Democrat candidate will have a few ideas on how to positively engage with our Middle Eastern, Russian, and Chinese neighbors.

Gerard Nolan looked around at them and declared, ` Just to let you know, I pressed the trigger minutes ago, while I was speaking. There is a timer, and it should be just about finished counting down to zero now`.

In the comfortable chair opposite Nolan's seat, President Stamp incredibly had that smug grin on his face again. He pointed a finger at Gerard Nolan, ` screw your history lesson, you lying asshole; you didn't bring a bomb on board my plane. But you have messed up your big move with your disrespecting of us. Your limey ass is getting deported straight back to the shit-hole country you came from as soon as we land at Andrews air-force base. `

Stamp was still smirking when Gerard Nolan clapped his hands sharply and yelled, `BOOM`, causing President Edwin Stamp to throw his own hands in the air with a loud scream. Gerard Nolan's action had the effect of finally knocking the annoying smirk off his face. And Stamp was sitting fully upright in his chair. His slumping problem had been fixed. There was that, at least.

Up and down the length of the Presidential plane, conversations ceased abruptly, and heads turned towards the President's lounge. Most people on board had not heard the words spoken by Gerard Nolan, but they realized there was some sort of tense situation unfolding in the enclosed area in which were seated the President and his VIP guest. Some guests could see there were several agents standing in that small area. Maybe somebody was drunk and getting unruly. There had been a shout from someone and then a scream. It seemed to have all gone quiet there now so maybe all was ok, probably just some kind of joke. Stamp was not renowned for his sense of humor and did not appreciate pranks unless they were cruel in nature and directed against others.

In the cold space of the cargo hold, inside packaging in the crate that Harris Feldman failed to open, the numbers on a digital timer silently moved from two to one to zero. Relays switched and an electrical circuit was complete. BOOM, indeed.

Heathrow airport.
Air traffic control.
Present day.

Air traffic control in London Heathrow had more than the usual number of staff in the tower. Due to the arrival of Air Force One earlier that evening, two senior controllers had a long rest, and were ready for a long evening. They took the previous shift off and had come in to run the control station while the American behemoth was on their tarmac. George Thompson and Peter Linton had fifty years' experience between them. Both were cool, calm, and collected under any amount of pressure. They had delegated the coordination of other air traffic to their junior colleagues so they could be fully focused on The US President's plane. From the moment it landed, through its time parked at the stand, and up to the moment it went wheels-up and began climbing out of the crowded air space over Heathrow, they watched the radar. Or they looked at the actual plane, standing big and proud in the lights below them.

The air crew on Air Force One radioed their readiness to depart. George replied that the exit door was open, the way was clear. After they crossed Ireland, the Atlantic Ocean would be the only thing between them and the good ol' USA.

In reply, Air Force Colonel Frank R. Olson radioed back that he would return to England in the Summer with his wife for their vacation. He promised he would try to come in on something a bit smaller than his current transport. He thanked them for their hospitality and wished all a good night.

The aircraft rolled down the runway, got up to speed and dragged itself up into the sky. On ATC radar screens, the Air Force 1 call sign showed as a prominent track across UK airspace. George and Peter, up in the tower and outwardly calm, did not take their eyes off the USAF1 track. They could see the horizon line on their screen where technically at least, the huge plane would leave the patch of sky covered by their radar and would be out over international waters. In truth, ATC towers at every airport in Western Europe would have attentive eyes and ears on that track until it was safely over American territory, and they could finally hand off responsibility to the FAA.

Approximately one hour and twenty-five minutes after the plane left the ground at Heathrow, the glowing line snaking across the radar screens and being closely watched on screens at over a dozen airports, abruptly disappeared.

There one moment, it was just gone.

A sudden absence of American accented radio chatter underlined the lack of movement in the relevant section of the radar screen. The junior ATC personnel in the control tower, although kept occupied with their own sections, were of course aware of the VIP so recently departed from the runway beneath them. There was an instant outbreak of both live and radio chatter in everyone's headphones and George Thompson swiveled in his seat to roar across the room to ` shut the hell up, every one of you! Tend to your own sections, you've got planes in the air. `

He turned back to his console, aware that his colleague next to him, Peter Linton, had lost all the tan he had gained on his recent Portugal holiday. Peter was adjusting the focus on their screen while also switching through the radio channels. George took over at the radio to allow Peter full access to the computerized radar search. They worked perfectly in tandem because the procedures were written in stone and seared into their memory. They had first to establish the missing radar track was not due to equipment fault or failure. So, they used a second set, and they checked other planes that were known to be in the airspace. There were a couple of passenger jets on outgoing paths either further west or east of the flight path taken by AF1 and it was these other flights to which Peter directed his radio checks now.

One was an Aer Lingus plane and Peter made contact with its crew to ask if all was ok. The strong Cork accented voice came back instantly with confirmation of everything being fine in their little corner of the sky. Next, Peter called up the Air Canada flight whose lights could still be seen as it climbed away from Britain, towards its Northwestern destination. Again, the reply of all ok came back with zero delay. Two further checks with other aircraft were answered cleanly.

A similar check call to Air Force One was met with ominous silence.

At the same time, they were scanning radio frequencies in the hope of hearing from the US Secret Service agents who would be first to have any information pertinent to the situation. Along with these checks, George had activated an automated notification system that would send messages, both voice and text, to relevant levels of the British government. Once these messages were received, confirmation and verification to make sure the alert did indeed originate from ATC in Heathrow, and it hadn't been sent by mistake or due to some glitch in a computer would be requested and received. A meeting of the COBR emergency response committee would be convened to decide on the next course of action.

In the event of worst case, search and rescue services would be alerted and scrambled from relevant bases. Although these crews would be aware how low were the chances of them finding survivors from a plane flying at an altitude of several thousand feet and passing over nothing other than freezing cold ocean. Military over-flights would begin in the area where the Presidents plane was last recorded, and shipping in the area would be made aware of a possible problem.

Publicly, this would be descried as a rescue. Emergency crews would be privately calling it a body recovery exercise.

If this turned out to be worst case scenario, George was very glad he would not have any active part to play in the aftermath. He had avoided developing an ulcer or other health problems after twenty-nine years in this highly stressful job and he rather felt this might be his final twelve months. Retirement, collection of his pension and a trip to visit his daughter in Australia sounded like a good idea right now. He looked at Peter and asked, `anything yet? `. Peter shook his head, reached into his shirt pocket, and removed a foil blister pack of antacid tablets. Pushing three of the little squares out of their plastic nests, he popped them into his mouth and began chewing. He had reached the last of any possible fault finding checks he could perform. He was now sure the absence of radar track was not due to a system failure.

Which only left one conclusion, which was that there was no sign of Air Force One on the radars scanning the sky because Air Force One was no longer in the sky.

There was a very tiny hope that the USAF was testing a new electronic camouflage system as part of the defenses on Air Force One. It was technically possible they might somehow have managed to make a seventy-meter plane disappear from the sight of one of the most advanced and powerful radar systems in the world. Peter voiced this possibility to George in a voice they were both aware sounded perilously close to breaking. To comfort his colleague, George agreed that it was possible. Of course, it was possible, anything was possible. They would await official confirmation before they got upset. Or rather, before they got more upset.

All the relevant government department secretaries had been notified and the various strands of the official response had been pulled together in the basement of designated buildings in

Whitehall. There was nothing to do now but wait for the inevitable official confirmation.

Official confirmation was what everybody got an hour later when a phone call was put through from the airport police office half a mile away on the other side of the Heathrow complex. The Irish police service, the Gardai, in a small coastal town in Northwest Donegal had been summoned to their local port by the harbor master. They got there to be met by the crew of a fishing boat. The crew were local men, and all were well known to the police officers. They had been out on the icy waters off the Northern coast since early that morning. The boat had developed minor engine trouble a few hours into the trip which delayed the trip with the result that it had become fully dark, and they were still finishing up their days work, putting away nets and stowing equipment.

While out on the water, the crewmen were aware of planes passing overhead. There was very little other noise out on the water so planes sounded much closer than they would when heard from land. They all heard this one, although it was far enough above the cloud cover so they couldn't see its running lights. Boat skipper Ian Fox said he remembered thinking the plane above might be carrying the US President. He had seen the news on his phone earlier that day that Stamp and his entourage had stopped off in London after leaving Paris. Ian had mentioned this news to his crew, and they were still talking about the US President while they worked. They wondered what his possible reasons for might be stopping in the UK.

Their conversation was interrupted when a large orange glow bloomed silently in the night sky, high above their heads. There was no sound for a second or two following the light and then they heard it. A hollow booming noise swiftly followed by high-pitched, whistling sounds.

They were all looking up into the darkness trying to decipher what these sounds meant, when from out of the black sky, debris began raining down around their location on the dark water. There was a loud thud on the deck down behind the pile of netting they had gathered earlier. It was too dark at that end of the deck to see what had caused the noise. Ian Fox was first to understand what the disturbance in the darkness meant, and he had run to the wheelhouse and started the boats engine, praying his earlier engine repairs would enable a quick escape while yelling over his shoulder for the lads to get under the scant cover of the wheelhouse immediately.

Ian got the engine up to maximum power and sped away from their position as fast as the boat could travel. When he had moved a safe distance away from their original spot, Ian slowed the boat and turned it in a wide circle to face back towards the area from which they had just fled. There were objects tumbling from the sky and there was now fire on the surface of the sea. Confusingly, the flames appeared to be in the water, and it was the youngest member of the fishing crew, Jamie Connolly, that figured out what they were seeing. There was fuel mixing with the waves. The fuel was floating on the surface while continuing to burn. They were seeing the aftermath of a midair explosion at altitude.

Destroyed parts of both humans and machine were raining down. There were burning chair covers, flaming luggage and clothes fluttering like oversized fireflies from the impenetrable darkness above all the way down to the flickering surface of the sea. There were multiple heavy splashing sounds among the other noises and Ian felt sick when he understood what was hitting the water with such force. It's all the dead people, folk that were sitting in comfy chairs sipping a drink just a few minutes ago. They are now dead and falling from the sky. He called to his crew and told them they were heading back to port at their fastest speed as they had a duty to report what they had seen and heard.

Before departing the location, the fishing crew had the presence of mind to mark off the area with floats and buoys and they recorded the GPS coordinates so the site could be located accurately later.

Kyle mc Entee took some pictures with his phone camera, using the glow of the burning fuel to illuminate the photos. They had then fled towards shore `as if all the devils of hell were chasing them` the phrase used by Paul Carrick, the oldest member of the crew looking visibly shaken and close to tears.

Kyle handed his mobile phone to the Garda officers who met the boat crew at the small dock. `Look at the photos I took out there, it's what Ian thought. About whose plane it was that passed over our heads and blew up. If he was on that plane, he's well dead. Along with everybody else with him`.

In the photos, even in the bad light and with a strong fire-glow blurring part of the picture, it was obvious what was in the strangely flickering water. It was a large section of an airplane, and though it was partly submerged in the dark, oily water, clearly visible on it was the Seal of the President of the United States.

Mexico City.

Same day.

In the National Palace in Mexico City, Vice President of the United States of America Lance Worth was enjoying an informal chat with Mexican President Lopez Salazar. They had completed two days of productive talks and agreement had been reached on several issues. These were issues upon which US President Stamp had previously stumbled badly, both personally and diplomatically. President Salazar enjoyed dealing with Lance Worth because the man did not play the sort of games his boss seemed to be consumed by. Worth was a deeply religious man and was guided by his faith. No lying, no unjust treatment of his fellow man and his handshake was his bond. Lopez Salazar wished to only do business with straight talking people, otherwise valuable time got wasted and people suffered. Salazar was pouring a second cup of the very good local coffee for them both when the ornate doors to the meeting room were abruptly opened without the grace of even a simple knock.

Three US Secret Service agents stormed in, two of whom got either side of Lance Worth and lifted him bodily from his seat. The third agent, said `excuse us please` to President Salazar, turned on his heel and hustled back out, holding the still swinging doors open for his colleagues hurrying behind him with a shocked and acquiescent US Vice President supported between them. Worth did not even get the chance to say goodbye to his Mexican host and his feet barely touched the floor all the way out to the courtyard where three massive SUVs stood waiting. The engines were idling on all three vehicles and there seemed to be armed agents in sunglasses with earpieces wired to their ears at every corner and in every doorway.

The agents carrying Lance Worth did not hesitate as they reached the cars, they simply continued moving their boss through the open rear door of the vehicle until he was seated in the rear of the middle SUV. They then buckled his seat belt like a child that has been removed from a family event for bad behavior. The remaining seats were swiftly occupied, and Worth felt himself pushed back into the plush upholstery when the short cavalcade accelerated away into the Mexican sunshine.

The cars headed directly to a small airfield outside Mexico City where a privately owned Gulf-stream jet was waiting, engines already whining. Again, there was no waiting or hesitation at the steps. The Vice President was pushed up the airplane steps, guided to a seat and strapped in. Almost immediately, the small jet began rolling down the airstrip, accelerated until it seemed it would crash into the shabby looking sheds and outhouses clustered together at one end of the field. At the last possible moment, the plane lifted smoothly up into the air and away. Barely a couple of thousand feet from the ground, the pilot banked the aircraft sharply to the North and pointed the plane's nose towards Washington D.C.

Lance Worth sat in silence, hunched over in his seat, deep in thought. He managed to maintain his calm facade until they were just over an hour into the flight and then his nerve broke. He fumbled his seatbelt open, flung the buckle away from himself and bolted from his chair to the spotlessly clean toilet cubicle at the rear of the plane. Putting his face barely an inch or two above the swirling blue water in the stainless-steel toilet bowl, he vomited up the breakfast and the coffee he had enjoyed in the Palace in Mexico City. His stomach clenched again and again until he feared he was suffering a seizure. When he felt sure he had finished, he turned away from the smell wafting from the toilet. There was an agent standing in the aisle with a packet of scented face wipes and a glass of water. Agent Brian Reynolds smiled sympathetically at the Vice President. `Are you ok Sir? I'm assuming by now you have guessed the reason for our snatching you from under the nose of the President of

Mexico`. Lance Worth nodded weakly and asked, ` God help us, something terrible has happened to our President?

Washington DC.
Inauguration day.

The day of the Presidential inauguration ceremony was not the joyous occasion it would normally be. Journalists spoke to the cameras in somber tones. Americans being interviewed on the streets and in the parks of Washington DC tearfully pledged to support their new president in these trying times. This was unknown territory for a huge number of Americans as many had not been alive when John F. Kennedy had been killed while in office. There was an air of shocked acceptance that this was how the world is now. Not even a President is safe anymore.

In the few days following the blowing up of Air Force One, private gun sales in America had increased by four hundred percent. Private security firms were recruiting extra staff to handle the increase in calls for patrols in affluent neighborhoods. There was huge demand for metal detectors to be placed in schools and colleges amid fears of an increase in mass shootings. The whole nation was on high alert. Police patrol officers were counselled by force psychologists in response to orders from above to restrain their usual bullish behavior on the street. With tensions so high everywhere, trigger fingers would be more likely than ever to twitch at the wrong moment. Body armor was in high demand by every officer due to the renewed fear of being shot at on the streets. Sergeants did roll call inspections to ensure all body cameras were switched on and working and there were quiet words advising restraint for certain cops who might have been heavy handed in Black neighborhoods in the past.

At the Capitol buildings in Washington D.C. large numbers of Federal agents moved through the crowds trying to look in every direction at once through their mirrored sunglasses. The agents were paying particular attention to anyone that wore a backpack or indeed any sort of bag at all. Canine units roamed the area, getting close to any small clusters of people. The dog handlers were openly and unapologetically allowing the dogs to sniff at coats and baggage. Once all the bag checks and identity card scanning had been completed, and there was no longer a line of people at the barriers waiting to enter the grounds, the pomp and ceremony began.

The main reason for the massive gathering had commenced. The Chief Justice of the US Supreme Court stood waiting to perform the simple swearing in of the new President. Vice-President Lance Worth approached the podium, blinking in the bright sunlight and looking almost reluctant. He did not feel ready for this, even after all his years in public service. Being vice-President had been a big enough responsibility for him, he had never wanted to be President. Unbeknownst to Lance Worth, at that moment, in the humility of his abject need for wiser heads to guide and counsel him, he was exactly the President that Jim Needham and Gerard Nolan had wished for America. They had assassinated the sitting President and murdered everyone on the Presidents plane to achieve their objective but there was now a decent, humble person in the highest office in the nation.

With the formal procedures and the Presidential prayers completed, newly inaugurated President of the United States Lance Worth turned to the steel forest of microphones sprouting from the glassed-in stand and prepared to address the nation for the first time as President.

Before he began speaking though, he made the mistake of looking down at the swarm of TV and print media correspondents from every nation in the world, milling around in the press area front of him. They looked as if they wanted to attack and devour him. Not one of them smiled or nodded at him, they just stared back as he looked at them. Just like caged predators, they would be as happy to have him fall among them in the cage as they would be to get out to where he was.

Quite a few of the journalists had been in Heathrow when Gerard Nolan was collected by President Stamp. Bored by the end of the briefing, they had left immediately afterward. They were still sick over not being at the airport when the Presidents plane went missing. They had little interest or sympathy for this bland, unexciting new President in front of them. There was only a faint, unvoiced hope that somebody might take a shot at Lance Worth today. That would at least create some excitement around the man.

In trying to divert his gaze away from the terrifying vision below, Worth looked out over the crowds of spectators instead. It appeared to be a never-ending sea of people stretching so far into the distance, he couldn't see where it ended. Every single one of the faces seemed to be screaming, in terror of this crazy world or in anger at the new President, he could not tell. It did not auger well for his Presidency if he inspired only fear or wrath in the citizens. He forced himself to look down at his notes and to focus on the typed words his speech writers had hurriedly composed. The advisers had told him to keep it simple, do not deviate from the script, you will be fine. Sweat from his forehead, rolled down into his eyes, blurring the words. In large upper-case letters, the underlined print of the first three words stood out from the page. These words were supposed to help calm him and to bring him peace of mind. He managed to speak the opening three words into the microphone calmly enough, ' GOD BLESS AMERICA. '

President Worth risked another glance down into the media area and now that he was a tiny bit calmer, he could recognize some well-known journalists and news reporters from various networks. Lance Worth looked away and saw himself displayed on one of the big television screens erected so that people at the outer edges of the park would be able to see the President and the other speakers and guests as they appeared up on the stage. As he watched the screen, the camera angle changed and now it showed the assembled journalists in front of the speaker's podium. Lance Worth could now see the media people that he had just been looking down upon in front of his location.

As the President gathered his thoughts and got ready to begin his prepared speech to America and to the world, he continued to watch the screen. Among the reporters and camera crews in the media area, one man stood apart from the other media people. While most of the people in the press enclosure were busily doing their jobs, this man was simply standing there, gazing up at the President, as the President cleared his throat. This man was well dressed, with a neatly clipped beard and wearing tinted spectacles. He seemed to realize he now had the eye of the American President as he reached into his jacket. He withdrew his hand holding an object and using both hands he unfurled a black cloth. Printed on this cloth was a line of Arabic letters and beneath these was a line written in English. The man put his finger on the line of English letters, while maintaining eye contact with the President, who was standing four feet above the man's position. While President Worth watched, the man moved his finger along the line of print, mouthing the words to emphasize their importance.

By now, secret service agents had become very concerned at the exchange between the man and the President. They couldn't see or hear what was being said, but they could see the President was transfixed by the man, like a small animal caught in the glare of oncoming vehicle headlights. Armed agents were pushing through the crowd from intersecting directions to apprehend the man in the press area. Onstage, two agents were being sent out to get in front of the President, to break the connection between him and the unidentified man. And to get the President out of there if necessary.

One cameraman, Glen Franks from Minnesota, bored filming crowds and politicians, had been looking around to see if there was anything newsworthy to catch on film and he noticed the President had stopped his speech and was simply standing there, staring down into the media enclosure. Glen pushed his way through a few of his equally bored colleagues to see what the President was locked onto. He threw the mini camera onto his shoulder when he saw the man holding what looked like a black flag with white printing on it. Glen moved slightly forward of the man to get the writing into focus and as he did so, the man broke eye contact with the President and turned his head to look at Glen. The guy did the same pantomime for Glen that he had done minutes before, for the President. Drawing his finger along the English words, he then mouthed the words for the camera. "DEATH TO AMERICA, THE GREAT SATAN".

Behind the man, Glen's camera feed had gone main-screen and the mans printed message could now be seen by everyone, both those in the park and around the world. As people realized what it said and meant, there was a sudden movement of bodies away from the stage and towards the park exits. The secret service agents, trying to get close enough to the man to stop him doing whatever he was intending, were swept away, along with the thousands of panicked citizens trying to escape what was coming. The two agents on stage had just reached the President and were speaking to him, telling him there was an alert, he was to come with them, right now. President Lance Worth, having lost eye contact with the man below the stage when the man turned to face the camera, reacted as if awakening from a nap on a warm afternoon. For just a moment, he wasn't sure exactly where he was and had a fleeting hope that he hadn't been forced to assume the Presidency, that it was a bad dream and was now over.

In the seconds before the agents dragged him away from the podium, Worth looked back at the man that had made that strange connection with him. The man had dropped the black cloth and was now lifting a canvas hold-all from where it had lain on the ground at his feet. He hoisted the bag up and holding it on a raised thigh while balanced on one foot, he reached inside the bag. Lance Worth saw the man withdraw his hand and now it held an object. The man dropped the bag back to the ground.

The secret service agents, Bill and Phil, were physically bigger men than Lance Worth. Bill, looking over his shoulder as they moved the President, had seen the same thing that Lance Worth had seen, that the man below had made a move for the bag. Bill shouted to his partner that they really needed to move now. Phil yelled back, "on two!" and they picked The President up by his arms and began running towards the rear of the stage.

Glen was still filming the man. Glen hadn't run away like everybody else. He wasn't suicidal and he wasn't a hero. He had simply looked around at his current location and realized he was hemmed in by the railing around the media area. Beyond the railing, was a fast-moving river of people. The crowd was pushing toward the exits, but those gates had never been intended to accommodate the sheer numbers of terrified people that were attempting to exit now. Glen decided he preferred to face whatever this guy was going to do, rather than trying to escape and getting hit in the back when it came. Plus, it was important to get the whole thing on video, somebody would be able to learn something from it and maybe they would be able to capture the people responsible for this man being in Washington DC.

The man looked at Glen and his camera, he glanced out at the crowds, much reduced in numbers now, still pushing past the media enclosure. He returned his attention back to the object in his hand. Holding it in one hand, he used his other hand to push a switch on the top panel. The man's lips were moving again, and this time Glen reckoned he was praying. The man looked around himself once more, and then he pushed his thumb down hard on the box.

President Lance Worth, being carried at running speed across the stage and towards safety to the rear area, had never wanted to be President. He hadn't wanted to be in high level politics at all really, he had been involved in local councils for years and somehow had gotten chosen to run in the State Governor elections a few years ago. His political career had gone from strength to strength and soon he found himself in the running for the Vice-President role. His wife had encouraged him to be ambitious and when President Edwin Stamp got assassinated, Worth's wife had kissed him and said she always knew he was destined for high office. At this moment in time, he regretted every single vote cast in his favor.

The agents carrying him to safety were running flat out now. Bill, the agent on the left of the President, was reaching out with one hand to push open the stage door at the rear. They were almost safe, nearly to the door now.

A powerful, warm hand pushed the running agents from behind. They were lifted and thrown at over one hundred miles per hour, hitting the steel and wood stage framework in a bloody tangle of bodies. President Lance Worth, having been President of the United States for just a couple of hours, was killed instantly along with secret service agent Bill. Agent Phil remained alive in the wreckage for a few minutes but bled to death while the remains of the stage scaffolding collapsed around him and while lots of others died around him.

The original crowd attending the inauguration and the attending festivities, had numbered at approximately two hundred and fifty thousand. The remnants of that crowd, still streaming towards the exit gates when the device in the bag exploded, numbered around twenty thousand. Almost one thousand of those closest to the stage area died in the initial blast with a further two hundred dying of their injuries over the following hours and days. Twelve agents of the secret service died along with their President.

Later investigations found that the bomb had been brought to the venue disguised as sound equipment under a forged permit copied from a genuine permit that had been stolen from one of the tv studio technicians. The bomb had consisted of eighty pounds of high explosive in a core, surrounded by a large volume container of steel ball-bearings, nails, and screws. The effect was that of a massive shotgun blasting in every direction at once.

Of the cameraman Glen, not a trace could be found. The video he shot was being recorded on a remote server and the film survived intact. His work won a Pulitzer Prize, posthumously awarded.

Virginia, U.S.A.
Next day.

In a farmhouse in Virginia, a young man was watching television with his mother. They were absorbed in watching the inauguration of a new American President as it was broadcast live from Washington DC. When the footage of the man with the bag, filmed by Glen, came up on the big screens in the park, and was subsequently shown on television, Ibrahim Mahmoud leapt to his feet in excitement. "it's Uncle Maamar, he is ok, he is alive!!", he yelled. His shouting brought two federal agents running from their post at the front and rear of the house. They had been bored to tears with guarding Ibrahim and his mother and they couldn't wait for the orders to come that their prisoners were being transferred to their new home.

The agents hurried into the tv room to find Ibrahim dancing around singing and shouting happily that Uncle Maamar was alive and hadn't died after all. Unbeknownst to the young man, behind him his dear mother had collapsed onto the sofa.

Upon seeing her `dead` brother appearing live on television, and realizing he was in the process of blowing everybody up, Emani instantly knew her own, and her sons' dreams were over, their lives in America were at an end, there was no way the Americans would allow them to stay. She fainted dead away. Ibrahim, true to form, hadn't even realized she wasn't dancing with him.

Forced regime change, so often visited on other nations by America, had twice come to America.

And the weapons makers began gearing up for a new war on terror, rejoicing in the fact that governments change, but people rarely do.